MW01233710

By JACOB Z. FLORES

Published by DREAMSPINNER PRESS
http://www.dreamspinnerpress.com

When *Love* Comes *to* Town

JACOB Z. FLORES

Dreamspinner Press

Published by
Dreamspinner Press
5032 Capital Circle SW
Suite 2, PMB# 279
Tallahassee, FL 32305-7886
USA
http://www.dreamspinnerpress.com/

This is a work of fiction. Names, characters, places, and incidents either are the product of author imagination or are used fictitiously, and any resemblance to actual persons, living or dead, business establishments, events, or locales is entirely coincidental.

When Love Comes to Town
© 2014 Jacob Z. Flores.

Cover Art
© 2014 Michael Breyette.
www.breyette.com.
Cover Design
© 2014 Paul Richmond.
http://www.paulrichmondstudio.com

Cover content is for illustrative purposes only and any person depicted on the cover is a model.

All rights reserved. This book is licensed to the original purchaser only. Duplication or distribution via any means is illegal and a violation of international copyright law, subject to criminal prosecution and upon conviction, fines, and/or imprisonment. Any eBook format cannot be legally loaned or given to others. No part of this book may be reproduced or transmitted in any form or by any means, electronic or mechanical, including photocopying, recording, or by any information storage and retrieval system, without the written permission of the Publisher, except where permitted by law. To request permission and all other inquiries, contact Dreamspinner Press, 5032 Capital Circle SW, Suite 2, PMB# 279, Tallahassee, FL 32305-7886, USA, or http://www.dreamspinnerpress.com/.

ISBN: 978-1-62798-785-1
Digital ISBN: 978-1-62798-786-8

Printed in the United States of America
First Edition
April 2014

To Pilar:

I didn't know what love was until you came to town.

Chapter One

BRODY O'SHEA logged off his phone and ran around his apartment to do a quick cleanup. He only had about fifteen minutes before Dan showed up, and he wanted the place to be presentable. Why the fuck didn't he just pick up his shit instead of leaving it strewn all over the damn place?

He bolted toward the pile of dirty clothes in the corner of his bedroom, tossed them into the closet, and shut the door. What next? His unmade bed, the stack of paper plates sitting on the coffee table in the living room, or the pods of water bottles that littered almost every surface of his apartment?

Fuck! This place was a pigsty. No, it was worse than that. No self-respecting pig would deign to step foot in this place. What had happened to him? He'd always made sure things were in their proper place before, but ever since he moved to Provincetown, he'd given up on housekeeping.

Why was that?

Irene, who'd stopped by last week, claimed he had poor life-management skills when she eyed the growing stack of audition manuscripts he'd been reading and for which he'd never actually auditioned. She even threatened to turn him in as a hoarder. They were supposed to be on the road to being friends again. So much for that! After her comment, he escorted her out the front door. He could manage his life just fine. He'd been doing so for almost thirty years.

His general state of chaos was a relatively new problem, but it was one he couldn't find the solution to.

No matter how hard he might try to pick up after himself, he grew bored and instead jumped on his computer or phone to see if he had any bites on the many social dating sites he subscribed to. Yes, it had recently become an obsession, logging onto Cyber, Manhunt, Scruff, Growlr, Mister, or any of the other apps that clogged up his phone and laptop. But what if he missed the message from the Mr. Right he'd been waiting to find?

Okay, now he was starting to sound like his mother. That was a frightening thought. She'd always believed she needed a man to make her complete. That was probably why she'd been divorced four times. Well, that and the fact that she was a drug-addicted, alcoholic, fame-obsessed has-been who'd been unable to recreate the brief success she enjoyed in the '90s with her grunge band, Square.

But he wasn't like his mother, trying to find happiness in heroin, booze, or men. He wasn't like his father either, who seemed concerned only with women or work. He'd worked hard over the years to be someone better than either Joy or Patrick O'Shea. Sure, he'd not been in a real relationship since college, and he had managed to screw that one up out of fear. Who could blame him? He'd never seen a real relationship, and he had no clue what love was about.

But then he came here. To Provincetown.

Everywhere he looked there were happy couples. Men and women who'd devoted their lives to each other. Like Gary and Quinn, who'd been together almost twenty years, and Zach and Van, who were getting married later that week. Even Teddy, the man he'd loved in college, lived here with his new boyfriend, Nino.

Why couldn't he have that too?

That was when he decided it was time for him to find a man to call his own, and he couldn't just leave it up to fate. He'd never done that before in his life. Let some unseen force work its hocus-pocus and bring him what he wanted. What he had was hard earned. If he wanted something, he went for it. What made love any different? It didn't. Not in Brody's book.

Since last year, when Teddy had rejected him in favor of Nino, he'd decided to be more proactive and weed through the many men out there until he found the man for him. He'd already been on dates with most of the single men who lived in Provincetown, at least those who met his high standards of hot, sane, single, employed, and childless.

Snagging the dates had been easy enough. He was a pretty attractive guy. Not to sound vain or anything, but he appreciated his own aesthetic qualities. But pretty much every single guy out there who met his standards was only interested in finding Mr. Right Now. They'd spend time with him and flirt, but when it came down to really getting to know each other, to moving past the bedroom, none of them were interested.

While he had no problem with tricking—because, well, it was fun—why wasn't anyone more interested in him beyond a fuck?

It was enough to start giving Brody a complex. Was there something undateable about him? He sure as hell didn't think so. Which was why he'd asked Teddy to come over a couple of days ago. They might not be together anymore, but they were still friends. He could always count on Teddy to be honest with him.

Luckily, Teddy had validated Brody's self-assessment. There was nothing so wrong with him that would put guys off. What Teddy had said next, though, threw him for a fucking loop. He wasn't "desperate." One thing Brody O'Shea was *not* was desperate.

Yes, he was singularly focused. He was a man on a mission, but that didn't make him desperate. Did it? He sure as hell didn't think so.

But according to Teddy, Brody was not only desperate but also unhappy. Brody's disgustingly dirty apartment reflected that unhappiness, in Teddy's opinion. He couldn't have disagreed more. While it was true he wasn't over-the-moon in love like Teddy was with Nino, he wasn't exactly suffering from depression.

He had a lot of things on his mind. He hadn't snagged an acting job in far too long, which was starting to piss him off. The number of clients he had as a personal trainer was steadily growing, which helped pay the bills. He was also trying to get the male lead in *Poke-a-hunkus*, which was Brian Long's parody of the Disney classic *Pocahontas*. If he could get Brian, who had many connections to the various Provincetown acts, to cast him in the play, he might be able to land his own show at one of the many venues around town.

So he wasn't unhappy. Just very busy.

He had a lot on his plate, and he had to work on finding himself a man.

That took a lot out of a guy, and that was why he didn't have time to clean up his apartment regularly. What he needed was to slow down. Perhaps find a maid. Maybe his mother's housekeeper, the one she could no longer afford, could hop a jet from New York City and get here in time to clean up this shithole before Dan arrived. Yeah, and maybe singing monkeys would come flying out of his ass too.

Now, *that* would make a good show for the average P-town audience.

What the hell was he doing? He didn't have time to stand around with his thumb up his butt. He needed to clean before Dan got there. A quick glance at his watch told Brody he had maybe five more minutes until Dan, who he'd been chatting with on Cyber for the past two days, knocked on his door.

Ignoring the bed, which would likely just be messed up again in a few minutes, Brody headed for the water bottles on his nightstand. He scooped eight of them off the table, then noticed four more lying on the floor. He kicked those under the bed. How much damn water did he drink in a day?

He couldn't answer that now. After rushing to the kitchen, he deposited the water bottles in the recycling container. He then ran around picking up paper plates and as many water bottles as he could carry before heading back to the trash basket. After five more armloads of trash, he'd finally managed to clear the apartment of most of its detritus.

There were still some spots of clutter, but it wasn't as bad as before. At least now there would be a place for Dan to sit. Their conversation over the last few days had been promising. Dan was tired of the hookup scene too and only logged onto Cyber occasionally, just to see who was out there. Luckily for Brody, he had happened to be online during one of Dan's rare Cyber appearances.

Since then, they'd been messaging almost nonstop. They sometimes talked about serious subjects like their jobs or their childhoods, but Dan preferred to flirt, which was important. There had to be that sexual attraction before things could go anywhere. He wasn't about to end up with someone who didn't enjoy a good flirting session. Done right, they could make Brody breathless.

A light knock on his front door interrupted his thoughts. Dan had arrived.

Now, it was time to see if Dan lived up to Brody's expectations.

WHEN BRODY opened his front door and got his first real-life glimpse at Dan, who leaned against the outside doorframe, he couldn't help the grin that traveled across his lips. He was perhaps the hottest accountant he'd ever laid eyes on. Although height wasn't a huge hang-up for Brody, he preferred tall men, and since Dan stood eye level with him, he was just the right size at over six feet. His brown hair was clipped very short, and he had stunning dark brown eyes. If Brody had to, he could stare into those eyes every day.

What he liked most about Dan was his smile. It hitched up at the left corner of his mouth. It made him look masculine and confident. Two traits any man he planned on spending the rest of his life with had to have.

So far this good-looking accountant met two of Brody's requirements—hot and employed. Only three more to check off the list.

"You gonna invite me in, or we just going to do this here?" Dan asked. The right corner of his mouth tugged into a grin until it stretched wide across his thick lips. Fuck, that was sexy!

"Sorry about that," Brody laughed as he motioned Dan inside. "I'm just *very* pleased that you look like your profile picture."

Dan nodded as Brody closed the door. "Yeah, I hate false advertising. That shit just pisses me off. If you don't have a nine-inch cock and a muscular body, don't tell people that you do. Own up to your tiny dick and fat ass. There are people out there who get off on that shit."

"That's true," Brody hesitantly agreed. "There's someone out there for everyone." What was this guy's problem? He might be hot, but his abrasive attitude wasn't making a good first impression. Did that mean Dan might be crazy? Nothing was sadder than an insane hot man. Talk about wasted potential.

He took a deep breath to center himself and then led Dan over to the couch. A hint of smoked leather lingered in the air around Dan. Was he a smoker? If he was, this was going absolutely nowhere. Smoking was disgusting. He definitely needed to add nonsmoker to his list of requirements.

"You're fucking hot," Dan commented. He studied Brody as Brody sat down. He could practically feel Dan's eyes roaming over his body, and by the slight increase in his breathing, Brody could tell that Dan liked what he saw. Mutual attraction was good, but there was more to a happily-ever-after than looks. He still needed to find out if Dan was sane, single, and a childless nonsmoker.

"Join me," he said while he patted the couch.

"Don't mind if I do," Dan answered before he settled next to Brody. Dan sat on his right hip so that he faced Brody, then extended his arm around Brody's shoulders. "You are most definitely my kind of man," Dan growled.

"Thanks," he answered as he eyed Dan's extended arm suspiciously. Dan obviously wanted to get down to business, but he had yet to pass the interview process. Not that Dan realized he was about to be interviewed. Brody had to find some way to get him to slow down, so he could ask the questions he needed answered. What better way to put a gay man at ease than with a compliment? "You're pretty hot yourself," he finally responded.

"I know," Dan replied.

A grimace unfurled across Brody's lips. Confidence was one thing. Cockiness was an entirely different animal. Brody wasn't a fan of arrogance. In fact, he needed to add humility to his list of expectations.

Before he could tell Dan to rein in the attitude, Dan scooted closer until his right thigh pressed against Brody's. Dan's skin radiated more warmth than the sun. He was obviously hot for Brody's body, while Brody's initial desire for Dan had all but cooled.

"I'd almost given up on finding someone like you." Not that tired old line. His afternoon lunch rose into his throat. Originality most definitely needed to be added to his list too. "When I booked this week in P-town for my vacation," Dan continued, evidently completely oblivious to Brody's declining interest in what he had to say, "I had no fucking clue it was Family Week. There are far too many fags and dykes pushing strollers up and down Commercial."

Really? Fags and dykes? What the fuck was the matter with this guy? Those derogatory labels pissed the shit out of Brody. Gay men who called other gay men fags needed to look in the mirror when they were munching on cock or shoving a dick up their ass.

It was time for Dan to go.

Brody stood up and headed for the front door.

"What's the matter?" Dan asked as he stood from the couch. He stared blankly at Brody as if he had no clue he was the biggest douche in the world.

"It's time for you to go now."

"What?" Dan asked. The hot and cocky motherfucker wasn't so smug now. He'd turned into a child who'd just had his dessert taken away. "Why?"

"This isn't going to work out," Brody said as he opened the front door.

"I've been here like five minutes," Dan complained. God, he hated whiners. That was another characteristic to add to his list. "It took me longer to get here."

"Sorry about that," he said, and he meant it. He was sorry he had wasted two days and the past five minutes chatting with Dan. While he was doing that, he might have not been paying attention to the man he was meant to fall in love with.

Maybe he needed to speed up the process. Less chatting online and straight to coffee or something. There had to be some way to cut out the middleman.

Dan stomped over to where Brody stood in front of the open door. "You're a dick, you know that?" he asked. He stopped in front of Brody and sneered. "Are you one of those fags who just teases and never puts out? Is that what you are? A cock tease?"

Brody settled his gaze on Dan's crazed eyes. If he were any more like a rabid dog, his lips would be covered in a white froth. This guy was definitely insane. Pity. "Actually, I'm a gay man who doesn't have time for fags like you," he responded before gently pushing Dan past the threshold and slamming the door shut.

"Fuck you!" Dan screamed from the other side before his footsteps stormed down the stairs.

Brody rolled his eyes. What a loser! He needed to reevaluate his screening process. It obviously wasn't working correctly, and contrary to what Teddy had said, he was *not* desperate. A desperate man wouldn't have just kicked a hot trick out of his apartment, no matter how crazy the motherfucker was.

What was he going to do now, though? Spending the afternoon alone wasn't how he'd imagined passing the next few hours. If Dan had worked out, there would have been a lot of naked time. Not to mention the customary grunts and groans of a successful date.

But that wasn't going to happen. Unless he gave himself a happy ending. He might not have Mr. Right, but he did have Mr. Right Hand. Who else was better at getting him off? But one quick glance around his apartment told Brody what he really needed to do.

He needed to clean up this shithole. If he started now, he could be done by the time he needed to head over to Gary and Quinn's.

So which was it going to be? Clean or jerk off?

He eyed the piles of crap around his apartment and then his slutty hand.

Who was he kidding? Within seconds, his clothes were off and he was on the couch with that five-fingered whore clutching at his goods. He pounded his cock furiously as his hips thrust into his grip.

He'd only been jacking himself for a few minutes, and he was already close to unleashing. He was either seriously horned-up or he had the best hand ever! Whichever it was, he wanted the sensation to last. Floating between orgasm and release was the closest thing there was to heaven on earth.

So Brody closed his eyes. As he pulled on his dick and played with his heavy balls, he searched the countless images of naked men from his past. Perhaps there, he'd find the man he was meant to be with. The one who would free him from the loneliness that filled up his days.

All he saw was a sea of naked flesh, bare asses, and throbbing cocks. How could he tell one apart from the other when all he'd ever noticed was the pleasure they'd briefly given him? No matter how hard he tried to recall a particular sexual encounter, he only glimpsed the hairy chest that he buried his head into or the cock that serviced him.

How fucking sad was that?

When he opened his eyes again, his hand no longer held wood. It gripped a wet noodle.

Great. Not only did he suck at finding a man, he couldn't even please himself anymore. As if he needed another reason to be depressed. He should just get up and clean. That would take his mind off his troubles.

Instead he curled up into a ball and closed his eyes.

THE IRRITATING and constant chirping of crickets woke Brody from his peaceful slumber. What the fuck was going on? He'd been having a wonderful dream. He'd been walking hand in hand with a man on the beach. Although he couldn't see the man's face, his heart soared at just the warm weight of his hand inside his own.

It was beautiful, as if their touch was something spiritual, a joining of not only bodies but of souls that were destined to be together for a lifetime. Brody often tried to see the face of the man whose touch sent electrical current shooting through his body, but every time he gazed up at him, the sun was too bright, and he couldn't see. Or the wind blew sand in his eyes. Whenever he finally wiped his vision clear, the man was then looking the other way, pointing at something or someone running down the beach toward them.

Did they have a dog? If so, he hoped it wasn't a precocious Frenchie like Teddy's Louie. He saw himself with a more amiable breed, like a Golden Retriever with a name like Buddy. Yeah, that was what he wanted.

But what he wanted even more was to see the face of the man whose presence made him feel loved and safe and cherished. Just as the man was turning around to look at him, a chorus of crickets exploded within his room.

"Goddammit," he cursed as he reached for his phone. He'd changed the default text tone to crickets, thinking it was the least harsh tone on his phone, but when someone sent a million texts within a span of a few minutes, the soothing chirp turned into the buzz of an approaching plague of locusts.

When he rubbed the sleep out of his eyes, he was able to read that the texts were from Gary.

Brody O'Shea, where are you?

Brody sighed. Even in texts, Gary used his full name. He found that a rather annoying personality quirk of his new friend.

Why aren't you here yet? Standing up your friends isn't like you. At least not the Brody O'Shea I first met. We have mountains and mountains of things to do.

Yeah, and he didn't want to do them. He was happy that Zach and Van were getting married. He just wasn't in the mood to celebrate a happily-ever-after at the moment. Much less decorate for the bachelor party, which would be filled with *other* happily partnered couples.

Humberto and Theodore just got here, and they're usually late to everything. Yet still no Brody O'Shea.

Why couldn't Gary just call them Nino and Teddy like everyone else?

Theodore claims that you are hooking up again. I hope that's not the case. Mama Travers would be very disappointed in you.

Oh Lord. Not the Mama Travers thing again. Gary was a nice guy, but he definitely wasn't his mother. And he wasn't hooking up. Well, he would've been if Dan hadn't turned out to be a complete waste of space. But Gary didn't need to know that.

Gary was also right. Standing up his friends wasn't like him at all. What was that about? He'd always been a proponent of bros before homos. But lately he'd been so consumed with finding Mr. Right that he'd let everything else fall by the wayside.

He had to rectify that.

I'll be right there, he texted to Gary before getting off the couch.

He wasn't abandoning his search for Mr. Right. He just wasn't going to let his friendships suffer. The people who'd embraced him since he moved here were important to him. It was time to stop being ridiculous, to stop trying to force a connection with a man.

What he wanted was what he experienced in his dream. Anything less was unacceptable.

Chapter Two

HAD BRODY stepped into a party preparation scene or a minimilitary base? Who could tell? Party decorations covered almost every surface of Gary and Quinn's condo, but that was where the festive atmosphere ended. Gary was in full commandant mode, barking orders at everyone who had come over to his place to decorate the condo and the patio outside for Zach and Van's bachelor party.

Gary was currently instructing Irene and Tara on how to properly hang and twist the streamers so they hung just right. They didn't have the appropriate eight-inch arch Gary looked for in hanging decorations, and their twisting of the black-and-white paper ribbons had been subpar.

Tara listened intently to Gary's direction. Her kind, beautiful face was hidden underneath a mass of brown, wavy hair. How did Tara always manage to keep so calm? No doubt being best friends with Gary for years had caused her to build up immunity to his particular ways. Irene, on the other hand, had no such resistance. A curl rose from her upper lip that he recognized from their days in college, back when he had dated her best friend, Teddy. Underneath Irene's blonde hair, blue eyes, and big boobs roiled a temper capable of blowing this place sky-high. Luckily, Tara saw the steam coming out of her lover's ears and calmed her with a kiss and a hug.

Could Gary be any more oblivious to the crap storm Tara just saved him from? Brody got his answer when Gary took the streamers out of Irene's hands to demonstrate exactly what he wanted. That boy was playing with fire.

No doubt about it. This place was more Guantanamo than Party Central. Perhaps he could slink away unnoticed.

"There you are!" Teddy exclaimed from amid a nest of wires that snaked from behind the television set. So much for a quick getaway. Thanks to Teddy, Gary had spotted him. There was no escaping now. He was doomed. "You finish with your trick already?"

"He mustn't have been very good," Nino snickered. "Either that or it was you. Which was it?" Nino's tone was playful, but the wry grin that sat on his perfectly symmetrical lips revealed more caustic intentions. Although he and Nino had worked through their difficulties from last summer, their relationship remained cool at best. Nino had yet to completely forgive him for his failed attempt at winning back Teddy. Could he really blame Nino? Not at all. But did Nino really have to constantly paw all over Teddy in his presence? It was difficult enough seeing the man he loved and lost with another man. Nino didn't have to consistently rub salt in his wound.

"He was a jerk," he replied as he approached where they busily worked. "Not worth my time."

"Aw, I'm sorry about that," Teddy commented. The sincere smile that sprang to his lips lit up his bearded face and dark brown eyes. Brody missed waking up next to that man and his furry little body. When Nino wrapped his arm around Teddy's shoulders and drew him close, the action spoke volumes. Brody had been staring at Teddy for too long. Good Lord! What did Nino think he was going to do? Snatch Teddy from his side and run off with him? It was obvious to everyone how much they loved each other.

That was what made being here so difficult for him. Everywhere he looked these days, blissfully happy couples surrounded him. He certainly didn't begrudge his friends their happiness, but did they really need to flaunt it in his face?

"No biggie," Brody finally replied to Teddy with a shrug. "I've got high expectations."

Nino and Teddy glanced sideways at each other. There they went again. Talking about him without saying a word. He hated when they did that! "Stop it," he told them.

Teddy's arched, bushy eyebrows and wide eyes expressed his mock confusion. He'd done that ever since they dated in college. Pretending he had no idea what Brody was talking about when he clearly did. "Don't give me that look. You know damn well that the two of you just had a conversation about me."

"I didn't say a word," Nino announced with a smirk. He even punctuated the statement with a slight shake of his brown locks. It was one of Nino's standard model moves that somehow set his mass of curly hair into textbook alignment. How the hell did Teddy fall in love with such a cocky little shit?

"Not with your mouth," Brody finally agreed. "But you said a whole shitload with that look you gave each other."

"All right, simmer down," Teddy said. His voice was low and calm; it was the same tone he'd used when they'd been together. Teddy had always been able to bring him down from the rafters. No one had been able to do that since. "We're just worried about you."

"We?" Nino asked. "Brody's a big boy. He can take care of himself."

"Nino!" Teddy chided.

Even though Teddy's concern still offered him comfort, Brody waved it away. "Nino's right. I am a big boy, and I've been taking care of myself for a long time."

"See," Nino said.

Teddy rolled his eyes at Nino before he turned back to Brody. "I just want you to slow down. You've been going ninety to nothing in search of a man, and I can tell you're getting frustrated. You need to let it occur naturally. It's not something you can force. It's just something that happens."

"That's the way it happened for us," Nino chimed in. Naturally, Nino would add that last part. Open wound. Insert salt. If it wouldn't totally cheese Teddy off, he'd strangle Nino with the wires he'd been working on.

"I appreciate your concern," he told Teddy. "But I think I've got things covered. I know what I'm looking for, and I'll know him when I see him." His thoughts drifted to his dream from earlier. Even though he hadn't seen the face of the guy he'd dreamed about on the beach, the emotions from the dream came back with him to the waking world. It filled him with wistful longing and with an unprecedented need to hold that man in his arms and never let him go. It was so overwhelming that it made him anxious, as if the man of his dreams was out there right now, either walking down Commercial Street or on his way to town.

Why was he standing here when he should be out there searching for him?

"Brody O'Shea!" When he turned in the direction of the screech, Gary was suddenly at his side. His twisted features clearly communicated his disapproval of Brody's late arrival. "I have half a mind to bend you over my knee and spank that perky little bottom of yours."

He turned around and presented his ass, which Gary playfully swatted. He'd quickly learned how to interrupt one of Gary's tirades. An ass presentation, crotch grab, or anything completely inappropriate usually did the trick.

"While I thank you for that, a little ass play will not get you off my list." Gary crossed his arms and snarled, "It's going to take much more than light BDSM to get you in my good graces again."

Brody grinned and unbuttoned his shorts. "How about a peek at my junk?"

Gary considered the offer for a moment before his powder blue eyes glanced over at Nino and Teddy. "And why are you two just standing there?" Gary asked them. "This isn't a peep show. You're supposed to be hooking up the speakers in the condo and running lines to the ones I set up on the patio. Are you forgetting that we're playing Zach and Van's favorite show tunes all night long? We can't do that without proper audio connections."

Nino and Teddy opened their mouths to speak, but Gary shot them a piercing glare. They immediately closed their mouths and stood at attention. Gary Travers was definitely in command of this stalag. "Now, move!"

The two men quickly went back to work while Gary grabbed Brody by the elbow and led him out to the patio. "Here is your work space." On top of the deck furniture were scattered tons of pictures of Zach and Van as a couple and with numerous friends and family members. Gary then picked up a glue gun and scissors and placed them in Brody's hands. "You're in charge of making the decorations that will chart Zach and Van's path to love. I've organized the photos by date. You'll find the oldest ones stacked on the left, and then as you proceed right, you'll find the more recent ones. When you're done, I'll show you where to place each poster board."

Without another word, Gary turned around and left him. He had already set his sights on Quinn, who was in the kitchen preparing food for the party. No doubt Gary had some critiques on his lover's culinary skills.

When Brody looked down at the glue gun in his hands, he wanted more than anything else for it to be a regular gun. That way he could shoot himself and be granted the sweet release of death.

Why couldn't he have gotten audiovisual detail? He didn't need to make a collage of a happy couple about to be married. All it did was remind him of the one thing he didn't have.

JUST AS Brody finished putting the final touches on the last poster, a van with psychedelic colors painted along its sides rolled down the gravel driveway. Where the hell did this monstrosity come from? A Scooby-Doo cartoon?

He immediately recognized the driver from his pale skin and flaming-red hair. Zach Kelly, groom number one, had arrived. Although he couldn't see Van, he guessed that groom number two sat comfortably in the passenger seat.

Who else was in the car with them, though? Shaggy and Velma?

"Are they here?" Gary asked as he trotted out of the condo with Quinn in tow.

"Looks like it," Quinn answered. His perennially cheery face parted into a wide grin. "I see they borrowed Hector's van like I told them they should."

That explained the van. Hector was a fifty-year-old local hippy with three young children he'd named Rain, Moonbeam, and Starshine. But that still didn't explain why the Funk Van, as Hector called it, was parked in the driveway. "Who's here?" Brody finally asked.

"Who do you think, Sherlock?" Nino asked. He and Teddy had joined them on the patio. Arm in arm as usual. Couldn't they go five minutes without touching each other? "It's Zach and Van."

"No shit," Brody snapped. "Who'd they bring with them?"

"It's Zach's family from Texas," Tara replied. Brody stifled a laugh. Hicks from Texas in a van? That sounded about right. When he turned to share his humorous observation, the words died on his lips. Tara and Irene stood to the far right of Nino and Teddy. They, too, had their arms around each other. He hated being the fifth wheel. Well, in this particular case, he was the seventh wheel, but who was counting?

"Hey, everyone!" Van called out as he exited the vehicle Brody would never be caught dead in. A huge shit-eating grin had seemingly taken up permanent residence on his lips. Van had been that way since the start of the week. Being in love seemingly turned people into grinning idiots. What he wouldn't give to join their ranks.

Zach, too, waved up at them. "You ready to meet the Kelly clan?" he asked as he stared up at them dubiously.

"Ready?" Gary squealed. "I've been counting down the minutes to your arrival."

"I hope you're just as eager once you finally meet them," Zach said before sliding open the vehicle's door.

Brody half expected to see Scooby-Doo leap from the interior, begging for a Scooby Snack, or even a line of cowboy-hat-wearing country folk doing the do-si-do. He was *not* prepared for the ordinary people who poured out of the van. So much for stereotypes!

Thankfully, since he'd been working on Zach and Van's photos, Brody was able to identify each family member. Zach's mother, Donna, was the first to exit. She wore a tailored suit and a string of pearls around her neck. The ensemble was topped off with perfectly coiffed silver hair.

After Donna came her boyfriend, Cliff, the only one who fit the southern stereotype with his flannel button-down and cowboy boots.

Cliff looked far too rugged to be involved with someone as prim as Donna Kelly. According to Zach, though, the relationship had more legs than anyone gave them credit for. Zach's father, Gil, and his new husband, Tom, who just happened to be Zach's childhood best friend, emerged. How the hell did Zach handle his father marrying his best friend? Although he couldn't do it, it seemed to work for the Kellys. Gil and Tom had huge smiles on their faces, and of course, they were holding hands. What else would they be doing?

Next to exit the car was Zach's sister Sami. Her hair was just as red as her brother's, but instead of Zach's brown eyes, Sami's were a sparkling green. Her husband, Frank, followed Sami out of the vehicle, and in his arms, he held Zach's niece, Sophia.

Just what he needed to make this day even better. Not only was Brody surrounded by a total of seven happy couples, but now there was a child too.

He didn't like kids. They made him uncomfortable. Partly because his childhood sucked worse than Gary Coleman's. He didn't need the reminder or the aggravation.

What he needed was to find a way to get out of here as soon as possible.

"Where's Eric?" Quinn asked the advancing horde of guests.

"He's coming in on the ferry," Van replied as he helped Donna up the steps to the condo. "I'll have to go get him in a bit."

"Who's Eric?" Brody asked.

"He's Van's cousin," Zach replied.

"And the only member of my family to come to my wedding," Van added. The ever-present smile on his face faltered for a moment as Van obviously recalled how his parents had sent back his wedding invitation unopened and with no response. That had been a hard day for Van, and as they typically did, the entire group rallied around Van to lift his spirits. Even though their constant coupled happiness worked Brody's last nerve, when one of them needed comfort, there were multiple shoulders readily offered.

"It's their loss, son," Gil said as he patted Van on the back.

"Indeed," Donna added as she grabbed hold of his hand. "You're a good boy, and I'm proud to call you my son."

"That's right," Sami chimed in as she took Sophia from her husband's arms. "You've got a family with us now. As dysfunctional and crazy as we are."

"Samantha!" her mother chided with a displeased frown. While Donna appeared to be a loving woman, he'd heard stories about her biting tongue. According to those tales, she was capable of castrating a man with one snide remark.

"What?" Sami asked. "We *are* dysfunctional and crazy. But I wouldn't have it any other way!"

Sami's comment didn't cause Donna to unclench her jaw.

"I'm afraid Sami's right, Donna," Tom added. "How many families are like ours?"

Brody couldn't think of any that included what had assembled before them. Talk about a modern family. But if it worked, who really cared?

Donna finally sighed in resignation. "You're right. We are dysfunctional and proud of it," she announced to Brody and the rest of Zach and Van's friends. In response, the group cheered.

"Who's ready to get this party started?" Nino asked while he lifted Teddy into his arms.

"I will be," Van said as he leaned into Zach, "after I go retrieve Eric from the ferry."

"I can go get him," Brody offered. He'd been looking for an excuse to get away from all these happy couples. Talk about a prime opportunity. After all, Van hadn't said Eric and some other name. That meant Eric was coming alone. Perhaps he would be able to find some solace in another single person while the couples continued their lovey-dovey crap.

"You wouldn't mind?" Van asked.

"Not at all," he replied. "As long as I can use…." He paused and looked at their vehicle. Did he really want to get out of here *that* badly? The answer came back a resounding yes. "…the van."

"It's yours," Zach said. He then tossed the keys to Brody. "The ferry gets in at seven."

Brody glanced at his watch. He had about thirty minutes, but that didn't mean he had to wait here. "Okay, I'll head on over now if that's okay. Sometimes parking can be a bitch." Especially since he planned on parking as far away from people as possible.

"You don't fool anyone," Gary told him. "You just want to get away from work detail."

He smirked. "And that too."

Before Gary could respond, Brody bounded down the steps, hopped into the bitchin' van, and drove away. This was exactly what he needed. Some time by himself and away from all the craziness.

Hopefully, Eric would be a cool guy to hang with and not a stick-in-the-mud. It would suck if the only other single guy at this party turned out to be a bore.

Chapter Three

IF HE could punch himself in the face without looking like a complete nut job, Eric Vasquez would do just that. He'd been fighting that desire for most of the almost two-hour ferry ride. What had been his reason for not flying into Provincetown for his cousin Van's wedding?

Well, the airfare was too expensive. That was for sure. How the hell did a flight across Massachusetts cost over four hundred dollars? His budget was too tight to justify such an expense. Even though Van had managed to get him free room and board at a condo his friend Gary managed, he still had to pinch pennies he really didn't have to be able to afford the weeklong stay at a rather pricey destination.

What else could he do, though? Van was family.

It wasn't like Van's parents were going to show up. Harding and Charlotte Pierce weren't exactly accepting of their son even *before* they found out he was gay. Now that he was a gay ex-porn star about to marry another man, well, they hardly even acknowledged his presence. Which was not only sad but also seriously pissed Eric off.

Family should be there for each other. No matter what. That was what his parents taught him. If they were still alive, they'd have been there to show their support for Van. Just like they were always there for him. God, how lucky was he that his mother had turned out nothing like her brother Harding? And that she fell in love with a man who believed an open hand and an open heart made the world a better place. He couldn't even imagine how his life would be if she had been anything like her overbearing, judgmental, bigoted prick of a brother.

The Vasquez family always stuck together. Through thick or thin. Without them, he would have never survived the horrible tragedies that seemed to constantly fall upon him.

Eric's gut wrenched. Thinking about the painful losses he'd lived through always did that to him. That was why he did his best not to dwell on them, which was sometimes very difficult. They seemed to linger over his head like unseen nuclear missiles, just waiting to rain down upon him and reduce his world to one giant-size mushroom cloud of devastation.

No, he couldn't think that way. Down that path lay only the darkness of depression, and he'd worked hard to fight his way back from its viselike grip. He had to stay in the present. Not the past. Just like his therapist advised him to do.

Now, what had he been thinking about before he traveled down Gloom Avenue?

The ferry ride. That was it. He'd been bemoaning his decision to take the ferry.

When he'd been planning the trip, driving to Boston from Petersham, the small Massachusetts town where he worked as a local deputy, and catching the ferry seemed the best option. The ferry tickets weren't expensive, and it would get him into P-town just in time for the big bachelor party.

When he told Van that, his cousin shouted in glee. That had warmed his heart, especially since he didn't have much family left. But now, as he eyed the many gay men packed even more tightly onto the fast ferry than they were packed into their skimpy outfits, he mentally kicked himself in the head.

What had he been thinking? Well, that had precisely been his problem. He hadn't been thinking. He'd been so concerned with arriving in time for the celebrations that he completely overlooked the fact that this boat would be loaded full of horny men, lusting for each other up and down the aisle.

The couple to the left needed to take their tongues out of each other's mouths. Had they even known each other prior to boarding the ferry in Boston? Then there was the group of guys sitting right behind him. They'd been talking nonstop about the fact that they needed to find a place with a hot tub. Because, apparently, all the condos in Fire Island had hot tubs, where they evidently entertained the entire population of the island getaway. That didn't sound very hygienic at all. Who wanted to sit in a stew of virulent bacteria and random body fluids? Not him, that was for sure.

The worst, though, was the guy who sat in front of him, talking to his friends about how hot he was for just hooking up in the bathroom of the ferry. Really? The bathroom? Where people with queasy stomachs from the boat ride had been emptying their stomachs and their bowels? Yeah, real hot, dumbass.

If he were still at home in Petersham, he'd take Mr. Not-So-Hot in for public indecency. Unfortunately, the middle of Cape Cod Bay was a bit out of his jurisdiction.

When had he become such a stick-in-the-mud? He hadn't always been that way. Well, that wasn't necessarily true. He'd been that way until he met Charlie, who told him he needed to lighten up and live a little. And he'd done that. For as long as he had Charlie.

But he didn't have Charlie urging him to move out of his comfort zone anymore. There was no Charlie to get him to step out of the shadows that sometimes overtook him. He didn't have Charlie to light the way with his beautiful smile or his gentle touch or with the kisses he sometimes went to bed dreaming about.

There was no more Charlie.

Eric gazed down to his right at the little nine-year-old girl with dark brown hair tied back in a ponytail, tiny freckles spotting her cute little nose, and the most amazing green eyes he'd ever seen.

No, he didn't have Charlie anymore. But he did have Madison, their daughter.

That was why being here amid all these sex-crazed men was inappropriate. Especially since his daughter took in everything she heard or saw like a sponge.

"Maddie," he warned her again for the millionth time. She just couldn't stop herself from turning in the direction of the conversation she just happened to be listening to at the time. "It's not polite to stare. Or to eavesdrop."

She let out a long-suffering sigh before she turned her big green eyes to him. "I'm not eavesdropping. I'm observing."

Eric rolled his eyes as Maddie reluctantly turned back around in her seat. Even though she faced forward, her ears were noticeably tuned into the conversation Mr. Fire Island Hot Tub was having behind them. He could tell by the way she chewed on her lower lip while her eyes moved slowly from left to right. It was her standard I'm-listening-when-I-shouldn't-be pose.

"Madison," he scolded. Whenever he didn't use her nickname, he got her complete and undivided attention. "You're doing it again."

"I can't help it," she admitted. "I find this whole situation intriguing."

Intriguing? When did the average nine-year-old start using words like intriguing? Well, that was easy enough to answer. Maddie was anything but average. Not many fourth graders he knew read as much as she did or listened to classic rock music. His daughter was anything but average.

"How so?" he finally asked as she peered up at him, just dying to have a conversation about what she'd heard. If she started asking about hookups or hot-tub orgies, he would likely kill all the men in their general vicinity.

"As you know, I've lived a very sheltered life." She gazed up at him accusingly. As if being a good father and protecting her from all of life's evils was somehow something he should apologize for. "I've never really been around gay men. Other than you and Daddy."

That much was true. Petersham, Massachusetts, wasn't exactly a gay mecca, and he was fine with that. He enjoyed their sleepy little town. He didn't care if he was the only gay in the village. It wasn't like he wanted another relationship. As far as he was concerned, that part of his life was over. His only purpose in life was raising his daughter and keeping her safe. Not much else mattered to him.

"It's not like I haven't seen other gay people on television," she added. "But the networks only show gay people as no different from anyone else. Which they really aren't, I know. But gay men aren't all fathers just wanting to be happy with each other and their kids, are they?"

"No, they're not," he agreed. "Some are happy being single. Just like there are some straight people who are happy without being married with children."

"Makes sense," she said with a tiny nod. "I guess what surprises me is that I always thought that more gay men were like you and Daddy." She motioned her head to the guy behind her, who was still going on about the hot tubs. "But based on my observations, you and Daddy seem to be more of a minority within a minority."

Where the hell did she get all this stuff? Based on her observations? A minority within a minority? Was she nine or nineteen?

"You think too much," he finally told her. "Don't worry about what other people are doing or not doing. Just enjoy yourself."

"Why should I?" she asked. "You don't."

Ouch. When did Maddie's astute observations turn on him?

"Please don't be angry with me," she said. Although Maddie never begged or pleaded, since she saw that as being far too childish, her wide eyes clearly communicated her sincere apology and her wish for him not to be mad. "But I worry about you as much as you worry about me."

"What are you talking about?" he asked. "Why do you worry about me? I'm a big, strong guy. I can take care of myself. I even carry a gun. There's nothing for *you* to worry about."

She stared blankly at him as if he was completely missing the obvious. "Seeing all these guys here. How much fun they are having and how they're living their lives. Some rather irresponsibly," she stated as she shot a disapproving glare over her shoulder at Mr. Fire Island Hot Tub. "But they're living. They're getting out there. Making friends and finding boyfriends." She pulled her knees up onto the chair and wrapped her tiny arms around his neck. "I don't want you to be alone, Papa. I don't want you to think about me all the time. It's okay for you to think about yourself sometimes too."

Good Lord. Was his life really that pathetic that his nine-year-old now saw fit to give him relationship advice?

"I'm your father," he told her as he hugged her tight. "My job is to take care of you."

She rose from his shoulder and locked eyes with him. Her face turned serious and determined. He'd seen that look before on Charlie's face whenever Charlie thought he was being stubborn, which was more often than not. "And my job is to take care of you."

He shook his head. "Your job is to be nine, do well in school, and mind your papa."

She rolled her eyes in feigned exasperation. "I can multitask, you know."

For that, he started tickling Maddie's side. She absolutely hated being tickled, which was why he was doing it. She screeched and carried on, laughing hysterically while her limbs flailed all over the place. Only when he tortured her this way did the nine-year-old girl step forward. That was who he wanted her to be right now. Not the observant little adult with far too much common sense and insight.

Maddie couldn't be worried about him and his lack of a personal life. Whether she was right or not, that wasn't her concern. He was happy with his life the way it was. And he didn't want anything or anyone to change it.

SHORTLY AFTER their tickle session ended, Eric took Maddie out to the deck, where they could watch their arrival into Provincetown. She had been reluctant to leave, since she wanted to hear how the hot-tub story panned out. However, he had managed to convince her that they might see a seal or a whale, although she recounted numerous facts about how whales rarely traveled this far toward land. Or that most of the seal population could be found on the other side of Provincetown at Race Point Beach or further down the Cape in Chatham or Harwich. Eventually, she allowed herself to be led out of the passenger interior. The mere childish hope of a whale or seal sighting overrode any of the facts she'd learned when she began researching their trip to Provincetown a few months ago.

Thank goodness there was *some* evidence of a nine-year-old housed in her tiny frame.

As they leaned against the rail together, watching the distance between them and the shore grow shorter and shorter, he took in the beautiful sight before him.

Dusk had started to descend upon the town, and hundreds of lights from boats along the dock or buildings along the shore reflected outward to the sea like beacons calling them home. Along the water's edge, a warm orange glow sparkled, surrounding the town in a welcoming aura that lit up the dark blue sky that hovered above.

The town looked peaceful and friendly. Endless friends resided on its shores; they would open their arms and embrace the wayward travelers who made their way to their sandy patch of land.

It was certainly different from Petersham. Not that his town or its inhabitants weren't pleasant. Good people definitely lived there. But Petersham was more of a town that time had forgotten. It still had the same rustic character of two hundred years ago, which wasn't bad. It was one of the reasons he'd moved there from Boston. Less crime and less of a chance of something awful happening to his daughter.

But it was a town that had embraced the past and didn't look to the future. That was part of the town's character. Provincetown was completely different. Even from this far out, he sensed it.

Underneath the New England structures that were similar to the ones he saw back home resided a more forward approach to life. Perhaps it was the sea air or life in the middle of the ocean, but change seemed to be what Provincetown was about, especially from the stories he'd heard from Van. It didn't shy away from reinventing itself. Provincetown thrived on it. He could see it in the throngs of people who walked up and down the pier, or who hung out on the decks of the many bars they passed, or who simply navigated kayaks through the channel.

Within them breathed life and a longing for what was to come.

It made him very uneasy.

He'd grown accustomed to the stale routine of his life. It offered him comfort. How was he going to survive seven days here?

"You know something?" Maddie asked from his side. She placed her small hand over his and traced her fingers along his knuckles. It was something she'd done since she was a baby.

"What?"

"Daddy would have liked it here."

Eric sighed. She was right. Charlie would have loved Provincetown. He was the adventurer. The one who let go of the past and jumped feet first into the future. He would have much rather moved to Provincetown than Petersham, but Charlie moved there anyway. For him. Because Charlie knew how much he wanted to protect them after everything he'd been through.

But bad things could happen. Even in sleepy towns like Petersham.

"I'm sorry," Maddie whispered. She gripped tightly onto his hand.

"What are you sorry for?" he asked, not liking the miserable look on her face.

"I didn't mean to make you sad by bringing up Daddy."

"Oh, angel," he said as he knelt down in front of her. "I love talking about your daddy. He was a good man."

She nodded and sniffled. "I miss him," she mumbled.

Oh God. Me too. He blinked away the tears that formed at the corners of his eyes. He had to be strong. Maddie needed him to be strong. "I do too."

"I know," she whispered. She then shook her head twice as if she was trying to shake the sadness from her body. "But I think being here will be a good thing."

"How's that?" he asked, skeptically. A plan brewed inside that small adult brain of hers, and he didn't like it.

She looked up at him and grinned. "We're going to have a good time," she told him. "Both of us."

"I always have a good time when I'm with you."

She pretended to gag. "Do you have to be so sappy all the time?"

"You just bring it out of me," he told her. He then scooped her into his arms and rained kisses upon her forehead and cheek.

"Stop it!" she screamed, pretending to be annoyed. Even though she believed herself too big to be kissed by her father, he did it anyway.

Because he loved it. And even though Maddie complained about it, she loved it too. He could hear it in her laugh, and it was a sound he'd never tire of hearing.

At that moment, the ferry blared its horn one final time as it drew closer to the pier. He set Maddie back on her feet and gazed out into the crowds of people waiting for the ferry. Their faces beamed in sheer joy.

Yes, Charlie would have most definitely liked Provincetown. Maybe, if he let himself, he would too.

Chapter Four

"WHERE'S UNCLE Van?" Maddie asked after they had disembarked. She set her black rollaway suitcase, which was covered with stickers from her favorite classic rock bands, by the pier railing. He wasn't as much of a classic-rock aficionado as she was. He enjoyed Queen and vintage Aerosmith, but Maddie loved them all. While most girls her age drooled over One Direction or Justin Bieber, Maddie's iPod was packed full of Led Zeppelin, The Doors, Lynyrd Skynyrd, Journey, Boston, and the Grateful Dead. If the music was made prior to the hair-band era, chances were Maddie had it on her playlist. And a sticker for the band on her suitcase.

She looked like a pint-size fanatic. Especially wearing her Rolling Stones T-shirt with Mick Jagger's big red lips and tongue wagging across the front. He hated that shirt, but what could he do about it? It was who his daughter was, and one thing he and Charlie had agreed upon when they first decided to start a family was to let their child be whomever he or she was.

He wouldn't go back on that now. Especially now that he no longer had Charlie.

"He's supposed to be here," she said. Her tone clearly convicted Van of gross negligence. She crossed her arms and furrowed her eyebrows. Maddie was pretending to be in indignant mode, but he wasn't fooled. He knew his daughter all too well. She was worried. "I am not amused."

Yeah, neither was he. Where was his cousin? He had given Van specific instructions to be there on time. He'd made it very apparent why that was so important. But as he glanced up and down the pier, there was not one sign of him. Droves of people scurried away from the ferry or into the arms of the loved ones who greeted them. Even Mr. Fire Island Hot Tub found his ride, hopped into the car, and drove away. Eric didn't cross half the state of Massachusetts, as well as Cape Cod Bay, in a ferry full of horndogs to be forgotten. And to have his wishes completely ignored. If Van didn't show up soon, he'd give him an atomic wedgie like he used to do when they were kids. Van might no longer be the scrawny little kid of their youth, but he still hadn't outgrown Eric.

"I don't see him anywhere," Maddie commented. Her eyes were wide and betrayed her true emotion. She was on the verge of a panic attack, which was evident in more than just her gaze. Her knees had locked, and her fists clenched and unclenched helplessly at her side. The precious lips that had been laughing a few moments ago on the ferry had pulled tight and pencil thin. If she lost it, it wouldn't be pretty, especially since she stood in front of the gangway, creating a bottleneck for the passengers who had yet to exit the ferry.

"Let's wait over here," he replied as he led her to the left of the exit. There were plenty of benches where they could wait until Van showed up, where they wouldn't block pedestrian traffic, and where Maddie could melt down in relative privacy.

"Perhaps you should call him," she whispered. Her voice was low and faraway. She was beginning to check out. She glanced down at the watch that was secured around her wrist with a tie-dye bracelet. When she saw Van was five minutes late, fear crouched at the corners of her eyes.

He reached out to stroke her hair, trying to give her the comfort she needed.

Punctuality was very important to Madison Warren-Vasquez. Most people thought it was some weird personality quirk, sometimes poking fun at her for needing to be at least thirty minutes early for everything. It drove her teachers crazy when they went on school field trips, but after he explained the genesis of her particular idiosyncrasy, they had all quickly understood and did their best to accommodate her.

Although it was a pain in the ass to leave early for school, trips, or doctor's visits, he had to do it for her. It gave Maddie peace of mind. It kept her from worrying. The last time someone was late she hadn't been concerned.

She was never making that mistake again.

"Will you call him please?" she asked. Her words were so soft they could hardly be considered a whisper.

"I will," he said while he fished his cell phone out of his pocket. "I'm sure there's nothing to worry about."

Although Maddie nodded, she didn't believe him. She chewed on her fingernails, as she did during moments like these, in an effort to rein in her outright panic.

After he entered Van's number and pushed the call button, he mentally thrashed his cousin. If he didn't get here soon, he'd do more than give him a wedgie. Van might just end up going for an unexpected dip in the ocean. As the phone rang and rang, his temper continued to flare. Where the hell was he? Eric understood Van was busy with wedding plans and the bachelor party, but did he have to be ignoring his calls too?

When he glanced down at his daughter, she peered up at him, her eyes overfull with dread. If Van didn't have a good excuse, he might not make it down the aisle at all.

BRODY CLOSELY scrutinized the passengers as they exited the ferry. Perhaps one of the men who now scurried down the ramp might be the man of his dreams. Stranger things had happened. It was Provincetown after all. If someone like Nino Santos could find love, why couldn't he?

Nino wasn't exactly the kind of guy who partnered up. He'd always been the fuck-'em-and-leave-'em type. That was how they'd met last year. As a trick. Yet somehow Nino—with his model-perfect body, asshole attitude, and vain, self-absorbed ways—managed to find true love with Teddy, the nicest and sweetest man to ever walk this planet.

Just how the fuck did *that* happen? How could Nino have someone, and he be alone?

That just didn't make any sense whatsoever.

What was he doing wrong? Not a damn thing as far as he was concerned.

He just had standards he wasn't willing to sacrifice. For anyone. Sure, plenty of guys made exceptions. Most of his friends had. Quinn had to deal with Gary's penchant for drag, and Gary had to put up with Quinn's more serious approach to life. Zach looked past Van's old porn career, and Van got over how Zach treated him. Teddy saw beyond the many awful qualities Nino possessed. As for Nino, well, he couldn't find one bad characteristic Teddy had that Nino would have to overcome. The only negative Teddy brought with him to a relationship was his best friend Irene. Which was bad enough.

He wasn't willing to overlook things that bothered him. Why should he? He wasn't going to change himself for someone else and let someone else call the shots.

That wasn't love. That was a dictatorship, and his dick wasn't going to be ordered around by anyone. Well, except him, of course.

It was entirely within the realm of possibility that he would find someone who met his standards, a list that had grown exponentially after his encounter with Dan, and whom he wouldn't have to change for. After all, that was the entire reason for the list. Surely, the man who met all his requirements would not only be perfect for him, but those standards would make Brody perfect for his ideal man as well.

It was a win-win situation for everyone.

Now, all he had to do was find that one perfect guy.

The group that now made its way down the pier didn't have anyone to his liking. They were all smoking and blowing their cancer clouds all over the damn place. How could making out with an ashtray be hot? Behind the Future Cancer Patients of America strolled an attractive group of guys, but they had a little too much swish in their hips. What were they trying to do? Wash their clothes as they walked? He pictured himself with a manlier man. So they were definite no-nos.

Then he spotted a dark-skinned, ruggedly handsome man step off the metal gangway and look up and down the pier. He had a soft spot for dark skin. Especially on men with a bearded and good-looking face. And there didn't seem to be another man with him.

This guy had *definite* promise.

Not only did he appear single, but he also had a thick head of black hair that wasn't so long that it made him look grungy and wasn't so short that he looked like a carbon copy of every other man who came to Provincetown. It was longer on the top, especially toward the front, but trimmed perfectly at the nape of the neck and on the sides. His unique hairstyle marked him as someone who was his own man, an original. He liked that.

Brody also enjoyed the way strands of hair fell in front of his eyes, which looked light in color. He couldn't tell what hue they were from this distance, but they looked to be a mixture of yellow, gold, and copper. How much more unique could a man get?

He also wasn't immediately lighting up a cigarette. While it didn't automatically make him a nonsmoker, it showed promise that he wasn't. His clothes also didn't look dated or filthy, and he carried himself with an air of confidence. Only the gainfully employed could pull that off in his opinion. That was yet another requirement met.

And he hadn't even talked to him yet!

All this man had to be was a sane, humble, nonwhining, childless man, and *eureka!* He'd have struck gold.

But in order to find that out, Brody would have to go up and talk to him. He just didn't have the time. What if he missed Van's cousin Eric while he was chatting up the dark-skinned hottie who might be his potential new love?

There was no reason he couldn't do both. All he had to do was go up to the man and talk to him while he kept a watchful eye for some guy who resembled Van. He'd always been a great multitasker.

Brody began his approach, and then he noticed the small problem that ruined everything.

The guy had a kid. Fuck! Right now, he was reaching down to stroke her hair. While it was a sweet gesture, since she seemed to be out of sorts, it killed the man's chance of being with Brody.

There was no way in hell he'd ever get involved with someone who had a kid. While the guy could just be traveling with the little girl, the loving look in his eyes clearly communicated that if this guy wasn't a parent, he definitely wanted to be.

Why was it so damn hard to find just one guy who'd be perfect for him?

Thanks to his parents, having a child was the biggest deal breaker there was for Brody. They had fucked him up royally. There was no way he would return that favor to any other impressionable little person. With his parentage and genes, wasn't he destined to just repeat that cycle?

He sure as hell thought so.

The little girl was cute, though, with her Rolling Stones T-shirt. He loved the Stones and most of the classic rock-and-roll bands. Even though she'd totally ruined his chance with her father, Brody had to give her props for her taste in music.

Then an idea struck that sent waves of dread coursing through his body. Could this guy be Van's cousin?

He appeared to be waiting for someone to pick him up. Most everyone else had already departed with their friends or left in a taxi or pedicab. They simply waited, and the guy was now pulling out his phone. Was it Van he was calling?

No, it couldn't be.

This guy was clearly Latino. How could he possibly be related to Van by blood?

But as more and more people departed the pier, the odds were no longer stacked in his favor.

Why the hell did his luck have to suck worse than a broken vacuum?

Just what he needed. A hot man he would love to get it on with but couldn't because of a kid he might now have to shuttle over to the party and spend an entire evening with.

Wasn't that just fucking fantastic?

ERIC ALMOST tossed his phone into the ocean when Van's cell phone switched over to voice mail for the fifth time. There was no doubt about it now. He was going to kill Van.

"Nothing?" Maddie asked. Her nails had all been chewed off. She was now biting at the skin along the edges. If he didn't hear from Van soon, she was going to lose it.

"Cell service is bad here," he said. Van had warned him that calls were often not connected or dropped because P-town didn't have enough cell towers. Something to do with nesting birds and species protection. Damn birds! "I'm sure he's on his way and is just having trouble contacting us."

"I hope you're right," she muttered. She didn't appear relieved. Now, she was not only gnawing on her skin but also picking at her shirt with her free hand. They were definitely on a countdown to a meltdown.

"Excuse me," a voice to his right said. "Are you Eric?"

The voice caught Eric by surprise, something most trained police officers didn't appreciate. He spun around and reached for the gun that wasn't in its holster because he wasn't wearing it. It was safely packed in his suitcase. The move, however, caused him to drop his phone, which crashed onto the dock. Pieces of the casing exploded everywhere.

"Jeez," the man with dirty-blond hair replied as he backed up. He held his hands in front of him, which told Eric he wasn't a threat. He even moved backward three additional steps. "Calm down. I'm not mugging you or anything. I was just wondering if you were Eric."

Who the hell was this guy? And how did he know his name?

"I'm sorry about your phone," the stranger said as he surveyed the broken bits. "I feel real bad about that."

Eric ignored the guy's concern. As he bent down to pick up his phone, he kept his eyes on the newcomer. Although he didn't think he posed a threat, it was better to be safe than sorry. Once the phone was back in his hand, he inspected the damage. It still turned on, but the casing was broken, and a bloom of shattered glass spread across the face.

Just what he didn't need after such an expensive trip—to buy a new phone.

"You didn't answer my question," the man repeated. "Are you Eric?"

"Yes, he's Eric," his daughter replied. "And I'm Maddie." She was now standing at his side. She had stopped biting her fingers, and her eyes were wide and hopeful. "Did Van send you to pick us up?"

Eric shot his daughter a warning glance. He'd taught her better than that. While he didn't think this man was going to attack them, she shouldn't be identifying him, and most definitely *not* herself, to a stranger.

"Lighten up, Papa," Maddie told him. Like always, she read him like a book. And why was she constantly telling him to lighten up? When he wasn't on alert, things usually went from bad to worse. He had experience with that. "He doesn't look like a deranged serial killer to me."

After that comment, the man increased the space between them. "No, I'm not a deranged serial killer, and yes, Van asked me to pick you up. I'm Brody. A friend of Van's. I'm supposed to take you to Gary and Quinn's for the party."

Cool relief washed over his body. Since Brody knew about Gary and Quinn, that meant he was a legitimate ride to where they needed to go. When he stared down at his daughter, though, she took the news in a different manner. Maddie's eyes changed from relief to irritation. It was too late to warn Brody about what was coming next.

"Well, you're late," she told him. She crossed her arms and peered at him through eyes that had narrowed to slits. "You were supposed to pick us up at seven o'clock. Didn't Van tell you that?"

Brody stuttered. He was most likely unaccustomed to being chastised by a nine-year-old. Although Eric wanted to intervene, he just couldn't. He was a little miffed too. If Brody had been on time, Maddie wouldn't have been so worried.

"I don't like being late," Maddie announced. "And I don't like people who are. It makes me..."—she paused and looked up at him—"...uncomfortable."

"I apologize," Brody replied once he finally found his tongue. "Van didn't tell me about that, but I *was* here early. When I agreed to pick you up, though, I left pretty quickly to get here on time, and I forgot to ask Van what you looked like, and cell service su—" He cut himself off before uttering a word unsuitable for a nine-year-old.

"Well, let's just say it's not very reliable. So I had to wait to see who was left behind."

"You could've made a sign," she advised. "Or called out for my dad as people got off the ferry."

"I guess I'm just not as smart as you," Brody replied with a shrug. After that comment, his daughter nodded. She then dropped her arms to her side, and her narrowed eyes returned to their normal size.

That was well played. Maddie was susceptible to comments about her intelligence. This Brody guy was good with agitated children. He was also pouring on the charm. The way he talked to her and not at her, the way his lips parted into a rather striking smile, and the way his gorgeous pair of light green eyes twinkled as he spoke.

It also didn't hurt that he was very handsome.

But why did staring at Brody make him feel uncomfortable? It was like his insides had turned to quicksand, and he was in danger of collapsing into himself. What was that about?

That was when Eric realized he couldn't stop staring into Brody's eyes. They were beautiful, but it wasn't their beauty that had caught him so off guard. It was that they were so familiar to him.

They reminded him of Charlie, who had the most beautiful green eyes he'd ever seen.

No doubt Maddie saw it too. She kept staring at him in awe.

How was that going to affect his daughter?

BRODY LED Eric and his daughter Maddie down the pier and toward the lot where he'd parked the Funk Van. So far, the pickup had gone less than smoothly. First, he'd incorrectly pegged Eric as a potential mate. He would've been perfect too. As stunning as Eric was from afar, he was even more remarkable up close.

Dark hair, tanned skin, built like a brick shithouse, and the most unique amber eyes he'd ever seen in his life. Talk about a walking wet dream.

At least he would've been. If Eric didn't have a daughter. Which also meant that he was most likely yet *another* happily partnered man.

Just what he needed. When happy couples were together, they were impossible to be around. When happy couples were apart, well, they were even worse than lovesick teenagers pining over their high-school sweetheart who was away at summer camp.

It was pretty sickening. Even though he wished he had someone to pine for too.

As if meeting such a hot man who did not meet his standards wasn't bad enough, he had also upset the little girl, who had a serious hate-on for tardiness. Was she gunning for perfect attendance throughout life or something?

That had been pretty fucking peculiar. But then again, what kid wasn't strange?

He certainly was in his youth. He used to eat dirt and chat with his imaginary friend Jack.

By the time he turned nine, Jack had been upgraded from imaginary friend to imaginary boyfriend. And when he let his parents in on the change in his relationship with Jack, well, they weren't exactly thrilled that their son was a faggot. His womanizing father used to shove *Playboy* magazines into his hands on the weekends that he spent with him in Boston. He somehow hoped exposing his son to fake titties and shaved kitties would cure him of his attraction to other boys.

That had been an epic fail. It had only grossed him out and made him appreciate cock and balls more.

His mother tried an even bolder approach. She bought him a stripper for his sixteenth birthday party. A party to which she had invited all his classmates, thinking they were all his friends. She had no idea that they teased him daily for having a drunken, drug-addicted mother, whose exploits they followed on MTV. Unfortunately, as the lead singer for a popular grunge band at the time, her problems with the law were documented for all to see.

So naturally, they called her names and told him he'd grow into a loser just like her.

After the party, his life got worse. He was visibly uncomfortable with the stripper pushing her fake breasts into his face and gyrating on top of him. While the other boys in the class cheered her on, he made her stop. After that, they called him Grody, which was short for Gay Brody.

What made it worse was that Joy and Patrick O'Shea sometimes called him Grody too. Such wonderful parents he had!

That was why he did his best to make Maddie feel better about his being late. His parents would have just teased him or yelled at him. So he figured doing the opposite of what they would do would be the best possible thing.

And it had worked. Thank God.

"Is that yours?" Maddie asked. She pointed to the Funk Van, and her eyes sparkled like the stars overhead.

"Well, I don't own it, but yes, that's what I drove here." She squealed in reply. This kid got stranger by the minute.

"Oh. My. God!" she screamed as she bolted for the van, dragging her suitcase behind her.

"Maddie!" Eric called after her, but his daughter paid him no attention. His eyes grew saucer wide as he scanned the mostly empty parking lot. What was he looking for? Psychopathic killers? This was Provincetown, not New York City. Eric needed to chill.

"Don't worry," he told Eric. "She'll be fine. P-town's a pretty safe place." Eric glared at him as if he was the stupidest man in the world. "Besides, it's not like we can't see her from here," he pointed out.

Eric took three deep breaths before calming down. For a big guy, he was easily set on edge. Where was this guy's wife? Or husband? Or whatever he had. He certainly didn't want to have to bring him down from the rafters all week.

He signed on to pick him up from the ferry. That was it.

Once that was done, he doubted he'd be spending any more time with Eric and Maddie than was necessary.

"Sorry," Eric finally said. His voice was low but sturdy. He could probably hear this man whisper in a windstorm. What happened if he ever shouted? Brody definitely didn't want to find out. When he spoke again, Eric's eyes didn't meet Brody's. He kept them glued on his daughter. "I'm just very protective."

No shit! But he couldn't fault Eric. At least he cared for his daughter. His parents had tried, but they never really succeeded at anything when it came to him. "No worries," he finally replied. "She's your daughter."

"Yes," Eric nodded. A smile grew across his face, and that smile reflected a warmth that he had yet to see from the serious, easily startled, and overprotective man. It made him even more stunning.

Fuck! He *would* be attracted to a man there was absolutely zero future with.

"This van is awesome!" Maddie shrieked at them as they drew closer. "It's definitely my kind of ride."

"You like it?" he asked as he unlocked the door and let her hop inside.

"Like? I *love* it!" She spread out on the second-row bench seat with a smile plastered all over her face. "I imagine Jim Morrison rode around in a van like this. Maybe even Jimi Hendrix."

"You really like classic rock, huh?"

"Yeah, I do," she beamed. "It's the best! Much better than the cr—" She stopped and eyed her father as he arched an eyebrow at her. "Well, the stuff that girls my age listen to. I'm not a fan of bubblegum music. Music should have a soul. And a message. It should fill your whole body. Popular music just doesn't do that."

How old was this girl again? He glanced over at Eric, who just smiled and nodded. He didn't seem fazed by her in the slightest. "Well, although I do like today's pop music," Brody admitted, to which she groaned, "my favorite band is Lynyrd Skynyrd."

This immediately got Maddie's attention. She sprung upright in the seat. "What are your favorite Skynyrd songs?"

"Well, there's 'Sweet Home Alabama' and 'Freebird.'"

"Of course," she said, waving him to continue. "*Everybody* loves those. What else?"

Why did this feel like a test? If he didn't pass it, he would likely forever be relegated to doofus status, and for whatever reason, he most definitely didn't want that.

"Well, there's also 'That Smell,'" he admitted, to which she nodded agreeably. "I appreciate what Gary Rossington and Ronnie Van Zant were doing with that song. They were trying to own up to the horrible accident ol' Gary was in because of drugs. Trying to change his life. I think that song's got a great message."

"I agree," she replied. A grin spread across her cute little lips. He had succeeded in answering correctly, and he wasn't going to be a doofus for now and ever more. Thank God. She then began spouting all she knew about the band, from its original incarnation as the Noble Five in 1967 to the plane crash that virtually ended the band's career in 1977.

"Thanks," Eric whispered as he got into the front seat and closed the door.

"For what?" he asked as he started the vehicle.

"Just thanks" was all Eric answered before buckling himself in and interrupting Maddie long enough to tell her to buckle up.

Why did Eric have such a huge grin plastered on *his* face and just what was he being thanked for?

Chapter Five

THE RIDE from the ferry to the condo hadn't been a quiet one. His daughter chattered nonstop about Lynyrd Skynyrd with Brody. The two of them were seemingly becoming pals. Eric had never seen Maddie take to someone new so quickly. She wasn't an unfriendly girl. She was typically very polite. Just unwilling to open up. She'd lost too many people in her life to so eagerly jump into making new friends. Being cautious among unfamiliar faces had been her recent approach to the world.

That was why he'd thanked Brody for putting her at ease prior to driving away from the wharf. Of course, Brody had no clue what he had done, but that hadn't been important. After her almost meltdown at being picked up late, he'd imagined a very long evening of calming her down. Of reminding her that everything was fine and would be okay.

That nothing bad had happened and that nothing bad *would* happen.

Ever since... well, it had just become a part of their routine. Especially before and after he went off to work. She fretted that something would happen to him while he was out on patrol. He did his best to allay those fears, but she wasn't happy until she set her eyes on him again after his shift was done. Then she would calm down. At least until he had to drop her off at school and go to work again. Then the process repeated itself.

That was what he'd envisioned occurring tonight. Soothing Maddie, showing her that Van was okay, and making her see that everything was all right.

But he didn't have to do that. Brody had so easily taken her mind off her worries, without knowing what was going on and seemingly without realizing what he'd done.

How did Brody do that? Was it the green eyes, which reminded her of Charlie? It could definitely explain why she was treating him as if he was someone she'd known all her life.

What else could it be?

For Eric, the similar eye color didn't put him at ease. It made him uncomfortable. If that was truly the case, then why was he constantly stealing glances? Perhaps it was because he'd regretted not looking into Charlie's beautiful eyes one more time. But here he was, staring into eyes that were the same pale green that used to make his heart flutter and make him feel at home.

The problem was that Brody was *not* Charlie. And looking into Brody's eyes made him miss his husband even more than he already did. How was he going to handle an entire week around this man? With luck, maybe Brody wouldn't be around them much. Maybe he'd just drop them off at the condo and exit their lives, never to be seen again.

It was entirely within the realm of possibility. Wasn't it?

"We're here," Brody announced as he turned the van onto a gravel driveway. He parked the vehicle before the condo on the far right, which was teeming with people. Broadway music was also blaring from the structure. This was definitely the place. Van loved show tunes. From the sound of it, Zach did too. "Bachelor Party Central."

"Yay!" Maddie cheered from the backseat. "I can't wait to see Uncle Van." Her face twisted in displeasure. "But I'm not a fan of their choice of music."

Brody laughed. "Me either. But when you get married, you can play as much Skynyrd as you want." He turned off the vehicle and hopped out. Maddie scrambled out of her seat and out the sliding door that Brody opened for her.

She usually waited for Eric to let her out of a car. What was up with *that*?

"When *I* get married, I'll have the best classic rock cover band ever playing at my reception. And they will be under strict orders *not* to play 'The Chicken Dance.' I *hate* that song." As if suddenly remembering she had a father, she looked over her shoulder at him. "You don't think Van will play that song at his reception. Do you, Papa?"

Eric shrugged. "We'll just have to wait and see."

She scrunched up her nose, displeased with that answer.

"Thanks for the ride," he told Brody as he shook his hand. His palm was warm and inviting, just like his eyes. "But I think we've got it from here."

"No problem," Brody replied with a grin. His teeth were so perfect and white. When Eric realized he'd stared at them for a second longer than was necessary, an unfamiliar warmth spread across his cheeks. What the hell was the matter with him? He hadn't looked at another man in years. The only person he'd ever wanted was Charlie.

Yeah, it was definitely time for Brody to go home.

"Let me just get our bags and then you can be on your way."

"Just leave them," Brody replied. "I'm not going anywhere. I'm here for the party too."

Well, fuck! He wasn't getting rid of Brody that easily after all.

"Besides, the van's not mine. Zach borrowed it from a friend, so it's staying here till he returns it."

"Great!" Maddie grabbed hold of his hand and tugged him toward the party. "Let's go see Van, Papa."

Eric nodded and allowed Maddie to lead him up the steps to the laughter that thundered from the condo. He was just as excited to see his cousin as Maddie was, but at the moment, all he could focus on were Brody's kind eyes and his warm touch.

That had to stop. Immediately.

"ERIC!" VAN shouted as Eric and Maddie entered the party, which was in full swing. There were people everywhere, drinking and talking. Although most of them were now staring at them, since Van had yelled his greeting at the top of his lungs. When his cousin's arms were wrapped around him, delivering a powerful hug, Eric found himself lifted off the ground.

When had Van become so strong?

"I want you to meet my future husband," Van said after setting Eric back on the ground. "This is Zach."

"Nice to meet you," Zach said. He extended his hand and a broad smile in greeting.

Eric shook the offered hand and marveled at how red Zach's hair was. He'd seen pictures of Zach from the photos Van had shared, but he'd never seen hair so red or skin so pale before. On Zach, the combination made him look stunning. "Same here," he replied. "It appears as if my cousin has chosen well." He turned to Van and winked. It was time for the teasing to commence. It was something they'd done ever since they were kids. And it was a playfulness that hadn't come over him in years. "For once."

"Ah, family," Van said. "You can't live with them, and you can't chop them into pieces and feed them to sharks."

"At least not those who work in law enforcement for the great state of Massachusetts."

"Well, it would certainly make it more difficult," Van conceded. "Not impossible. I just don't know if you're worth the effort."

"I'm worth my weight in gold."

Van looked him up and down and nodded. "Yeah, you've definitely put on some weight."

"It's called muscle," Eric pointed out. "You know, what you didn't have until you turned twenty-one and puberty kicked in."

"Well, I might have been a late bloomer, but at least I didn't peak in high school," Van replied. "How sad for you."

Before Eric could let loose another barb, Maddie interrupted. "Are you two mad at each other, Papa?"

He smiled down at his daughter, who stared up at him in grave concern. Maddie wasn't used to seeing him banter with anyone. It was usually just the two of them at home. Letting loose and having fun was something new to her, and she hadn't ever seen his more playful side. Well, not since Charlie. "No, angel, I'm not," he told her with a pat on her head. "Your Uncle Van and I are just being boys."

Maddie frowned. "Boys are weird."

"Yes, we are," Van chimed in. "But enough of our teasing. It's about time you got here. I was beginning to worry."

"Blame Brody," Maddie commented. "He was late."

The previous merriment on Van's face melted away, and his eyes widened in obvious concern. If Van had forgotten what Eric had told him earlier, he most certainly remembered now. "I'm so sorry," Van said. His face contorted in absolute misery. "I should have told Brody about that."

Before he could say anything, Maddie answered for him. She seemed to have a knack for that these days. "It's okay," she said. She then grabbed Brody's hand and tugged him forward. "I got on him for that, but he likes Lynyrd Skynyrd. So he can't be *that* bad."

"Well, you don't really know him yet," Van told Maddie.

"Hey, now!" Brody pouted. "Don't be ruining my rep. I just spent the drive over here getting Maddie to like me."

Van rolled his eyes at Brody before turning back to Maddie. "Don't trust that guy," he warned while giving her a playful wink. He leaned down and whispered in her ear. "He likes Britney Spears."

Maddie's head snapped back around to size Brody up. "Tell me it isn't so. Tell me you don't like Britney Spears."

It was obvious from Brody's even stare that he wasn't very pleased with Van at the moment. He apparently wanted to stay in Maddie's good graces. How adorable was that? Wait, that wasn't right. He didn't mean adorable. No, he just appreciated the fact that Brody wanted to make a good impression.

Calling him adorable had just been a slip. That was all.

"I'm waiting for an answer." She tapped her right foot lightly on the wooden floor.

Brody exhaled. "Fine. I admit it. I like Britney Spears, but I told you earlier that I liked popular music."

Maddie frowned. "Liking popular music and liking Britney Spears are two totally different things." She stared up at Van and grinned. "You're right. I definitely can't trust someone who likes Britney Spears."

Brody groaned while Maddie and Van broke out into laughter. Maddie had obviously inherited her father's love of teasing and had found a conspirator in Van. Brody seemed oblivious to the joke. He seriously appeared worried that Maddie might no longer like him. He stared down at her with wide, hopeful eyes, as if waiting for her to release him from his agony.

Eric regretted wanting to get rid of Brody earlier. He seemed a good man who was great with kids. It wasn't Brody's fault that his eyes reminded him of Charlie. He had to look past that and judge the man for who he was, and so far, there was nothing wrong with Brody in his book.

Brody appeared to be a nice guy. So what if Eric found him somewhat attractive? He could be attracted to someone without doing anything about it. Cal, the new deputy back at the station, was hot, and it wasn't like anything was *ever* going to come of that. Especially since Cal was straighter than Mel Gibson and about as homophobic as the actor too. Eric wasn't exactly looking for another relationship anyway. He already had his shot at love. And while it had been great while it lasted, he wasn't making a return trip down that road.

He couldn't handle that kind of pain again. And neither could Maddie.

Besides, what could be wrong with just being Brody's friend? He was going to need someone to hang out with while Van was busy with wedding preparations. He certainly didn't expect his cousin to devote every single minute of the day to him. And one glance around the room told him that pretty much everyone else had brought a significant other along with them. Since Brody didn't appear to have anyone hanging on him, he might be the only other single person in the bunch. After being a single dad for the last few years, he'd learned that hanging out with happy couples got a bit tiresome.

Brody might just help keep him sane.

"Fine, I forgive you." His daughter's voice brought him out of his thoughts. She had finally granted Brody the clemency he'd been hoping for. "But no Britney for you while I'm here," she commanded.

Brody saluted her. "Aye, aye, Captain."

Maddie grinned. "I could get used to this captain business." She turned to stare up at him. "What do you think, Papa?"

"If you're the captain, then I'm the admiral."

"Never mind," she frowned. "I'm always outranked."

"Better get used to that," Brody told her. "At least until you have your own kids. Then you'll hold the power of grandchildren over him."

Her eyes lit up. "I hadn't thought about that!" She rubbed her hands together like the devious little schemer she could sometimes be. "Oh, the power I shall wield."

Before he could tell his daughter to bring it down a notch, Van grabbed him by the elbow. "Come on over here, Eric. I've got some people who have been dying to meet you." And as Van led him away, Eric was surprised that Maddie didn't follow him.

Instead, she stayed behind and chatted with Brody.

Over the last few years, whenever they were together, she was like his shadow. But after one meeting with Brody, she seemed to forget all about her paranoia and her constant need to be at her father's side. While he wanted to see this as a positive step in the right direction on her road to recovery, he didn't like the crushing weight of abandonment that dragged him downward.

What was he supposed to do if Maddie wouldn't constantly need him anymore?

AFTER BEING introduced to the entire Kelly clan and all of Van's friends, Eric required fresh air. He'd grown unaccustomed to so much socializing, and it was wearing him out. He hadn't been to a party in years. Not since he and Charlie had gone to poker night at the sheriff's house, where Charlie not only charmed the entire department but also walked away with the pot.

Charlie had always been good at bluffing, which was why Charlie had consistently been able to surprise him. It wasn't that his husband told lies. He was just very good at hiding what he was up to.

He had no clue that Charlie had planned a vacation getaway in Hawaii for their first wedding anniversary. When they had discussed gifts, Charlie made him promise not to be extravagant. So he hadn't. Eric had gotten him a book of poetry by Walt Whitman, Charlie's favorite poet.

Boy, did he feel like an ass when Charlie presented him with two round-trip tickets to Hawaii. Charlie claimed to love the first edition of *Leaves of Grass*, but how could a book compete with a tropical destination? There was no comparison in Eric's mind.

But Charlie was like that. He enjoyed throwing Eric off, making him think that nothing was going on when he had some grand plan. That was what he had been doing that night. Putting the finishing touches on the plans he'd made for their sixth anniversary, when, well, when it happened.

Life with Charlie had certainly been an adventure.

And being around all these people, all of them so full of life, and watching Maddie flitter about like a social butterfly he'd never seen before, it was just too much.

He missed Charlie, and more than anything, he wished his husband could be here with him now. Even though he hadn't seen much of Provincetown in the few hours since his arrival, he knew Charlie would have liked it here.

This was his element. Being surrounded by groups of people he could get to know better, and making preparations to celebrate what was likely going to be a spectacular wedding.

This was certainly more Charlie's cup of tea than it was his.

Eric had trouble getting close to people he didn't already know. Like Maddie had unfortunately learned, most forged relationships came to an end one way or the other. No matter how happy they were. He hadn't always been like that. He had once held his arms open to the world and had a come-what-may attitude.

But that had ended in middle school. After what happened to his sister, Kimberly.

And watching Maddie seemingly shed the cautious way she'd lived until now worried him. Was his daughter just setting herself up for more heartache? And what could he do to prevent it?

"Needed a break too, huh?"

The voice pulled Eric out of his thoughts and from the melancholy that too frequently swirled about him. As he turned to face Brody, who had joined him along the railing, the tentacles of depression tugged at him, wanting to pull him down beneath the familiar waters of gloom. "Yeah," he finally responded. The swirling arms yanked on him, refusing to be cast off. But he wasn't going to allow them to win. He had to be strong. Not for himself, but for his daughter. "I'm not a very social person."

"I got that," Brody announced after he took a sip of his beer.

"Really?" he asked. He shook the despair from his body and kicked the insistent limbs away. They wouldn't claim him. At least not today.

Brody nodded. A crooked grin sloped across his lips. If he looked any more like a mischievous devil, he'd have horns growing out the top of his head. "You seem to be having as much fun as I am," he whispered, as if they were coconspirators to some secret plot. "I can tell by the way people are constantly talking to you while you just mostly listen. I mean, you've barely said five words to me since I picked you up at the ferry. I guess you're just not much of a talker, huh?"

"Not really, no," he answered with a shake of his head. "I guess I'm just used to Charlie picking up the slack at events like this."

"I wish I had a Charlie to do that for me," Brody replied. His voice was wistful and faraway, as if he were in a dream. "But it's just me. And it's been just me for quite some time now."

"Why is that?" he asked. Brody immediately gazed into the contents of his beer bottle. The happy-go-lucky guy who chatted with his daughter and conversed with most everyone at the party disappeared. In his place stood a sad and lonely man.

What was he doing, asking such a personal question? That wasn't like him at all. He didn't poke his nose into other people's business. If they wanted to share, that was fine, but he didn't go digging around into other people's lives. When he did, he typically made a mess of things. What the hell was the matter with him? "Sorry," he said. "I didn't mean to pry."

Brody waved off the apology and took another sip of his beer. After a few moments the sadness lifted, and the man he'd met earlier once again stepped forward. "Just haven't found the right man, I guess. Well, that's not entirely true. I did find him in college, but I was stupid and let him get away."

"That sucks," Eric responded. What else could he say? Sorry you screwed up a chance at happiness? Yeah, that wouldn't have been inappropriate at all. "What about now?" There he went again, asking stupid questions. Was there no way to shut him the hell up? Maybe he could use the glue gun he'd seen on the kitchen counter while he was talking to Gary and Quinn. That might just do the trick.

"I don't really have an answer to that," Brody admitted. "It's not that I'm not looking. Because I am. Like, everywhere. But I just haven't met the right guy who's perfect for me. I have some very high standards, you know."

"No, I don't know. But if you're looking for perfection, chances are you'll never find it."

"Really?" Brody asked. "Your Charlie isn't perfect?"

Eric turned away. He didn't like talking about Charlie. Especially not with a stranger who had eyes that made him think of his husband.

"I mean, he made you come to P-town by yourself. Probably because he had to work or something, so I guess he can't be *that* perfect. Right?"

Eric turned back around and stared into Brody's smiling eyes. Evidently, Brody had no idea that Charlie was… dead. There, he said it. His husband, the man he loved more than anyone else, was dead and had been for the past two years.

God, he hated admitting that to himself, much less telling someone else.

He'd already gone through the process of condolences, and it had almost been as bad as Charlie's actual death. It tore him apart to greet other people as they stood in line after Charlie's funeral, just waiting to shake his hand and offer a hug or word of comfort.

A fat lot of good that fucking did.

They didn't have to go home with a bereft seven-year-old who couldn't stop crying. They didn't have to deal with her constant nightmares. Or with the dreams that plagued his sleep, where Charlie had never died and they were happy. Then when he woke up, he had to face the passing of his husband all over again. They didn't have to pick up the pieces of a shattered life or a broken heart and try to be human again because there was a child who needed him.

Their pity-filled words could do none of that.

He had to do it by himself. As he had learned to do over and over again.

"Jeez, Eric, I'm sorry," Brody said. The previous amusement had disappeared entirely. Brody now stared at him in concern. "I didn't mean to touch on a sore spot. I tend to do that sometimes. Speak before thinking. My mother used to call it diarrhea of the mouth. Look, I'm sure Charlie had a good reason for not being here. Even though you're pissed at him for *not* being here. But I'm sure he is a really good guy."

Not *is* a good guy. He *was* a good guy. The best man he'd ever known.

He'd never been happier than when he met Charlie. They went on a picnic in the middle of Boston Common for their first date the following weekend. Or when they moved into their shabby, run-down apartment. Or when he proposed to Charlie on the Alaskan cruise. Or when they danced their first dance as husbands, or decided to give surrogacy a try and conceive a child, or when they brought Maddie home for the first time, or any of the other scores of things they did together that were a mundane part of life. Like cooking dinner, watching a movie, or waking up on Sunday morning and having breakfast in bed, followed by a sweaty round of bed-breaking sex.

Those had been the best moments of his life, and Eric cherished each and every memory. But that was all they were now. Memories. There would be no more because Charlie had been taken from him, and he'd been left alone to raise the daughter that they were supposed to raise together.

So why couldn't he tell Brody any of that and just admit that his husband was dead? That Charlie's absence wasn't because of work. That he wasn't angry with Charlie for making him come to his cousin's wedding while Charlie stayed home.

Why couldn't he just say that he was angry with Charlie for being dead?

He couldn't do any of those things because, as insane as it sounded, for just a moment Charlie *was* alive. At least in Brody's perception. And for just a second he was alive again for Eric too.

"Are you okay?" Brody asked. He'd set his beer on the railing and was rubbing Eric's shoulder.

He needed to correct Brody. Tell him that Charlie was dead, not alive. "Listen, Brody, there's something you should know." But just as he spoke those words, laughter boomed from inside. A quick glance through the patio doors revealed how happy everyone was inside, and his daughter was a part of it. Right now, Van was giving her a piggyback ride.

How could he bring his grief here to a place with such happiness? This wasn't about him. This was about Zach and Van.

"What is it?" Brody asked. "What should I know?"

"You're right about Charlie," he said. "He's a good man."

"I knew it," Brody commented with a pat of congratulations on his back.

He didn't like misleading Brody, but now wasn't the time to have such a depressing conversation. That was for a moment much further away from the happiness that surrounded him. Besides, Brody would find out about Charlie eventually.

Someone was bound to tell him.

Maybe this was what he needed anyway. After all, this was supposed to be a vacation. Maybe what he needed the most was a vacation from Charlie's death.

"Thanks for the talk," he said. "I haven't felt this good about things in a while."

"You're welcome," Brody replied. He would have to be staring down the barrel of a gun to look more apprehensive than he did at that moment, looking back into Eric's eyes. "I'm not sure what I did that you're thanking me for, but you're welcome anyway."

"Well, you've started me on the path to having a good time. I think I'll be able to do that now. I'm not as stressed as before."

"I can see that," Brody commented. "You look almost chipper."

Eric couldn't help the grin that stretched across his face. "I feel chipper," he admitted. "I can't wait to explore the town with Maddie tomorrow. Got any recommendations?"

Brody nodded. "A few. If you want, I can show the two of you around. I don't have anything else to do, since tomorrow's my day off. And I know everyone else will be busy with wedding prep, so entertaining you and Maddie might just save me from work detail."

"You don't mind?" he asked. He certainly didn't want to be an imposition.

"Not at all. You've never worked under Gary's iron fist. It isn't pretty."

"Then let's do it," Eric said with a pat to Brody's back. What could be wrong with a guided tour through town courtesy of Brody? Maddie sure as heck liked him, and despite his eyes, which were a painful reminder of Charlie, Brody appeared to be a genuinely nice guy. It would be a great change of pace to actually have some fun for once. Lord knows he needed it. "Now, let's get back to the party and enjoy ourselves. And tomorrow, we'll let the fun continue."

Brody smiled as Eric led him back inside.

Although his therapist might call what he was now doing denial, he didn't care. For this moment, he was married to Charlie again. And thinking that way made living each minute a little more bearable than before.

What could be wrong about that?

Chapter Six

WHAT THE hell was he doing? It was a beautiful sunny morning in Provincetown, he had the day off, and instead of sleeping in or continuing his search for the perfect man, here Brody was with Eric and Maddie, taking them on a guided sightseeing tour.

Why had he agreed to this again?

It couldn't just be that Eric was one hot motherfucker, could it? But as Brody glanced to his right, where Eric strolled beside him on their walk over to the Pilgrim Monument, he had to admit that it was a pretty big reason. Eric's white T-shirt clung to his broad chest and his biceps bulged nicely even in their relaxed state.

Fuck! He was one hot man. And those amber eyes? Damn!

He needed to get a serious grip.

They had a good time last night, once Eric unbunched his panties after their talk on the patio. Although he still didn't understand how he had helped Eric work through whatever the hell had been going on, he'd been glad to see Eric's mood change. And it had lasted for the remainder of the evening and still persisted this morning, when he dropped by their condo to pick them up.

Instead of a distant stare through which he appeared to simply observe the world go by, Eric seemed to actually be in the here and now. But he wasn't fooled. No matter how hard Eric tried to act as if everything was okay, something dark hid just beneath the seemingly perfect calm.

It wasn't anything dangerous. He'd learned to spot trouble after living with his mom, whose best friends were all junkies or drug dealers. So it wasn't anything bad like that. It appeared more like all-encompassing sadness. As if Eric was drowning in a tidal wave of pain, just looking for an outstretched hand to pull him to shore.

But how could he know that or see it when no one else appeared capable of noticing? Like his cousin, who definitely knew Eric better, yet Van seemed oblivious. Why wasn't Brody?

Maybe that was because his childhood had been an exercise in torture. He'd never been happy as a kid, traveling in the tour bus with his mom and her band and most often ignored and overlooked. Like that time they forgot him in Seattle and he had to spend the night in the bus station, a little boy of ten, freaked out and scared to death his mother wouldn't show up.

He had to watch his mother go through detox and then fall off the wagon numerous times. He'd seen their belongings repossessed and then regained after his mother's stint on *Celebrity Rehab*.

Most of his life had been like one bad movie, and he'd often disconnected himself from it. So he could survive.

Was that what Eric was doing? Putting on a front so he didn't have to deal with whatever crap he preferred to ignore? If that was the case, it wasn't going to work.

No one knew that better than he did.

It wasn't until after he'd dealt with the crap in his life and confronted his parents that Brody was able to truly live. Had he gone about it the wrong way and made some mistakes? Most definitely. He gave up a chance at happiness with Teddy out of fear that he would just make the same mistakes his parents had. That was why he'd never really pursued a relationship since.

But now, well, now he was secure enough in himself to see that he'd never be anything like either of them.

That was exactly why he shouldn't be here, climbing the hill toward the Pilgrim Monument and playing tour guide. No matter how hot Eric was—and he was un-*fucking*-believably hot with all that tanned skin and muscle—there was zero to gain from this effort.

Eric was married *with* a kid.

Then why was he wasting his time?

He'd already squandered away enough of his life while trying to figure out what he wanted. Now that he had, did he really want to waste a day off on some hot guy with a kid? Even if that guy looked like he *really* needed someone to save him?

"We're almost there," he told them.

Evidently so.

Why the hell was he doing this? Eric had already found his perfect husband, Charlie. They even had an adorable little rug rat. Brody should be focusing on *his* needs, not altering his plans to entertain two people he'd likely never see again after the wedding.

"It's so pretty," Maddie commented as they drew closer to the Pilgrim Monument. "It looks like a giant rook. I sure wish I could play chess with it."

"You know how to play chess?"

She stared at him as if that were a silly question. "Of course I do." Her tone was a combination of incredulity and boastful pride. "I'm pretty good too. I beat Papa all the time."

"That she does," Eric said. "I don't like to play with her anymore. She's ruthless."

Maddie rolled her eyes. "I play to win. Or else why play at all?"

It was hard to disagree with that completely honest appraisal. Especially since Maddie allowed a precious little smile to light on her lips before skipping toward the front steps of the building's entrance in her Queen T-shirt.

Why did he find Maddie so darn cute? Well, besides the fact that she was completely adorable and brighter than most adults he'd met. He'd never liked kids before. Much less hung out with them. Not only were they constant reminders of his lost youth, but they tended to be whiny pains in the butt.

But Maddie wasn't like that.

She'd actually grown on him rather quickly. He hadn't seen that one coming. When he first saw her and Eric on the pier, he naturally assumed she'd be a snotty little shit like most kids were these days. But she'd surprised him.

She had a good head on her shoulders and a quick tongue without being a smartass. He found that impressive. She also loved classic rock about as much as he did, yet he probably knew less about his favorite bands than what she had stored in her adult-size brain. How'd that happen? Most girls her age drooled over teenage pop icons. Not Maddie. She preferred her music with an edge. Just like him.

Maybe that was why he liked Maddie so much. She represented what he could have been if he'd had better parents.

"You okay?" Eric asked.

He nodded, forcing the could-have-beens from his mind. "Just marveling at your daughter."

"Join the club," Eric replied with a lopsided grin. "She amazes me every day."

"I bet," Brody said as he started up the steps. Maddie was already at the top, waving them up. She was champing at the bit to begin the journey up the over-two-hundred-foot-tall structure.

"Thanks for giving us the tour," Eric told him as they made their way up the stairs. "I appreciate it."

"Not a problem." His comment surprised him because it was true. No matter how much he had just complained to himself about doing this, he enjoyed their company. He had since he first picked them up at the pier. Yes, today detoured his quest, but maybe that was what he needed. Some time away from the man hunt. Taking a day off might give him some perspective. Let him see why he'd been unable to find someone when everyone else around him already had a significant other. Besides, making new friends had never hurt him before. He used to thrive on it.

This might end up being exactly what he needed.

THIS WAS exactly what Eric needed. Spending time with someone who didn't know what he'd been through. Why hadn't he thought of this before? Ever since last night, he'd been able to release some of the grief he'd carried around with him. He actually had a full night's sleep. No nightmares about Charlie caused him to spring out of bed. And when he woke up, the usual dread of another day without his husband didn't immediately weigh him down.

He actually looked forward to getting up and exploring the town.

That surprised the hell out of him. When had he last awoken to the sound of chirping birds and actually whistled along with them? The fact he couldn't remember told him it had been too long. Even Maddie had been surprised. She had stared at him with wide eyes. It was as if she couldn't believe what she was hearing. For his daughter to be so dumbfounded by his good mood told him he'd been wallowing far too much.

He needed to get a grip and change his perspective. That was exactly what Brody had unknowingly helped him do.

For as long as he was with Brody, Charlie remained alive because Brody didn't know any differently. That meant he wouldn't be greeted with eyes filled with sorrow. Or with the sympathetic head tilt and deep sigh. It was as if people saw only heartache when they looked at him.

That had to change, which was why he still hadn't told Brody the truth. Brody was probably the only person he knew who didn't know the whole horrible story, and while it didn't bring Charlie back, it was what he needed right now. Was it the most honest thing he'd ever done? No. But he wasn't trying to deceive his new friend. By remaining ignorant of the reality, Brody was actually helping him.

More than he even realized.

"It's a beautiful day, isn't it?" Brody asked, at his side.

Eric lifted his face to the sky, and the sun's rays reached out to him. It was as if hundreds of warm fingers were caressing his face and welcoming him back to the land of the living. All around him were families, both gay and straight, with their laughing children. They scampered around on the expansive lawn on which the Pilgrim Monument sat, their arms open to the gorgeous day that shone down upon them all. A slight breeze swept around the hill the monument perched on, bringing with it the sweet scent of the flowers that bloomed around the gated perimeter. Eric inhaled deeply before finally replying, "Yes, it is."

Brody's sunglasses hid his green eyes from view, but they couldn't prevent Eric from noticing the big smile that stretched across

Brody's face. The expression clearly revealed Brody was feeling a bit better too. Last night, when they'd been talking about Brody's search for the perfect man, he'd detected a crushing sadness inside the happy-go-lucky man who had picked them up from the pier and charmed his daughter.

That melancholy was nowhere to be found. Eric was glad. There was enough sadness in the world already, and they both undoubtedly needed to get over themselves. Perhaps today wasn't just good for him. Maybe it was what Brody needed too.

"Are we going all the way to the top?" Maddie asked as she sprinted toward them. She had run all the way to the base of the monument and then ran back to them when they weren't keeping up. The slight slant of her lips revealed that she wasn't pleased by their snail's pace.

"Yes," Brody replied. "It's a requirement for everyone who visits here."

"Well, if we keep going at your current rate of speed, we'll make it to the top by sometime tomorrow afternoon."

Brody laughed. Eric just rolled his eyes. "Don't encourage her," he said to Brody. "She thinks amusement gives her license to be a smarty-pants."

"Who? Me?" Maddie asked. She pointed to herself with a look of complete innocence plastered across her face. If this were Broadway, her performance might snag her a Tony.

"Yes, you," Eric replied. He rubbed his hand roughly across the top of her head. The gesture elicited a playful scowl from his daughter. While she wasn't a girly-girl, she had enough girl in her to absolutely hate for her hair to be messed up. She definitely got that from Charlie, whose hair *always* had to be perfect.

"You know I hate when you do that." Maddie took her hair out of her ponytail and tried to smooth out the misplaced strands.

"I do," he replied. "Which is why I do it so often."

"I'm going to start pretending that nothing you do bothers me. Maybe then you won't do them anymore."

"That'll never happen. I know you too well."

Maddie studied him closely. Her eyes narrowed, and she looked him up and down. She only ever did that when she was about to make an observation. But when she opened her mouth, no words came out. Instead, she looked from him to Brody and back to him. What was that grin for?

"What?" he asked.

"Nothing." Her smile broadened. Turning back around, she hauled ass back to the monument.

"What was that look about?" Brody asked.

Eric shrugged. "Your guess is as good as mine."

"Come on, ladies," Maddie yelled from under the arched stone entryway that led into the Pilgrim Monument. A mischievous grin tugged the left side of her mouth upward. "Take off your pumps and put on your sneakers."

"Did your daughter just call us out in front of all these people?" Brody asked.

Eric went mute. Unfortunately, he couldn't say the same thing for the parents who milled around them. Most of them chuckled, clearly used to being embarrassed by their children as well. Some of the older kids snickered at them, though. They even pointed at them while repeating the word "ladies."

"Are we going to let her get away with that?" Brody asked. A devilish smile snaked across his face.

"No, we aren't. Let's get her."

He and Brody took off at top speed toward Maddie. She shrieked in surprise before disappearing into the monument and up the stairs.

MADDIE HAD made it about halfway up the monument before he and Eric had caught up to her. She'd been giggling uncontrollably the entire time they chased her, taunting them about how their high heels were holding them back. But when they finally overtook her, she'd surprised Brody by not pleading for mercy.

Instead, she accepted her fate, which happened to be an extended tickle session doled out by her father, who held her upside down by her legs. Unlike most kids, she didn't beg for him to stop. She reminded him, through fitful bursts of laughter, that excessive tickling was once thought to be the cause of stuttering.

Was that even true, and just where did she get all these facts?

Right now, though, finding out whether there was a connection between tickling and stuttering was the furthest thing from his mind. Eric's white shirt had ridden up his chest while he'd been torturing Maddie. His muscular, tanned stomach was exposed, as well as the patch of dark hair that encircled his belly button. It charted a delicious path down to the waistband of his tight shorts before disappearing beneath the fabric.

Fuck! What he wouldn't give to follow that trail to its treasure.

"You're killing me here," Maddie screeched.

Eric continued his playful assault. "Maybe next time you'll think twice about calling me a lady."

What the hell was he doing? Eric was a married man. Brody shouldn't be lusting after some other man's man. He'd never done that before meeting Eric, and he most certainly was *not* a home wrecker. It was one of the character traits he planned on not inheriting from his parents, who had more affairs than they had marriages. Which was saying a whole hell of a lot.

His lustful thoughts needed to be reined in. But why couldn't he stop looking at Eric's furry stomach? Or his biceps, which bulged outward as he held his daughter to his chest and continued to tickle her sides?

What he was doing was inappropriate, and he was more than a little ashamed.

"What's wrong?"

Eric's question pulled him out of his thoughts. When he met Eric's gaze, he noticed that Eric had placed his daughter back on the stairway, and the two of them were staring at him. Oh God. Had he been caught ogling Eric?

"Nothing," he said. His cheeks were on fire. They couldn't be as red as they felt, could they? "I was just watching the two of you be silly."

"Yeah, right," Maddie teased. The mischievous glint in her eyes revealed she didn't believe him. But if she'd caught him staring at her father, then why wasn't she upset with him? If the grin that spread across her face was any indication, she was pleased. What was up with that?

"Shall we continue to the top?" he asked, needing to distract them both from the uncomfortable silence that settled into the stairwell.

"Sure," Eric answered. He pulled his shirt back down, covering up the chiseled abs Brody desperately wanted to lick. "We've come this far." He started up the stairs with Maddie following him. After a few steps, she peeked over her shoulder and winked at him.

What the hell did that mean?

IT TOOK them about another twenty minutes to make it to the top of the Pilgrim Monument. They would have made it sooner if his daughter hadn't stopped at every dedication stone along the way. The names of each town and the town's incorporation date were etched into the walls of the monument at various points during the ascent, and Maddie was never one to pass up a historical moment.

As they climbed their way to the top, she explained that the Pilgrim Monument was the tallest all-granite structure in the country, and there was much controversy around the monument's design, which was modeled after some tower in Italy.

Eric appreciated his daughter's curiosity, but did she have to research *everything*? It made him feel stupid. He didn't know half the things she did, and he was more than three times her age.

When they finally exited to the observation deck, the sheer beauty of the panoramic view of Provincetown finally silenced her. There were some things that didn't need to be explained.

Before them, Cape Cod Bay sparkled in the blazing sun. It was as if millions of diamonds had been spread across the surface. Dozens of boats also spotted the harbor. Their white hulls intensified the sun's glare and made Eric regret forgetting his sunglasses at the condo. He shifted his attention away from the pristine blue ocean to the grandeur of Provincetown spread out around them. To the right stretched the west end, where he'd heard most of the shops and clubs were located. On the left was the art district, which was much quieter but also more out of the way.

"Papa, look over here."

Eric followed his daughter around the left corner, where a large and rather old-looking cemetery, judging from the timeworn headstones, was visible. From this distance, the grave markers resembled a smattering of gray teeth, which jutted out at rakish angles.

"You've found the cemetery, I see," Brody said to his left.

"Sure did," Maddie replied. "How old do you think the oldest tombstone is?"

"I actually know this," Brody said. He sounded as pleased as a contestant on *Jeopardy!*

"You do?" The surprise in Maddie's question made Eric laugh. Brody didn't find it amusing. He crossed his arms over his chest and stuck his tongue out at her.

"Real mature," she replied before turning her attention back to the cemetery.

"Do you want me to tell you what I know or not?" he asked. Brody remained in his faux angry stance, and Eric caught himself staring at Brody's lean, muscular arms. Brody's biceps weren't as big as his, but they were well-defined. And his shoulders were broad without being overdeveloped. Just the way he liked them.

Wait. What? The way he liked them? He was on a sightseeing tour with a friend, not at a gay club inspecting some grade-A beef.

"Okay, fine," Maddie finally replied. "Enlighten me."

"The oldest grave belongs to a woman named Desire."

"Desire?" Maddie turned from the cemetery back to Brody. "Really?"

Brody nodded. He took off his sunglasses and kneeled down at Maddie's side. His green eyes glinted in the sunshine as if the diamonds from the ocean had all been transferred to his gaze. "Her maiden name was Hawes, and she was born in Yarmouth. That's about forty miles or so from here."

Maddie's brow furrowed. That typically meant a question was coming. "But she died here in Provincetown?" When Brody said yes, she asked, "Why did she come here?"

"She moved here with her second husband, John Cowing."

"Second husband? What happened to her first?"

"He died," Brody said. Eric couldn't help but wince. He didn't like talking about death, especially with Maddie. She'd experienced far too much death already. As Maddie usually did, she sensed his unease and glanced over her shoulder at him, smiling reassuringly before Brody continued his story. "His name was Josiah Hatch, and he was a carpenter. They had seven children before his death."

"Wow! That's a lot of kids, but that was pretty common back then. They needed to have helping hands around the farm somehow. Kind of like the way Papa makes me do chores."

"I can always make you do more," he said. "The lawn doesn't mow itself."

Maddie shot him a blank stare before returning her gaze to Brody. "Did her children move with her and her new husband?"

"Not all of them," Brody replied. "Some died before she remarried."

Eric winced again. This story needed to stop now. Dead children wasn't a favorite topic of discussion. His sister Kimberly had only been fourteen when she died. Maddie crossed over to him and grabbed a hold of his hand. It was her MO. She wanted him to know that everything was going to be okay. Since when did she become his consoler?

"That's sad," she finally said. Her big green eyes gazed up at him lovingly.

"Yes," Brody replied as he stood. Eric narrowed his eyes in concern; something had changed. "Maybe I shouldn't be telling this story."

"It's okay," Maddie responded. "I'm a big girl. I can take it." Why did it seem as if Maddie was speaking to him instead of Brody?

"Eric?" Brody asked. "Do you want me to stop?"

Yes, he did. But Maddie wanted to hear the story for some reason. Just because he didn't like talking about death didn't mean he had to deprive his daughter of her curious nature. "It's fine," he finally replied. "What happened to Desire when she moved to Provincetown?"

Brody shrugged. "Not too much is known about her. All that can really be found are public records that involve her being the administrator of her first husband's estate. I do know that her second husband died before she did, and Desire finally passed when she was forty."

Maddie studied Brody in that way she normally did when she was processing information. She looked him up and down for several seconds.

"What?" Brody asked. "What did I say?"

Eric had already figured out what his daughter was now thinking, and he was confident she'd arrive at the same conclusion.

"You're a descendant of Desire Cowing, aren't you?"

Brody's eyes went wide with astonishment. Eric had never been prouder of his daughter's deductive skills than he was at that moment.

"You're one smart kid," Brody said. "I am. My mother's maiden name is Cook, which was the family Desire's eldest daughter married into."

"You must really be into genealogy," she said.

Brody nodded. "I am. I find it fascinating."

"Me too," Maddie added. "It's history. But family history. I think it's important to know our roots."

Brody chuckled. "Me too, kiddo."

Why did Eric want to rush over to Brody, take him in his arms, and kiss him? Was it the way Brody interacted with his daughter? It certainly made him far more attractive than his lush green eyes, lean muscles, or fair skin. And his ass? Damn, it was round and delicious in those tight shorts. He could make a meal out of that any day.

No. This wasn't right. He had to stop thinking this way. Charlie had been the only man he'd ever wanted. Lusting after some other man's body was a disservice to his husband and their relationship. Would it be nice to experience the comfort of another man again? Hell yes. But he'd promised himself that part of his life was over. He lived for Maddie now.

That was all he really needed.

Chapter Seven

WHAT WAS Brody doing? He'd already taken Eric and Maddie to the Pilgrim Monument. They'd had lunch and trekked up and down Commercial Street for some shopping. They spent over an hour in Shop Therapy, where Maddie fell in love with the seventies atmosphere and snatched up even more classic-rock tees to add to what was most likely an already expansive collection.

After all that, he should have called it a day and gone home.

Is that what happened? Of course not. He had to go and open his big, fat mouth and suggest they rent bikes and ride the biking trails over to Race Point. What the hell was the matter with him?

Yes, he enjoyed their company. Maddie was a riot and probably the most fun little person he'd ever been around, and her father? Well, Eric was hotter than Ricky Martin, Enrique Iglesias, and Joe Manganiello combined.

But he couldn't go there. For obvious reasons.

So why was he cruising down Cornwall Street and crossing over Route Six on his rented bike? Because he was a dumbass. What other reason could there be?

He needed to put distance between him and Eric, not spend all day with him. What would that accomplish? Well, besides the fact he had a perfect view of Eric's muscular butt as he rode in front of Brody on his bike. That ass could feed a group of sex-starved gays for weeks. And, oh hell, did Eric's crack really need to be peeking out from the waistband of his shorts?

Fuck! It was extremely difficult to pedal with a boner. Right now, his hard cock was bent at an uncomfortable angle, and it hurt like a bitch. Dicks shouldn't be bowed at ninety degrees. They needed to be handled with care.

Well, most of the time. It was okay to abuse them every now and then. Especially if Eric was the one abusing it. How fucking hot would it be to see his hard cock sliding between Eric's lips? Or sucking Eric all the way to the root of his dick?

A passing car honked at him when he absently swerved into its path. He quickly corrected himself and waved an apology at the vehicle. Eric glanced over his shoulder, his wide amber eyes expressing concern about what had just happened. Brody smiled and gave a reassuring nod.

What else could he do? Tell Eric that his sweet ass made him so hot and horny that he almost had a head-on collision with a Hyundai? Yeah, that would go over like a ton of bricks.

See, that was what he was talking about. He couldn't be sporting wood for Eric. Especially around Maddie. Even though he didn't like kids, Brody liked her. He didn't want to piss her off, and being insanely attracted to her father while her other father was at home waiting for his family to return would certainly do the trick.

His hormones had to be brought under control. It wasn't like he couldn't go out and get laid afterward. There were plenty of hot guys in town, even though it was Family Week in Provincetown. Hell, some of the hottest sex he'd had was with couples looking to add some spice to their lives.

But that wasn't him anymore. He'd sworn off his usual slutty ways when he began looking for a relationship. He craved more than the come-and-go life he'd once led. What he wanted was what all his friends had with their partners. And what Eric had with Charlie.

God, did he have to sound like such a loser? Maybe that was part of his problem. Maybe his search for true love had turned him into a pathetic and desperate version of himself. That was what Teddy had told him. Of course, he'd told Teddy that he was bat shit, but he hadn't been. Teddy had been right. He wasn't letting the relationship come naturally. He was forcing connections that couldn't be forced.

That had to be the reason he was so lonely and depressed. And it quite possibly explained why he was so enthralled by Eric. Because liking him had come easy. Never mind that there was no way in hell they could be together. He had a kid, for one. Which was the biggest no-no there was on Brody's list of requirements. Plus, he was married. That one was the nail in the proverbial coffin of their potential together.

So then why did he continue to spend time with Eric and Maddie if there was no future in it? He certainly had no problem throwing Dan out of his apartment yesterday for being a complete douche and a big waste of time.

What made Eric any different? Well, first of all, he was far from a douche bag. But no matter how hot he was or how easy liking him had been, Eric was a waste of his time, and he needed to get off this crazy train at the next stop.

He'd already committed himself to this bike ride, but that was it. When they were done, it would be hasta la vista to Eric and Maddie. He'd see them again at the wedding. He wasn't going to go out of his way to ignore them or anything. He wasn't a complete asshole.

But he wasn't going to spend time spinning his wheels with Eric. This was the deadest of all dead ends, and once he accepted that, he'd be back on track.

Except this time, he'd be a little wiser. He wouldn't force a connection. He'd let it happen on its own.

Just like it had started to happen with Eric.

AFTER BIKING for several minutes, they finally arrived at the start of the Race Point trail. Brody was anxious to get the ride to the beach over with. Then he could go home and take a cold shower. Maybe that would get his cock to finally release its stranglehold on his blood supply. He was getting a little light-headed.

"Look at the geese!" Maddie quickly scrambled off her bike and jogged over to the waddling goose family.

The parents led the way, and their four little goslings trailed behind. The little geese carried on a hearty conversation with each other through their constant chirps. Then the little gosling in front stopped to peck at a passing insect. The move proved disastrous. The siblings behind the hungry little goose piled onto him. They became a feathery heap of beaks and tail feathers. As they got up, his brothers and sisters chirped at their offending sibling in disgust, and one of them even snapped at his behind in retaliation. The parents squawked at their children in reprimand. The goslings quickly got back in line but not before delivering one final irritated chirp to their brother, who caused the pile up.

Maddie laughed so hard she was doubled over. Even Eric was howling.

Why wasn't he? It had been pretty damn funny, but for some reason he wasn't in a laughing mood.

He was more irritated than anything else.

"Why aren't you laughing?" Eric asked between breaths. "Did you not see the way they got on that poor little guy?" His strong lips, surrounded by the dark beard that covered his cheeks and chin, parted into a radiant grin. The light of his smile reflected in his eyes, which were more yellow than amber at the moment. Eric was having a good time. The sadness he'd noticed yesterday had been blown away by the merriment of this new day. He was glad Eric was happy. For some reason, he believed it had been a while since a smile had lighted on Eric's lips.

Yesterday, he was a man who needed to be saved. Today, Eric stood on firm ground. He might have contributed to that glow in some small way. That should be a positive, right?

Only it wasn't. It wasn't his job to make Eric smile. Or play tour guide. Eric had a husband for that. No, Charlie wasn't in P-town to do those things, but that wasn't Brody's problem. That was Eric's. Brody was already far too attracted to a married man. Becoming personally invested in his happiness was not exactly a way off a train speeding toward disaster.

Was that why he wanted to punch a tree right now?

He really was a loser. Only a pathetic, desperate loser would find a potential mate in a man who already had a partner.

Brody finally faked a laugh in response to Eric's question, but it wasn't very convincing, as revealed by the suspicion in Eric's eyes. "Typical sibling behavior, huh? If I'd been unlucky enough to have a brother or a sister, I'd have likely waled on them all the time too."

"I suppose," Eric replied. The yellow tint to his eyes drained completely. They were darker now. Almost copper. And he gazed off in the distance, as if his eyes were piercing time and space and looking somewhere into a troubled past. What horrible events were a part of Eric's story?

From the gloom that had quickly descended upon him, it was not a pretty tale to be told.

Damn those sad coppery eyes! Before he could stop himself, he dismounted his bike and crossed the distance separating him and Eric. "What's the matter?" he asked. Eric had turned pale, which for someone with his tan was saying something.

Maddie noticed the change as well. She left the geese and ran over to her father's side. "Papa, are you okay?"

"I'll be fine," Eric replied.

Maddie's eyebrows stitched together when she gazed over her father's shoulder at Brody. "What did you say to him?"

"I didn't say anything," he answered. Why did he suddenly feel the need to apologize? He hadn't said anything that would have caused this change in Eric. "At least I don't think so."

"He didn't do anything," Eric said. He shook his head as if he were trying to shake off an irritating fly. "I was just thinking about Kimberly."

"Oh." The quiet tone of Maddie's response told Brody that Eric's comment explained everything to her. Would someone now enlighten him?

"Who's Kimberly?"

"She was my sister." Eric attempted a grin, but it failed even worse than when Brody had tried to fake a laugh a moment ago. "She died when I was a kid."

"Shit! I'm sorry," Brody said.

"That's not very appropriate language to use in front of a nine-year-old," Maddie reprimanded.

"Sh—" he began before stopping himself. "I'm sorry for that too. And I'm really sorry for talking about beating up on any siblings I might have had. I didn't mean to offend you. Or bring up unpleasant memories."

"You didn't offend me. Memories of Kimberly just sneak up on me sometimes. Sure, it makes me very sad, but I try to remember the good times we had together." Eric's eyes once again gazed into the past, but this time they settled on happier times. The return of the yellow tint told Brody that much. "We used to go for ice cream together every Sunday. She always paid for it too. With the money she earned through babysitting. We'd play games together, and she'd always let me win. She was the best big sister a guy could ask for."

"Yes, she was." Maddie then put her hand on top of her father's and traced his knuckles with her fingertips. The gesture seemed to soothe him, as he took a deep breath before blowing a lungful of air out. "I'm better now. Shall we continue?"

Maddie nodded, and Brody agreed.

The three of them then hopped back on their bikes and pedaled down the tree-lined trail. As he took his spot behind Eric, who followed Maddie, Brody regretted his previous decision. He couldn't abandon Eric now. Even though he had a husband and wasn't the man for him, Eric needed him. It might just be for the week, and it would just be as friends, but he liked Eric enough to look past the wasted potential they might have together.

Eric didn't deserve to be cast off simply because there was no future for them. He had to stop seeing men and relationships as though they were all about him. That wasn't how the world worked. Sometimes he had to just be there for someone else.

With no strings attached.

THE RIDE through the trails had been going great until Eric almost killed himself.

They'd been pumping their legs up the many hills and then coasting down the other side. The three of them hollered like fools on a rollercoaster. The more serious cyclists who graced the trails didn't appreciate the noise they made. They shook their heads at them as they passed.

If Brody could have, he would have rammed each one of them off the trail. Couldn't those sourpusses see they were having a good time? And after the sadness that had descended upon them after Eric talked about his dead sister, a good time was what they all needed.

Thankfully, the beauty of the rolling trail had seemingly eased their spirits. How could it not? They flew past lush greenery and sand dunes, and every now and then the dark blue of the Atlantic peeked into view as they drew closer to the trail's end. All around them birds chirped and butterflies danced. Not even the occasional pesky swarm of mosquitoes could bring him down, but what made him the happiest was the laughter that drifted back to him from Maddie and Eric, who zoomed along the path in front of him.

When was the last time he'd biked the trail to Race Point? It had to have been shortly after he moved here last year. Teddy and he had gotten permission from Nino to spend the day together, which hadn't been an easy task. Nino still believed that Brody wanted to steal Teddy from him, even though he had no such inclination.

Only Teddy's promises of hours of sweaty hot sex after the bike ride convinced Nino to let him go. That boy had always thought with his cock, so it was a good move on Teddy's part.

The two of them had enjoyed a nice ride and even got to work through some of their lingering issues about their shared past. After that, he hadn't returned to the trails. Even though the day had been fun, it served as one final reminder of the life with Teddy he'd thrown away because of youthful stupidity.

But today, none of those depressing memories returned. How could they? He was too busy rocketing through the trail.

Then it happened.

After one deliriously long downhill ride, Eric pulled over to the side of the trail to tie his dangling shoelaces. Unfortunately, when he stepped off the path, he failed to notice that the ground immediately sloped downward, and down he went.

As he fell, Maddie shrieked, especially since Eric's head came within inches of missing a broken tree trunk that resembled a wooden spike more than anything else. But before Eric came to a stop, Brody had somehow managed to dash to his side.

"Fuck, Eric! Are you okay?" He gazed down at Eric, who lay flat on his back amid the overgrown grass and weeds. No broken bones were visible. Thank God. That would have made him vomit. Further scrutiny revealed Eric to be free of serious injury. All he spotted was a small cut on his left shin. Considering how far he skidded down the hill, Eric was lucky.

"No," Eric whispered. His eyes remained closed, and he refused to move.

"Is he okay?" Maddie asked. The tremor in her voice clearly communicated her concern. He turned back to see her at the top of the hill, wringing her hands in evident worry. She clearly wanted to come down and help, but the pitch of the hill would prove too steep for her small legs.

"He's fine," Brody lied. What else was he going to say? Telling her that her dad had said he wasn't okay was definitely not the answer. "You stay there, and we'll be up in a minute or two."

"Okay," she replied rather tentatively. She was most likely unconvinced of her father's safety. The only thing to convince her would be to have her father standing by her side at the top of the hill.

"So what hurts?" he asked after he turned back to Eric. He ran his hands across Eric's legs, arms, chest, and head, looking for any spot that might cause Eric to wince in pain. "I need to know, so I can tell the paramedics."

Eric opened his eyes and stared at him. God, even after taking a spill down the hill, he was absolutely stunning. Why did the bastard have to be happily married? The saying used to be that the good guys were either gay or married. This one happened to be both. His luck fucking sucked.

"My pride," Eric finally answered.

If Eric hadn't already tumbled off the trail, he would have pushed him. "Are you fucking serious?" he asked. Even though he was trying to sound angry, his stifled laugh gave him away. "You scared the shit out of me!"

"Sorry," Eric said. He held out his hand for Brody to help him up. When he took Eric's hand in his, the contact almost caused Brody's knees to buckle. Eric's flesh was a combination of rough calluses along the joints and velvety smoothness at his palms.

Masculine and rugged, yet soft and tender.

His cock, which had finally calmed down, once again stood at immediate attention, and what made it even worse was that Eric just happened to be sitting up at crotch level. Perhaps Eric was too embarrassed by his fall to notice the obvious tenting of his shorts.

As he pulled Eric up, however, Eric stared for a moment longer than was necessary at Brody's basket. Fuck! Had he noticed? By the time he had Eric once again on firm legs, though, he couldn't get a clear read of Eric's expression.

Was the grin the result of being happy he hadn't died or because he was somehow pleased that Brody had a boner for him?

"Papa!" Maddie shouted at the top. "Are you okay?"

"I'm fine, sweetheart," Eric replied before climbing back to the top.

"Thank God." The relief in Maddie's voice was apparent. "But are you sure?"

"Yes, we'll be right there," he said before turning back to Brody. He held out his hand. Were they going to hold hands back up the hill? "For balance," Eric replied.

"Oh." Brody took the offered assistance. Had Eric somehow read his mind? The only other person who'd been able to do that was Teddy. But as they scaled back up to the top, Brody forgot all about how he and Teddy used to be able to sense each other's needs or concerns. All he could focus on was the warmth of Eric's touch, and the fire that scorched across his flesh.

"You made it!" Maddie immediately rushed into her father's arms once they were back on the trail. "I was so scared."

"I'm fine," Eric replied. He held her close and stroked the back of her head. "And I'll always make my way back to you. That's a promise."

Maddie smiled. Her father's word seemed an unbreakable covenant. "Good." She walked around her father and glared at Brody.

Her crossed arms and stern expression clearly told him she wasn't pleased about something he'd done.

"What did I do now?"

"Your language is horrible," she said. "I know my dad's fall scared you too, but did you really have to use the F-word and the S-word multiple times in a span of about three minutes?"

"Did I?" He didn't even remember cursing. Those words just seemed to naturally fly out of his mouth.

"I'm so disappointed in you," she said with a slow shake of her head. Why did he feel like he needed a time-out or something? Damn, this girl was good at pouring on the guilt.

"Don't be too hard on him," Eric said. "He did help your old man back up the hill."

Maddie hesitantly agreed, but there was a playful glint to her glare. Was she pulling his leg? "That's the only reason we're not washing his mouth out with soap right now."

"You're teasing me, aren't you?"

She rolled her eyes and looked up to the sky. Clearly, she was so frustrated by him only God could feel her pain. "Duh" was all she playfully said before she rushed into his arms. Her tiny limbs squeezed him tightly around the waist. She whispered, "Thanks for being there for my Papa."

"Not a problem, kiddo," he said after he returned the hug. "We all need someone to help us up every now and then."

She nodded, and although her eyes appeared wet, he didn't detect any sadness. There was something else. Something more than relief that her father was okay and that Brody had helped him. It was like she'd found an answer to some previously unsolvable equation.

But after a few seconds, she blinked the look away and headed back for her bike. "Now, if the death-defying stunts are at an end, how about we finally make our way to the beach?"

"Sounds like a plan," Eric said before he mounted his bike.

Brody once again followed Eric and Maddie down the trail, but he couldn't get that look in Maddie's eyes out of his head. What did it mean and why did it fill him with hope?

Chapter Eight

WHEN THEY finally made it to Race Point and had properly secured their bikes, Maddie turned tail and sprinted down the long walkway toward the beach before Eric could call her back. The call of the ocean most likely proved stronger than her father's need to keep a watchful eye over her.

Brody had initially believed Eric went a bit overboard with his protectiveness. When they first met, he'd been on edge when she ran ahead in the parking lot toward the Funk Van. Then, on the bike ride over here, Eric constantly warned Maddie not to get too far ahead of him. Having her in his sights was plainly priority number one.

But he understood the genesis of his overprotective nature now. It likely had something to do with his sister Kimberly. Whatever happened to her, Eric probably feared the same thing might happen to Maddie.

Eric couldn't watch her the rest of her life, though. Eventually, she'd have to be given some space. How else was she going to grow into her own person? She certainly couldn't live in her father's protective shadow forever.

Once Maddie's tiny pigtailed head disappeared from view, worry immediately descended on Eric. His eyes went wide, and his mouth hung agape. If he were a deer, he'd be bounding into the thicket after his missing fawn. But this wasn't the forest, and there were no hunters in sight.

"She'll be fine," Brody said. "There's nowhere for her to go but the beach."

Eric shot him a piercing stare. His amber eyes had once again turned copper. That didn't bode well. If he didn't calm Eric down, he was likely to descend into full-blown panic. His broad chest heaved up and down as his respiration increased exponentially.

"Or we could go after her instead of just standing here on the verge of a meltdown."

Eric's hard gaze softened. He no doubt realized how irrational he was being. But the lopsided grin couldn't hide the apparent worry that still lingered in his eyes. "I know I'm being silly," Eric said as they progressed toward the walkway down which Maddie had disappeared. Eric led the way, speeding up in order to round the bend as quickly as possible. If he didn't see Maddie when they reached the top, Brody was uncertain what would happen. "I just don't like Maddie being out of my sight. I have to know where she is all the time."

"That's not very practical." Brody had to quicken his pace to keep up with Eric. They were almost jogging. "How can you possibly know where she is all the time? When she's at school and you're at work, you don't know where she is."

"Not true. I know she's at a school."

"Well, yes. But she's still not in your sight."

Eric didn't answer. He was too focused on reaching the top of the walkway.

Once they crested the entrance to the beach access, Maddie was clearly visible. She stood about halfway down the path, which was lined with a slatted wooden fence, about fifty yards away. Eric's relief was apparent. His shoulders relaxed and his jaw unclenched. When Maddie saw them, she waved at her father and then pointed at the beach. Eric nodded, and Maddie continued under her father's watchful eyes.

"Feel better?" he asked.

"Much," Eric replied with a long exhalation.

They followed the trail after Maddie. The thick sand slowed their pace, but Maddie showed no signs of being deterred. She practically skimmed over the surface to reach the water's edge.

He glanced over at Eric, about to continue their previous conversation, but Eric's faraway look communicated he wasn't ready to speak yet. He clearly needed time to recover from his hysteria, so they continued on in silence.

Brody swept his gaze across the beach. The sand was so pale it was almost white and stretched for miles to the east and the west. Before them churned the Atlantic. Its typically strong waves slapped rhythmically upon the shore, where many children and their families frolicked around the edge. Normally turquoise in color, the water had turned a deep blue. No doubt a result of the blazing sun overhead.

On the far right, about two hundred yards away, extended a wooden boardwalk that cut through the beach. When he was last here with Teddy, they had taken that path up to the grassy hills at the top of the knoll. Up there sat a two-story, gray-shingled visitor's center, where almost the entirety of Race Point could be seen.

The white sand, the deep blue ocean, and the green grass made this place truly stunning. Just why did so many people prefer Herring Cove? Well, that was an easy answer. Because they could pork in the dunes without being bothered.

While Brody enjoyed putting on a public display in certain settings, sex on the beach wasn't at the top of his list. He wasn't exactly a fan of sand in his ass crack or the damn green flies that bit so hard they drew blood. Those pesky little fuckers swarmed all over Herring Cove. Plus, getting to Herring Cove wasn't exactly easy. Why so many guys trekked through the marshes and through swarms of green flies just to fuck in the sand was beyond him.

A good romp could be had at home without the sand or the flies.

That was what made Race Point ideal. It wasn't a cruising spot. It didn't have vampire-like flies, and it wasn't a bitch to get to. Those reasons, combined with the unparalleled beauty he currently observed, made Race Point his favorite by far.

"This place is stunning." Eric no longer watched Maddie like a hawk. She had made it to the ocean's edge and was currently dipping her toes in the water. When the usually frigid surf washed across her feet, she scrambled back to the sand. Obviously Eric didn't fear her wading into the water.

"Yes, it is. That's why I love it here. Much better than Herring Cove."

"Really?" Eric asked. "That's not what Zach and Van said last night. They raved about Herring Cove."

"Probably because they like to screw on the beach."

Eric's face twisted into a grimace. "That's definitely too much information about my cousin."

"I guess you've never seen any of his Hart Throb videos, then, have you?"

Eric glared at him as if he belonged in a straitjacket. "Of course not. That's disgusting!" He shivered, most likely at the mere thought of Van's previous career in porn and his cousin's former power-bottom notoriety. Not that he blamed him. If any of his relatives starred in skin flicks, he couldn't stomach seeing them be pummeled by random guys. There were just some sides of each other family didn't need to see. But then Eric had to ask, "Have you seen them? His videos, I mean."

Well, shit. Eric just had to go and open up that can of worms. "Um, well…." Should he lie about the fact that he owned all of Hart Throb's videos? They were pretty fucking hot, and Van certainly knew how to take a cock up his ass. Whenever he watched them, he envied Zach for snatching Van up.

"Never mind," Eric said with a roll of his eyes. "That response spoke volumes."

"What can I say? I like porn." He flashed his big grin to Eric. The one he usually reserved for trying to get out of trouble. It didn't seem to work too well. Eric glanced at him sideways before shaking his head. "What?"

"It's just extremely weird that you've seen my cousin naked. And in action."

"It's not like I was there while they were being filmed."

"Close enough," Eric replied.

"What are you two talking about?"

Maddie's voice startled him. Brody jumped about two feet in the air. Even Eric had been caught off guard, and resembled a rabbit about to bolt.

"Jeez, you two need to lay off the caffeine or something." Even though she was making fun of them, her crooked smile told Brody that she was pleased to have snuck up on them.

"What were you in a previous life?" he asked. "A cat?"

"I'm thinking more of a lioness than an ordinary cat," she replied after a few moments' thought.

"I've told you about sneaking up on adults," Eric said. "It's not very polite."

Her face scrunched up. "How else am I supposed to learn what adults talk about?"

"There are some conversations that aren't meant for children to hear."

Maddie gaped at her father, then over at him. "Just what were you two talking about?" A million topics no doubt ran through her mind as she searched for an answer.

Was it possible to keep *anything* from her? No doubt she had her Christmas presents figured out even before they were wrapped and under the tree.

"There aren't many topics you don't like to talk about in front of me, Papa. There's your work. Because you don't want to scare me." She looked up at Eric gratefully. She clearly appreciated being ignorant on that topic. "But I don't think you'd be talking about work here on the beach. It's really not the place. That leaves personal topics like dating and…." Her left eyebrow arched so far on her forehead, it about joined her hairline.

"Madison." Eric's voice, which was very deep and strong anyway, deepened even further. It was almost a low growl. Damn. He'd hate to be on the receiving end when Eric was pissed. His voice alone would make Brody quake.

Maddie, however, took it in stride. She'd most likely been there and done that. "I'm just curious. When I'm curious, I ask you questions. Unless it's about something like sex. I find those answers myself."

"You what?" Eric practically blew a gasket.

"I'm not a kid, Papa. I'm nine years old. If I have questions about something, I look it up. I thought about asking you, but I figured you'd act this way, so I didn't. It's really no big deal."

"It *is* a big deal. Why would you have questions about sex at your age?" If Eric didn't calm down, he was going to have a stroke. As it was, his face had turned beet red.

"Well, kids at school had been asking me how I could have been born if I had two fathers and no mother. I told them I did have a mom, but she was a surrogate. They didn't know what that was, and I wasn't entirely sure either. So I looked it up. You know how I hate not having the answers to questions."

The answer released much of the bluster from Eric's sails, but he hadn't settled down. His rapid breathing had yet to be brought under control.

"And you got all your answers from where?" he asked. "The Internet?"

"Mostly," Maddie replied. "From the library too. I don't trust everything I read online. Do you?" This last question was addressed to Brody.

"No, I don't," Brody said. "You're very resourceful."

"I am," she said, standing upright like a proud peacock with tail feathers on full display.

"But still, questions as big as that should probably be brought to your dad. Don't you think?"

Maddie sighed as she glanced over at Eric. He had returned to his usual tanned self, and he was no longer breathing like a raging bull. "I suppose," she finally conceded. She walked over to her dad and took his big hand in hers. "I'm sorry, Papa."

"That's okay. You just freaked me out a little."

"A little?" she asked, staring up at him in disbelief. "You just about hit the roof."

Eric chuckled and nodded in agreement.

"Next time I have a really serious question, I'll ask you. Okay?"

"Okay," Eric replied with a nod.

"But you're going to have to be okay with the question. You can't freak out on me. Is that a deal?"

Eric paused, no doubt thinking about his answer. "Well, depending on what you ask, I might freak out a little, but you can still ask."

"Sounds like a plan."

Eric and Maddie grasped hands and walked farther down the beach, quite content with the resolution of their slight conflict. Brody had never seen anything like it before. Whenever he and his parents had issues, World War Three usually erupted. Was this how normal families who loved each other behaved?

And why was he suddenly warm on the inside? Whatever it was, it reminded him of sitting before a fireplace on a cold winter's day.

"Are you coming?" Maddie asked. She still held onto her father's hand, but her free hand reached out for him. The warmth inside him grew more intense until it wrapped around him like a comfortable old blanket.

"Coming," he said. He trotted over to Maddie and took her hand. Then the three of them walked down the beach together.

IT HADN'T been but five minutes before Maddie said she had a question. Eric's low grumble revealed his immediate dismay. He clearly didn't appreciate his daughter taking him for his word earlier, and he was most likely regretting his promise not to freak out.

Brody was intrigued. Would Eric be able to hold up his end of the deal?

"What is it?" Eric asked. His eyes were half-closed, as if he were about to be hit in the face by a baseball bat.

"Well, it isn't for you," she said. Maddie turned up to stare at Brody with her precious green eyes. She batted them innocently. As if that was going to work. She was no innocent. No matter how young she was.

"It's for me?"

She nodded. "Is that okay?"

"Well, I guess that depends on the question, and if your father is okay with me answering it."

"He said he wouldn't freak out," she said as she turned her innocent routine on him.

Eric's blank expression revealed he wasn't buying the act either. "Why don't we hear the question first?"

"Jeez, the two of you are too high-strung," she said in complete exasperation. "It's not about sex. It's about Desire Cowing."

"My ancestor?"

Maddie mimicked her father's blank expression. She clearly didn't like stating the obvious.

Brody rolled his eyes. "What do you want to know about her? I've told you about all I know."

"Well, I've been thinking about her since the Pilgrim Monument. About how her first husband died. What was his name again?"

"Josiah Hatch," Brody reminded her.

"Yeah. Him. I know that sometimes when women remarried back then that it was because they had to. You know, they needed a man to support them. Which is something I will never do." Brody stifled back his rising laugh. From the twinkle in Eric's eyes, Eric was no doubt doing the same thing. But how could they laugh at such a serious statement? No matter how damn cute it was. "But I was wondering if Desire really loved her second husband. Did she marry him because she loved him? Or did she marry him because she had to?"

What could he say? He didn't possess such intimate information about his ancestor, but the question seemed very important to Maddie for some weird reason. "Well, I think she loved John Cowing very much. So much that she moved from her hometown to Provincetown. Why else would she have gone with him?"

"He could have made her," she answered. "Women weren't exactly free to do what they wanted, you know?"

Had he enrolled in a Women's Studies class that Maddie was teaching or what? She was too bright for her own good. It wasn't going to be easy to sell her on Desire's unwavering love for her second husband, but that was the story she craved. "That's true. But Desire wasn't your typical woman. The public records prove that."

"How so?"

Fuck. How was he supposed to know? He was just hoping she would buy what he said. He should have known better. "Well, let's see. If I remember my research carefully enough,"—which he didn't— "certain people in her hometown didn't like the fact that Josiah left everything to his wife. His estate should have gone to their eldest son." He had no clue if the crap he was spewing was true. He was winging it, but she seemed to be buying what he was selling. He couldn't very well stop now. "So she went to court and fought the charges that her husband wasn't of sound mind, and she won the right to inherit the estate."

"Okay," she said. So far so good, but he wasn't out of the woods yet. "But what does any of that have to do with whether or not she loved her second husband?"

"Well, when they were married, she handed over the estate to her husband. She could have easily transferred the inheritance over to her oldest son. Which meant that her new husband would have gotten nothing, but she didn't. I think that shows how much she loved him."

Maddie's brow furrowed. He'd been around her enough to know what that look meant. She was considering the logic of his argument. If she didn't believe it, what was he going to do? "Sounds reasonable enough."

Thank heavens. "Why did you ask?"

"Well, I'm sure Desire was very sad when her first husband died. Probably sadder than she knew what to do." Why was she looking at Eric? And why did Eric refuse to meet her gaze?

"I think that's a fair statement," Brody finally said.

"And I'd hate to think that Desire never felt loved again. That would be too sad. Life's too short to not have love. Don't you think?" Why was her question filled with such hope? This was getting very weird.

"I think you're right. Falling in love once is a blessing. To have it twice in one lifetime is a miracle."

The huge smile that broke across her face shone brighter than the sun overhead. His answer had pleased her.

But what were her questions about Desire Cowing really about? And why did Eric suddenly seem uncomfortable?

BRODY HAD wanted answers to his questions, but how was he supposed to ask them? Accusing a nine-year-old girl of having an ulterior motive wouldn't earn him any brownie points, and since Maddie was always at their side, he couldn't very well ask Eric what Maddie's questions had been about.

He had no choice but to leave them unanswered. At least for the time being.

Maddie's screech from down the beach got his attention. Right now, her father was chasing her around, trying to catch her and throw her in the water. They'd been playing that game since Maddie had finished asking about marriage, love, and second husbands.

It had come on so suddenly he couldn't help but see it for what it was—a diversion. But just what was Eric trying to avoid?

"Brody!" Maddie screamed. She zigged while Eric zagged and was able to increase the distance between them. "Help me!"

"I don't get between a father and his daughter," he called back. She replied by sticking out her tongue, but unfortunately that little gesture caused her to lose ground. Her father lunged at her and snagged her by her elbow. Eric then hauled her over his shoulder and headed toward the water.

Brody laughed. Whatever the reason for Eric's sudden interest in tormenting Maddie, it was working. How could he focus on finding answers when the two of them were being so adorable? He really needed to stop that. He'd already accepted that he and Eric weren't going to happen. They were destined to be friends. That was it. He was going to be here for Eric. Help make him smile. Especially since Eric appeared to be in dire need of a good time.

When it was over, Eric would go home to Charlie. That was an important point to remember. Eric would go home to Charlie.

Perhaps if he repeated that enough, he'd stop ogling Eric's muscular back and his perky, delicious butt.

Eric was going home to Charlie.

Maybe then he'd stop picturing what it would feel like to spend just one night wrapped up in those tanned arms.

Charlie. Eric's husband was Charlie.

And looking up into those amber eyes as Eric slowly eased his way inside him.

Charlie, Charlie, Charlie.

Yeah, his cock wasn't listening because it was rock hard again.

Fuck! What he really needed was to go home and rub one out. Maybe that would do the trick. Of course, he'd probably just end up fantasizing about Eric. Which would be hot. But guilt would probably claim him afterward. It wasn't exactly cool to lust after another man's husband.

There was even a commandment in the Bible that told him so.

Suddenly, Maddie rushed past him and sprinted down the beach. How the hell did she get away from Eric? Eric came lumbering after her. He had to do something to come to Maddie's rescue.

So as Eric ran past him, Brody leaped upon his back. The force unsteadied Eric, who teetered to one side. This caused Brody to fall off Eric and land on his back in the warm sand. Eric tried to catch himself, but the force of Brody's body first landing on him, then falling off sent Eric into a spin before he crashed on top of him.

In the distance, Maddie's laughter echoed back to him, but all Brody could focus on was Eric's heaving body pressed on top of him. His frame fit against him quite comfortably, as if they were missing pieces to each other's puzzle. Did Eric notice that too? Was that why his amber eyes, which had previously gazed down at him in wide surprise, no longer looked embarrassed? Instead, a sly grin caught the right corner of his mouth and hooked it upward.

Fuck, that was hot! And why did he have to smell so damn good? A heady mixture of sweat and aftershave drifted in the air. Then there were the hot pants of air that blew across Brody's cheeks. Each exhale fanned a fire that rapidly consumed him from within.

If not for his self-control, he would have craned his neck and stolen a kiss. But that was completely inappropriate. Especially in front of Maddie.

Shit. Maddie. What the hell was she thinking? Right now her father was lying on top of another man who wasn't her other father.

"I think it may be time to get up," Brody said. His voice was low and throaty. Did he really need to be speaking with a bedroom voice at the moment? His vocal cords seemed to think so. They were no doubt working in collusion with the erection that took up all the room in his underwear.

Oh great! He had an erection, and Eric was on top of him. There was no way he could hide that. But wait a minute. What was growing in Eric's shorts?

"I think you're right," Eric said before standing. He held out his hand to Brody, and when Brody took it, a wave of déjà vu washed over him. He'd done this before. But when? He'd never been to the beach with Eric before today.

After Eric pulled him to his feet, the sun's reflection momentarily blinded him. He couldn't see Eric, but the reassuring weight of his hand in his own told him Eric was still there. The contact was wonderful. Emotions he couldn't understand flooded him from within. It was like he was a desert plant receiving the first drops of rain after a long drought.

Even though the emotion was new to him, at the same time it wasn't. He'd been here before, and the same emotions had been stirred within him very recently.

Eric's laugh brought him out of what seemed to be a memory but couldn't possibly be. Although the blinding sun still kept Eric from his view, he followed Eric's pointing finger down the beach.

For some reason, Maddie was doing the cabbage patch dance.

What the hell was she celebrating?

When he turned back to Eric, the sun dipped behind the clouds. Eric's tanned and rugged face greeted him once again.

That was when it dawned on him. This was just like his dream. The one he'd had after he kicked Dan out of his apartment and before he headed over to Gary's to help set up for Zach and Van's bachelor party.

But how was that possible? How could he have been dreaming about Eric?

Chapter Nine

THEY RETURNED their rented bikes shortly after their visit to Race Point Beach, and Eric was glad the excursion had come to an end. Things between him and Brody had gotten weird after their little stumble on the beach. When he first landed on top of Brody, he'd been surprised and the wind had been knocked out of him. That had made it impossible to get up as quickly as he should have.

If he had, there wouldn't be this weirdness hanging over them like a patch of dense fog.

Maddie had noticed it too. She'd tried to force conversation between them on the beach and on the bike ride back to the rental shop, but he and Brody had only responded with one-word answers. That hadn't made Maddie happy one bit. Since they turned left on Commercial Street, she'd been sighing loudly with her hands crossed in front of her chest. Why was that exactly?

Eric didn't have time to figure out the source of his daughter's obvious frustration.

He was too busy replaying the event in his mind. Trying to find the cause of their silence and attempting to contain the nervous energy that roiled within him.

After scrambling off Brody, he'd tried to play it off. Thankfully, Maddie had been doing the cabbage patch. Something she only did after accomplishing some tough task, like an extremely difficult crossword puzzle.

What had prompted the dance? Well, Eric had no clue, but he'd hoped that it would somehow stop Brody from mentioning the fact that he'd gotten hard after falling on top of him.

That had been embarrassing!

What was his body thinking? Quite clearly, it hadn't been. Or the wrong head on his body had briefly taken over. Brody was a handsome man and completely worthy of a boner or three. His smooth, white skin reminded him of satin. And when he'd looked down into his piercing green eyes, which were framed by his windblown, sandy-blond hair, well, Eric had been unable to speak. As for Brody's lean, strong muscles, it was best not to recall how perfectly they'd pressed against him.

The last thing he needed was to sport another erection as they made their way toward the Lobster Pot, where everyone was gathering for dinner.

Out of the corner of his eye, he glanced over at Brody. Although he was staring straight ahead, Brody had checked out of his surroundings. He looked beyond the mobs of people congesting Commercial Street. The many strollers and the packs of gay parents that had descended on Provincetown for Family Week didn't exist in his line of vision.

He appeared to be somewhere else.

And there was an unfamiliar expression on Brody's face. Was it embarrassment? It sure looked like it. After all, Brody had gotten hard too, and as far as Brody was concerned, Eric was a married man. But humiliation didn't seem to be the right answer. Although he was no expert on Brody O'Shea, he was good at judging a person's character. That was a requirement for his job as a deputy. Brody didn't strike him as someone who was easily mortified.

Brody seemed to be the type of man who was proud of his erections and wasn't shy about sharing them with those that made him hard.

Then what was going on?

Perhaps Brody had sensed his unease. Maybe that was what Brody was responding to.

That could definitely be it. Since Charlie, he was unaccustomed to another man making him hard. Only his husband had ever gotten Eric's blood pumping, and he'd been proud of that.

After Charlie died, well, the only men he ever really looked at were images displayed across his computer screen. His hand had become his sex partner, and he'd been okay with that. His life was about Maddie now.

Then why did he want to slam Brody against a wall, tear his clothes from his body, and ravage him? Maybe that was what Brody sensed. Perhaps he'd crossed a line Brody preferred not to cross with him. But if that was true, then why had Brody gotten hard too?

This situation was more confusing than playing chess with Maddie.

His pent-up anxiety swirled around inside him like a tempest. He needed to dispel it somehow before it consumed him.

"I sure hope the two of you don't ruin dinner."

The irritation in Maddie's voice couldn't have been more apparent. She might as well have been a bee buzzing about her disturbed nest. "Why would we ruin dinner?"

"You mean beside the fact that you're both grumpy?"

"I'm not grumpy," Brody replied. He gazed down at her as if suddenly realizing Eric and Maddie had been walking next to him. "Just thinking."

She glanced up at him, evidently unconvinced. "Then what's that scowl for? Decoration?"

The swirling emotions burst free.

Laughter bubbled out of Eric before he could stop it. He even had to stop walking and lean on the wall of a temporary airbrush tattoo store they were passing. This was damn ridiculous. Why did he have to chuckle like some inmate in an insane asylum? Maddie's comeback hadn't been that good, which her one raised eyebrow succinctly revealed. Even Brody stared at him in open-mouthed surprise.

Although Brody and Maddie were clueless as to why he was acting like a fool, Eric wasn't. He'd been overtaken by nervous laughter before. On his first date with Charlie. He distinctly recalled how Charlie had looked at him as if he'd lost his marbles. But Eric had been so enraptured with him and so concerned about screwing things up that his nervous energy had to be released somehow.

So he had laughed. At least until Charlie had grabbed his hand. Then the world had been set right again.

"What's the matter with you?" Maddie asked. She smiled nervously at the people who approached where they stood. The passersby eyed him before giving him a wide berth. They most likely believed he was insane. Or drunk.

"Just thought that was really funny for some reason," he managed in between fits of hysteria.

"I know I'm a riot, but your response is a bit much." She stared up at Brody, who nodded in agreement. That got Eric going again. He laughed so hard his stomach hurt and his lungs wheezed. If he didn't get himself under control, he was likely to pass out. Or puke.

Wouldn't that be a fine way to kick off tonight's festivities?

Then a hand affectionately rubbed his shoulder. It was Brody. "Are you okay?"

His laughter trailed off, cut short by the weight of Brody's hand pressed against his shoulder. Its warmth cut through the fabric of his T-shirt, sending ripples of heat surging through his body, until at last the churning waters deep within Eric calmed.

He couldn't speak. A huge knot had formed in his throat, so he nodded in reply.

"Good," Brody answered with a pat. The unease that had previously darkened his expression had vanished. Only a friendly, beautiful smile lit up his face. It made Brody even more stunning. "We should probably get going, then. We don't want to be late for dinner. After all," he said while looking at Maddie, "we left the beach early to avoid doing just that."

"Yes, we did," Maddie agreed. "Besides, we need to get there as fast as possible since both your moods have improved. Crazy is better than grumpy, I suppose." After grabbing Eric's hand, she led him through the intersection of Commercial and Standish Street.

"I was never in a bad mood," Brody replied. "And your dad's the one who was taking a stroll down Looney Lane."

While Brody and Maddie bantered back and forth, Eric's ability to speak had yet to return. He was too dumbstruck by the fact that Brody had managed to calm down his nervous laughter.

Just like Charlie had once done.

"IT'S ABOUT time you three showed up," Van said as they drew closer to where everyone from last night stood, in front of the white building that was the Lobster Pot. Naturally, a giant red lobster was painted on the huge sign that hung over the door. This restaurant was a must to eat at for anyone visiting town. At least that was what Gary had told them last night when he'd reminded everyone about dinner this evening.

"Sorry about that," Eric said. He crossed over to Van and gave him a big hug. His cousin's embrace helped dispel the waves Brody had stirred across his flesh a few moments ago. Right now, that was the last thing he needed to think about. "Brody's been showing us around."

"Really?" Teddy asked.

Eric hadn't had a chance to talk to him that much last night. Teddy and his boyfriend Nino with the model-perfect body couldn't keep their hands off each other. They were obviously newly in love. Or extremely horny. Either way, they appeared to have needed some space last night, and he was glad to let them have it. He certainly didn't want Maddie exposed to anything more than she had already been introduced to on the ferry. "All three of you spent the day together?"

Was that surprise in Teddy's voice? "Yes," he answered. "How come?"

"No reason," Teddy replied. Now why was Teddy lying? That much was evident. Especially in the way he glanced over at Nino. That look they shared communicated there was something going on that he didn't understand.

"Well, I'm glad you've been enjoying yourself," Van said. "I don't think you've left Petersham since—" He stopped, and his eyes grew wide.

His cousin had almost brought up Charlie's death. It wasn't a topic Eric enjoyed talking about. Especially in front of strangers.

Luckily, Van stopped himself before the words came flying out of his mouth. He still needed to tell Brody the truth, and Brody needed to hear it from him. Not someone else.

"Since what?" Brody asked.

"Since getting that promotion at the deputy's office," Zach answered. Eric was grateful for Zach's partial lie. He had received a promotion about six months ago, but that was definitely not the reason he hadn't left town. Most likely, Van had filled Zach in on Eric's tragic past and his preference not to speak about it.

"You're a man of the law?" Brody asked.

Eric nodded. "Guilty as charged."

"What else don't I know about you?"

"You've spent the entire day together, and you don't know anything about each other?" Nino asked. The corners of his lips curled into a Cheshire grin. "Just what have you two been doing?"

Before Eric could comment on the inappropriate question, especially since they'd been out with his daughter, Brody replied, "We've been to the Pilgrim Monument, the bike trails, and over at Race Point."

"That sounds like a full day," Teddy said. Why did a huge smile part the man's bearded face?

"It was fun," Maddie added. "We had a good time. Right, Papa?"

Eric agreed. What was going on with Teddy and Nino?

Just then, Gary exited the front door of the restaurant. His hair was akimbo and his gaze darted around the group. It wouldn't have surprised Eric if he'd starting crawling up the side of the wall. "Thank goodness you're here," he said when he saw Eric, Brody, and Maddie. The stress of being the unofficial wedding planner for the Pierce-Kelly wedding was clearly taking its toll. "I've been working all day, and I'm famished. Thankfully, our table is already ready. If you didn't get here soon, I was likely to make a meal of Bobby Quinn's leg."

"Just my leg?" Quinn asked with a suggestive arch to his eyebrows.

Gary swatted Quinn's arms in response. "Mind your manners," he said with a head tilt to Maddie.

Maddie looked around as everyone stared at her. She was still innocent enough to not catch on to Quinn's hidden meaning. Thank God. "What?" she asked.

"Nothing, kiddo," Brody said. "Remember, boys are weird."

"That's the God's honest truth," she replied.

Everyone laughed as they entered through the front door, where the hostess waited to show the group to their table.

She led them down a long corridor and toward the back, where a huge table had been set up along the far wall overlooking the bay. The view was spectacular. The sun had almost slipped past the horizon, and the water around where it set turned a deep orange. Halfway across the sky, the sun's fading light gave way to the shadows that heralded the rise of the moon. Darkness was encroaching, and the first stars staked their claim to the approaching night sky.

As everyone began to take their seats, Eric continued to gaze out the window. The warring colors of darkness and light splattered across the sky's canopy entranced him. It mirrored his internal conflict for the past few years, since Charlie died.

He probably would have stood there much longer if Maddie's question hadn't pulled him out of his thoughts. "Can I please sit next to Sophia?"

"Of course you can, sweetheart," Zach's sister Sami said. "She'd love company other than me and her dad. But I have to warn you, she's been a bit grumpy today."

"No. Not grumpy," Sophia said. The jutting of her lower lip proved otherwise.

"That's okay," Maddie said with a nod to Eric. "I'm used to dealing with grumpy."

"Hey, now!" Eric replied as everyone laughed.

"When she's right, she's right," Brody teased.

"Don't you start on me too. The two of you have been ganging up on me all day!"

"Have not," Brody replied with a vigorous headshake.

"Have too!" Eric answered with an equally hearty nod.

"Do you see what I've had to put up with all day?" she asked the table. She delivered the question with such perfect deadpan that the table roared with laughter.

"I feel your pain," Gary said to Maddie. He and Quinn took the seat across from her. "I think you need a break from those boys."

"Don't you know it!" she replied.

Eric was about to take the seat next to Maddie when Van took it from him and sat down.

"Hey!"

"You heard the young lady. She needs a break from you two." Van pointed to the seats at the farthest end of the table. "Why don't you two go sit over there?"

"I always sit next to Maddie."

"Not today," Van replied as he scooted his chair under the table. "Besides, I don't get to spend that much time with my favorite niece. It's my time with her now."

"I'm actually your cousin," Maddie announced. "Second cousin."

Van turned back to Maddie. "Do you want a break from your dad and Brody or not?"

"You're the best, Uncle Van!" She bared her full set of teeth at him.

"That's what I thought," Van replied. He turned back to Eric and Brody. "Now get!"

Eric crossed over to the chair his daughter had relegated him to. What other choice did he have? She apparently was fine with him not sitting with her, even though she'd always made it a point to sit next to him ever since Charlie died.

OVER THE course of dinner, Eric's anxiety about Brody and about his daughter's continual steps toward independence drifted away. It was difficult to be moody with this group. All they'd done since they sat down was laugh. Some of the tables closest to them didn't appreciate their raucous energy. In fact, some of the older patrons appeared downright irritated.

Typically, Eric would do what he could to quiet down his table. He was a deputy after all, and disturbing the peace wasn't something he typically practiced. But today, he let his usual tendencies go, and instead he embraced the joy that surrounded him.

"So let me get this straight." Maddie's voice drifted to him at the end of the table. She was currently chatting with Nino and Teddy. He cringed. Would they be able to rein in their bawdy behavior? From what he'd briefly witnessed last night, he had his doubts. "The two of you met at a party that you didn't even remember? I assume alcohol was involved."

"Madison!" he called from where he sat, but everyone else laughed at her evident incredulity. She'd been cracking up the entire table all night. It appeared he had a future stand-up comedian on his hands. "I think that's quite enough."

His tone had come in loud and clear. Her lips drew taut, and she sat back in her chair.

"It's okay, Eric," Teddy replied. "She's right. We weren't drinking very responsibly that night."

"I hope you weren't driving," she commented before quickly covering her mouth with her hand. She glanced back down the table at Eric. Her eyes were wide and apologetic. Although he had every right to be furious with his daughter's remark, how could he be mad at such a pitiful display of regret?

"No, we weren't," Nino answered. "Cross my heart."

Nino's response drew Maddie's attention, and she eyed him carefully. He didn't have to be in law enforcement to know what she was thinking. She'd obviously caught on to the fact that Nino's word wasn't always golden, and she was just about to call him on it. "Madison," he warned.

Thankfully, she placed her second hand over her first to keep the words from flying from her mouth. Her gesture made everyone laugh, but Eric didn't find it amusing. His daughter was one toe away from crossing over the line.

He was just about to remind her of her manners when Brody patted his forearm. His touch restarted the warm waves, and they once again rippled through his body. If they'd been alone, he might have devoured Brody in one gulp.

"Cut her some slack," Brody said. "Besides, she's just thinking what everyone else already knows. Nino's a big liar."

"I heard that!" Nino shouted from the other side of the table. He tossed a piece of bread at Brody, who caught it.

"Well, I said it loud enough," Brody replied. After dipping the bread in the remaining mashed potatoes on his plate, he popped it in his mouth.

Why on earth did he find that so sexy?

Something was definitely happening between them, and he suspected Brody felt it too. The lingering of Brody's hand communicated that to him.

"You've got quite the daughter there." The words yanked him out of his thoughts. Zach's father, Gil, had spoken then. Gil sat across from him, and he and his husband, Tom, who was also Zach's best man and childhood best friend, had been chatting with them through most of the evening.

When he heard their story over dinner, he'd been shocked into silence. Didn't fathers only fall in love with their children's friends on daytime soap operas? At least that was what he remembered. Charlie used to watch *Days of Our Lives* religiously.

"Thanks," he finally responded. "She's sometimes a bit much."

Gil chuckled. "She is a handful. Reminds me of Sami."

"I was actually thinking of Zach," Tom commented.

"I think she's a combination of both," Donna Kelly chimed in. She sat on the other side of her ex-husband. Even though they were divorced, Gil and Donna got along well. While that had not always been the case, according to some stories Van had shared, Eric was pleased to see the former spouses interact so easily. In his job, he often witnessed the other extreme.

"I think you might be right," Gil said with a nod.

"Aren't I always?" she asked. A pleased grin cut a playful path across her lips.

Gil just shook his head. "I'm not walking into *that* trap."

"I guess you *can* teach an old dog new tricks," Donna replied with a pat to Gil's head. Gil rolled his eyes, and Tom laughed. "I'm glad you housebroke him, Tom. Lord knows I tried!"

"He's a good boy," Tom commented before kissing Gil's cheek. "He does enjoy the leash I bought him, though."

Donna's face blushed seven different shades of red, and Tom's cheesy grin revealed how pleased he was with himself. From what he'd heard, getting one up on Donna was a difficult accomplishment.

"I can't believe you beat Mom at her own game," Zach chuckled. "Good for you."

"Thanks a lot, Zach," Donna said in pretend anger. "A son should come to his mother's defense."

"Since when do you need anyone to defend you?" Zach asked.

The wry grin that crept across Donna's lips revealed that she didn't.

"Let's change the subject, shall we?" Gil asked.

"To what?" Irene asked. She and her partner Tara sat to Tom's right. He'd gotten the chance to speak with both of them extensively at the party. Irene had a gruff personality and rather unique choices in clothing. She seemed to always be dressed in 80s-inspired clothes. Right now, with her crimped hair and denim jacket, she resembled Madonna from her "Like a Virgin" days.

"How about our trip tomorrow?" Tara asked. Her wavy hair was just as wild today as it had been last night. Evidently, that was part of Tara's style. He doubted anyone else but Tara, with her buoyant personality, could pull it off.

"What trip?" he asked.

"A bunch of us are renting a catamaran and taking it out tomorrow," Tara answered.

"When did that happen?"

"While you were out gallivanting around town," Gary said. "If you were helping us with decorations for the wedding, you'd have heard all about it." The playful twinkle in his eyes betrayed his irritated tone.

"So who's going?" Brody asked, artfully sidestepping Gary's attempt to discuss work detail. From what Brody had already told Eric, Gary was something of a taskmaster.

Everyone but Quinn raised their hands.

"Why aren't you going?" Brody asked.

"I've got to work tomorrow." Quinn nudged Gary's shoulder. "Someone has to bring home the bacon."

Gary shot him a look that would've made Eric's balls ascend into his body. "While I might not be presently employed, I've been working nonstop on the wedding." The typically effervescent Gary briefly disappeared. With his eyes now downcast, he resembled a sulking child.

"I'm sorry," Quinn replied before he placed a loving arm around his partner. "I guess it's too soon to joke about it, isn't it?"

Gary nodded.

"Joke about what?" Maddie asked.

If he'd been sitting next to his daughter, he'd have covered up her mouth. It was obvious that Gary's lack of a job was a sensitive subject. He didn't even realize that Gary was currently out of work. If that was true, it probably explained why he threw himself into planning the wedding.

"I, unfortunately, lost my job a few weeks ago," Gary said.

"I'm sorry," Maddie replied.

"I'm not," Quinn chimed in. "You weren't happy with your work. You need to find something else. Something that excites you."

"Penny's always done that," Tara replied with a chuckle. Who the hell was Penny? And why would mentioning her cause Quinn to glare at Tara as if he hated her?

"My dear Tara Tebow," Gary began. For some reason, Gary enjoyed using a person's full name. Eric found that a bit odd. "You couldn't be more correct if you tried. Penny has always been a bright spot in my life. And I've thought about trying to start a show, but I'd need a gimmick. I haven't been able to think of one."

"Thank God," Quinn said as his eyes looked up to the sky. He certainly didn't like this Penny person too much, did he?

Maddie's eyes narrowed in confusion. She clearly wanted more information on this Penny person. She gazed over at him with a smile dangling from her lips. It was her way of asking permission to speak. Since he was just as curious as she was, he nodded once in reply. "Who's Penny?" she quickly asked.

Quinn groaned while Gary perked up in his seat. He obviously liked this Penny character much more than Quinn did. "Do you know what a drag queen is?"

She nodded. "A man who dresses up as a woman. I've read about it online. I can also tell you the difference between a transvestite and a transsexual if you'd like to know." Eric smacked his forehead with his palm. He should've known better than to let her speak. Maddie just didn't understand restraint or discretion. They would definitely be having a talk about that later.

"Thank you," Gary said with an amused sparkle in his eyes. "But I think I've got that figured out."

"Okay, so Penny is your drag name, then?" she asked.

"Penny Poison to be exact." Gary's face stretched into a big grin. Whatever negative emotions he'd been experiencing earlier had disappeared. The same couldn't be said for Quinn. His face contorted in pain.

"I think you should do it," Zach said. "Why not start your own show? You could give Suzy Wroughtinkrotch a run for her money."

"And I could do it too, Zachary." Gary jutted his chin forward, and his eyes burned with competitive fire. There was, no doubt, some history between Gary and this other drag queen. "La Wroughtinkrotch wouldn't know what hit her."

"Then why don't you?" Van asked.

"Well, I can't just waltz up and down Commercial Street knocking on doors in search of a venue. I need something to sell them first. While Penny is fabulous, she needs an interesting angle, preferably one that the other queens haven't snatched up already."

"Can we talk about something else, please?" Quinn asked. "Talking about Penny is giving me indigestion."

"Why?" Maddie asked. Oh, for heaven's sake! A muzzle tied around her head might be the only option left.

"Bobby Quinn doesn't appreciate the fine art of drag," Gary answered before patting Quinn's shoulder. "He prefers men to be men."

"I could wear a tuxedo right now but still be a girl," Maddie told Quinn. "The clothes we wear don't change our gender." Although Eric still wished his daughter would hush, there was no denying her logic.

"Exactly," Gary agreed with a nod. "I'm a man underneath my Penny accoutrement."

"See," she said to Quinn. "Problem solved."

Quinn's lips drew into a slant. His reason for hating Penny had been cut down by a nine-year-old, and he'd been rendered speechless.

"Now back to this boat trip," Maddie said. Since she considered the matter closed down by her logic, she saw no further need to discuss it. That had always been Maddie's way. "Are we not invited because we didn't help out today?"

"Of course you're invited." Van wrapped his arm around Maddie's shoulder. "I was just uncertain if your dad wanted to go."

He most certainly did not. Eric was terrified of the ocean, and there was no way in hell he was getting in a boat smaller than a ferry. If he did, he'd likely go insane from fear. "I think we'll bow out of this one," he finally said. "But you all have a great time."

Maddie complained loudly. Since when had his daughter grown fond of boating? She'd never expressed any interest before.

"She's more than welcome to come with us," Van said. "I know how much you hate the water, but that doesn't mean Maddie can't tag along."

"Oh, yes it does," he said. "If I'm not going, neither is Maddie."

"I've always wanted to go on a boat," Maddie said. "I've never said anything about it because I know how much you hate the ocean, but I would really, really, really like to go."

"It's not safe," he replied. "I don't like it."

Maddie turned to Sami. "Is Sophia going?"

Sami glanced from Maddie to Eric. The answer was obvious, and the pained expression on her face communicated that to him. Her response would not likely prove to be very helpful. "Yes. Sophia is going. And she'll be wearing a lifejacket. We all will."

"Boat!" Sophia interjected as she tried to mimic the sound of a motorboat with her tiny lips. She was clearly excited about the ocean excursion tomorrow.

When Maddie turned back to him, her face grew even more determined. She now had a logical argument in her arsenal. "If a five-year-old is going, I'd say that's pretty safe. Don't you?"

What could he say? No? That would be indicting Sami as a bad parent, and he wasn't going to do that. Besides, it was his fear that was holding Maddie back. Was that fair to her? "What am I supposed to do while you're gone?" he asked. If his paranoia wouldn't work, perhaps guilt would do the job. "I was planning out a fun day for us tomorrow."

"You can hang out with Brody," she quickly responded. A bit too quickly for Eric. Why did he feel as if he was playing right into his daughter's hands?

"I would love to," Brody said. "I do have some clients in the morning at the gym, but I should be free after that."

Brody worked at a gym? He didn't know that. Was he a personal trainer? That explained the lean build and flat stomach.

Maddie grinned at him, knowing full well she'd already won the argument. She just wanted him to admit it.

"We'll take good care of her," Van said. Everyone at the table nodded in agreement. "Besides, I'd love to spend more time with Maddie. I don't get to see her enough."

If he could, he'd kick the chair out from under Van. He wasn't helping Eric refuse Maddie's request. Neither were all the eyes currently awaiting his response.

"Fine," he said at last.

Maddie stood up from her chair and did the cabbage patch dance to illustrate how pleased she was. First she hadn't wanted to sit next to him, and now this. How else was his daughter going to change this week? He wasn't very eager to find out. She was supposed to stay his little girl forever.

After everyone applauded her breakout number, she walked over to him and kissed his cheek. "Thank you, Papa."

"You're welcome," he whispered. "But I don't like this. Not one bit."

She nodded. He wasn't telling her anything she didn't know. "But this way, you'll get to spend some time by yourself instead of always hanging out with me."

"I like being with you."

She smiled. "And I like being with you too. But it's okay to do things without each other every now and then, right?"

What could he say? That he planned on following her around for the rest of her life? While that was definitely something he'd considered, it wasn't very practical. "Right," he added reluctantly.

"Great! And you won't be alone tomorrow anyway," she said. "You'll be with Brody."

She flashed a grin at her father after looking over his shoulder at Brody. Then she turned around and returned to her seat.

If he didn't know better, he'd say that Maddie had planned this all along.

Chapter Ten

ERIC STOOD on McMillan Pier, waving good-bye to his daughter and everyone else as they sailed away on an all-day boat tour of the Cape. Why the hell had he let Maddie go again? It was completely unlike him to allow her out of his sight, especially on such a potentially hazardous jaunt as a boat in the middle of open water.

But as he gazed at her beaming face, which was almost hidden by the huge orange life vest, he quickly remembered why he relented. Besides the fact that she hadn't given him any other option, he couldn't let his fears dictate his daughter's life.

He was terrified of the ocean. She wasn't. She had even concealed her desire to go sailing because she knew how much he detested the sea. She had been denying herself because of him.

Were there other things she hid in order not to upset him?

He couldn't help but suspect there were. She had clung to him desperately since Charlie's death, but in P-town she practically leaped out of his arms every chance she got. Had she really been clinging to him or had he been the one holding on for dear life?

If he was the problem, he had to fix it. Maddie couldn't be responsible for his stability. It was supposed to work the other way around. Had that not been what he'd been doing?

Maddie blew him one final kiss before she turned around to join Van and the rest of the gang on the approximately thirty-eight-foot catamaran. The vessel looked sturdy and big enough for the crew. For Eric, it was about another fifty feet too small. At least.

Although he didn't like the ocean, with a father who was once in the Navy, his knowledge of boats was extensive. The multihulled vessel provided more stability than a standard monohull. Although catamarans could sometimes settle into a nausea-inducing hobbyhorse motion, such movement only occurred in excessively choppy waters. The bright sun overhead and gentle waters told him that was unlikely to happen this trip.

Plus, he'd checked the Weather Channel at least twelve times since he and Maddie had gotten up this morning. Even though he hoped a thunderstorm might delay their travel plans, the forecast for today and the rest of the week boasted abundant sunshine and no rain.

It was perfect for sailing. As much as he hated to admit it.

He had briefly entertained the idea of climbing aboard. He had even convinced himself that he'd surprise Maddie by announcing at the last minute he was going, but one look at the boat quickly cured him of those ideas.

He could get on the catamaran, but he'd have an awful time. He'd be moody and grumpy and ruin Maddie's adventure. Not to mention he'd probably white-knuckle the railing and puke his guts out. He hadn't done that on the ferry over to Provincetown because he'd taken a Dramamine. Plus, the fast ferry had been big enough that he barely noticed the motion of the ocean. On the catamaran, he'd definitely experience every wave crest they brushed against.

As hard as it was for him to do, considering everything, he had to trust that Maddie would return to him safely.

There was no other alternative, and Van had promised to guard Maddie with his life.

The catamaran rounded the bend at Long Point and disappeared from his view. There was nothing more for him to do. Unless he was going to sit here until Maddie returned later that evening. She'd made him promise to meet her at the pier at seven thirty. While there had been some changes in Maddie, she remained consistent on promptness.

For some reason, that made him breathe a lot easier.

Now, he had no choice but to go about his day and try not to obsess about his daughter. Yeah, that wasn't going to happen. Perhaps Brody could take his mind off his insecurities. After all, he needed to tell Brody the truth. He couldn't have Brody continue to think that Charlie was still alive. But how was he going to broach the subject? He couldn't just mention it offhand as if it was no big deal.

Because it was. And even though it had been what Eric had needed, he couldn't help the pangs of guilt that shot through him.

And then there was what had happened at the beach. That was something they should talk about. Or was it better to ignore it all together? If he did bring it up, how exactly did one work erections into casual conversation?

Maybe what he needed to do was just go with the flow for once. That was what Charlie would have told him to do. He was in P-town, after all, where anything was possible. If he and Brody were meant to have a serious conversation, it would happen.

If not, well, then that would be the universe's way of telling him to leave it alone.

ERIC ARRIVED about an hour early at the Provincetown Gym, where Brody worked. After dinner last night, they had agreed that he would show up after Brody's last training session, which was scheduled to end at noon, and then head out to the Boatslip to lounge around in the sun.

He hadn't sunbathed in years. Luckily, he had planned for such an occasion before leaving home. He brought the bathing suit he'd purchased for his and Charlie's last trip to Grand Cayman, and it still fit. Thank God. He hated shopping alone. Charlie had always been his style guru. Without him, well, Eric was likely to buy the first item he saw without trying it on. When it came to fashion, he really didn't care.

He didn't have to worry about that today. Even from the great beyond, Charlie saved him from fashion faux pas.

But why had he gotten to the gym so damn early? Well, he sure as hell wasn't going to sit alone in the condo or wander aimlessly down Commercial Street. That would only invite his mind to run rampant with worries about Maddie and her safety. It was better for him and everyone else if his thoughts remained otherwise occupied.

That was why he came dressed in his workout gear.

He could lift a few weights while Brody worked. That would clear his mind, and then he and Brody could depart for their date on the sundeck.

Eric paused before opening the door to the gym.

Was this a date? No. Of course it wasn't. Brody was just continuing to be kind by spending time with him. Just like he'd done yesterday. This was *not* a date.

If it wasn't, then why did the thought cross his mind? Did he want it to be a date?

That couldn't be it. Brody was attractive. His erection on the beach certainly established that. But his heart still belonged to Charlie. And likely always would.

Relieved, he opened the door and walked inside.

The first floor of the gym consisted of the changing areas and the entrance to the group fitness room. Through the small window in the door, he could see a group of men currently working on some yoga moves. Right now, they were all engaged in the downward-facing dog pose. As if they needed work on that position.

The music that drifted down the set of stairs to his left told him that the weight room was most likely on the next level, so up he went. At the top stood a desk where an extremely muscled-out man sat, drinking a protein shake. He smiled when he saw Eric and stood to greet him. "Welcome to Provincetown Gym." How big was his neck? It looked about as wide as a tree trunk. He half expected the guy to yell *Hulk, smash!* and then reduce the desk to splinters.

"Thanks," he said. Eric tried to force his gaze from the man's neck, but he couldn't rip it away. Did people really find such mass sexy? "I'm not a member here. But I'd like to get a one-day pass."

"Not a problem." The Hulk handed him a paper to fill out and told him the fee.

"Is Brody around?" Eric asked as he wrote his information on the form.

"Yeah," he said with a nod to a line of Nautilus machines, which sat before a mirrored wall that spanned about three-fourths the length of the room. "He's on the other side with a client. You have an appointment?"

"No. Just making sure he's here."

A smirk unfolded on his lips. "Gotcha."

What the hell did that mean? "I'm sorry?"

The Hulk laughed. It was even scarier than an angry Hulk. It made him look demented. "No worries, man. Happens all the time."

"I don't understand," Eric said. He handed the form back and paid what he owed. "People always ask if Brody's here?"

The Hulk nodded. His smirk turned into a grin that rivaled the Joker. A Joker Hulk? Now that was a terrifying combination. "He's *very* popular with the boys." Eric didn't like the way he said "very." It suggested that Brody was some common slut who slept around with countless guys. And maybe he was. He didn't really know Brody. Still, it bothered him.

"Well, that's not why I'm here," he said. He wanted to make it clear that he wasn't one of Brody's usual tricks. If that was what Brody did. "We're just friends."

"They usually are," the Hulk said with a wink.

If he'd had a dumbbell in his hand, he'd knock the Hulk across the head with it. Not that it would hurt the man much. But it would certainly make him feel better.

Okay, that wasn't a healthy response. Much less a realistic one. Like Maddie usually told him, he needed to chill out. "Thanks," he said before heading over to the free-weight area. He most definitely had a reason to work out now.

Since the gym wasn't very big, it only took him a few steps to cross the width of the room to the free-weight station. Of course, he had to weave around the many machines jam-packed into the available space. As he passed the preacher curl bench, the guy currently working out there winked at him and said hello. The lascivious grin that slid across his lips revealed his intent, but the wedding ring on his finger pissed Eric off. Why the hell did married gays think it was okay to play around? He and Charlie never did, and he wouldn't have had it any other way.

He was a one-man man.

So instead of returning the flirtation, Eric gave the guy his back. If the man didn't let it drop, he'd be forced to tell him to go home to his partner. He wasn't in the mood to be hit on by someone else's husband.

He placed his knapsack, which held what he'd need for the Boatslip later, next to the bench. Then he crossed over to the weights, where two other guys were working out while they admired their own reflections. How annoying was that? If they had to preen and flex, couldn't they do so in the privacy of their own rooms?

As he grabbed the forty-five pound weights from the rack, he spotted Brody with his client. The man, who looked to be in his late twenties, lay flat on his back with his right leg over Brody's shoulder. Brody was positioned on top of him, pressing his weight against the man's leg. He was most likely stretching his client after their workout, so why did he suddenly want to rush over to Brody and lift him off his paying customer?

He had no right to be territorial. He'd just met Brody, and it wasn't like they were dating or anything. They'd just spent one day together. It had been a good day. One he needed to escape his grief. But that was it.

The metal from the dumbbell cut into his hand. When he gazed downward, he was gripping the weight so hard he was shaking. Well, somebody needed to take a deep breath and regain control.

"Eric!"

Brody's voice drew his attention back to the spectacle that was Brody dry-humping his client. A grin settled onto Brody's lips as he waved to Eric with his free hand.

"I'll be with you in a minute."

He nodded. What else could he do? Besides throw Brody's client out the window.

Eric immediately sat on the weight bench, brought the weights to his chest, lay back, and commenced the dumbbell press that he hoped would clear the red haze from his vision.

Just what the fuck was going on with him? In a matter of seconds, he'd turned into some man he didn't even recognize. The last time he'd experienced anything close to what he felt now was when Charlie had told him someone at his work had made a pass at him.

Eric almost came unglued. He stormed out of their house and was about to go kick the man's ass before Charlie managed to talk him down. Charlie wasn't interested. Eric had never questioned that, but the mere thought of some sex-crazed idiot wanting his man drove him mad.

But Brody wasn't Charlie. So why did he still want to hurt someone?

"You're not doing that right."

Brody suddenly stood over him on the weight bench. His groin was about six inches away from Eric's head, and the bulge in Brody's shorts was clearly visible. It revealed that Brody packed much more than just six inches. The revelation almost made Eric drop the weights.

"Whoa there, big guy," Brody said. He moved quickly to rest his hands under Eric's as a spot. "You're gonna hurt yourself."

"I've lifted heavier."

Brody laughed. "No doubt. But your form is sloppy." He held his hands over Eric's and readjusted the weight in Eric's grip. "Your palms need to face up, and you need to move the weight directly over your shoulders." He grabbed Eric's outstretched arms and moved them back so they were where they needed to be.

"That's what I was doing," Eric replied. His voice was low, almost a whisper. Brody was just trying to help him. So why was Brody's warm touch turning him on?

"No, you weren't," Brody said. "You were over your chest. Not your shoulders. And you're not pulling in your abdominals." He patted Eric's stomach to indicate that they needed to be tauter. The contact definitely achieved that goal, as he immediately tensed. But it also had another effect. His cock was coming to life.

An erection in his gym shorts would be impossible to hide. He closed his eyes and imagined kittens being decapitated. Hopefully, that would stop him from pitching a tent there on the gym room floor.

Brody knelt behind him. His hands had moved from Eric's stomach to his shoulders. Damn, his hands were driving Eric crazy. "Then when you lower the dumbbells, roll your shoulder blades together and pinch. That will accentuate your chest more."

Eric nodded. Words were impossible to form.

"Now do a couple of reps and let me see if you've got it."

How was he supposed to do that? It was taking all his concentration to keep the blood in his body from surging into his cock.

"Come on, you big baby," Brody said.

He exhaled, hoping the move would take the wind out of his sails before he lowered and raised the weights as Brody had instructed.

"Good boy," Brody replied. A huge grin stretched across his face. "It's good to know you can take direction."

"I give as good as I get," Eric replied. Brody's eyes went wide and his mouth hung open. Oh shit! Why did he have to say that?

Brody winked. "That's good to know too." He turned around and went back to his client, who had finished the stretching routine on his own.

Eric sat up. Perspiration dripped from his face, and he'd only done two sets. He felt as though he'd been working out for hours. Plus, his cheeks were warm, and when he gazed at his reflection in the mirror before him, his face was flushed a deep red.

But what was worse was that the Hulk sat at the desk, grinning. He'd witnessed the entire scene, and the knowing stare told Eric he most definitely knew the score.

Now if only he'd clue Eric in on what had just happened.

Chapter Eleven

BRODY HAD to be a glutton for punishment or something. While he enjoyed the occasional spanking or the sting of a riding crop smacked across his bare blond butt, since when did he torture himself like this? Not in recent memory, for damn sure.

Yet here he was, once again spending his free time with Eric. Why did he have to agree to hang out with him while everyone else was out on the catamaran? Well, for starters, he just couldn't say no to Maddie when she suggested it. She wanted to go, and Eric was not going to let her. Eric's creased brow at dinner last night had been enough evidence of that. But when he'd begun to at least contemplate the idea, Maddie jumped at the chance to stick him with Eric so her father wouldn't be alone.

How could he have said no to that? He could have. But that would have made him a big doofus in Maddie's eyes. Why that mattered to him was a mystery, but it did.

So here he was, walking with Eric down Commercial Street and headed toward the Boatslip, where they would spend a few hours baking in the sun. He hadn't graced the pool deck in a few weeks. Work and wedding preparations had kept him busy, so it would be nice to just lounge around a bit. But what would happen when he saw Eric in his swimwear?

Was he going to have to spend all afternoon lying on his stomach to keep his erection from showing? He'd probably end up with a dark tan on his back while his chest and stomach remained white. Now wouldn't that be attractive?

Maybe Eric wouldn't have a skimpy suit. He could have brought board shorts, and Brody didn't find those attractive in the least. They were made for straight dudes who chased boobies and booty, not for gay boys who enjoyed putting on display what their mommas gave them. While not many gay men wore those long swimsuits with drawstrings, Eric just might be one of those guys. He lived in Petersham, after all. That place wasn't exactly a gay destination. So Eric most likely had a suit that was better fitted for Petersham than Provincetown.

Or so he hoped.

"Why so quiet?"

Eric's question drew him out of his musings. When Brody turned to face him, his bearded face parted into a wide grin. Long strands of his dark hair fell in front of his amber eyes. Damn! Did he have to be such a sexy fucker? Even if Eric did bring board shorts, he'd probably still get a raging erection.

"I don't mean to be," he finally said. He had to stop ogling Eric. "Just thinking about all the work that still needs to be done for the wedding. Gary will no doubt turn into a raving bitch after taking the day off today. He'll likely complain about it. Everyone will tell him that he deserved a break, but he'll just get pissy and start barking orders. Not really looking forward to that."

"Well, even though he's tough, you can't argue with his results. The bachelor party went well. I'm sure the wedding will be just as great."

Brody snorted. "Not before blood is spilled, I'm sure. You weren't there for the setup of the bachelor party. It was a bloodbath."

"I'm sure it wasn't that bad."

"Just you wait. Gary is lulling you into a false sense of security. When it's time to decorate for the wedding, you'll be sucked into the madness." He laughed like a comic-book villain to make his point.

"I'm sure I'll be fine," Eric replied. His jutting chin punctuated his confident tone.

"Don't say I didn't warn you."

Eric broke out into laughter that made his amber eyes sparkle. The sunlight glinted off the golden specks in his irises that turned his eyes into small, radiant suns. If Brody could, he'd spend the day sunbathing nude under such a glowing gaze.

Well, shit. There he went again. Was he ever going to get his head out of the gutter when it came to Eric? It was bad enough he got hard when Eric fell on top of him at the beach. Of course, Eric hadn't exactly been limp, either.

But he tried not to dwell on that. Erections happened. They were men, after all. No, worse than that. They were gay men, and gay men typically wore their erections as if they were clothing accessories. Besides, it wasn't exactly unusual for a man's cock to develop a mind of its own. It certainly had happened to him before, but Eric was married. He had no doubt been extremely embarrassed by it, which was why Brody hadn't brought it up.

What was he going to say anyway? Hey, Eric, care to explain the woody you popped on the beach? Talk about awkward conversations. No, the best thing to do was to simply let the matter drop.

But he really didn't want to. Especially after he realized that he'd dreamed about being on the beach with Eric and Maddie even before he'd met them. That was just damn bizarre. While he didn't have the answers, it confused him more than the plot of a David Lynch movie.

He'd spent most of last night trying to figure it out. Could he have been mistaken? Maybe the man in his dreams had been someone else. That was entirely possible. But the dream felt more like a memory, which couldn't have been the case. He would've remembered a scene as strong as the one he'd dreamed about.

Perhaps it had been a coincidence. Those happened all the time. His dream and his time on the beach with Eric and Maddie might have been happenstance. His subconscious might have just been trying to make sense of the dream still, and when he experienced an event similar to what he'd dreamed about, his fucked-up brain merged them together. That certainly made more sense.

Of course, it might have also explained his insanely intense attraction to Eric. Maybe it wasn't a happy accident after all. Perhaps

Provincetown had brought them together for some reason. But it was stupid to think that way. It wasn't like Eric was available.

No, it had to be a coincidence or a mistake. That was what he settled on after endless hours of tossing and turning. Only when he'd finally accepted that had Brody been able to fall asleep.

But now that he was with Eric again, he wasn't as sure as he'd been.

What was he going to do now?

WHEN THEY finally stepped onto the pool deck at the Boatslip, Brody couldn't believe his eyes. How many guys were here already? Typically, during Family Week, choosing the best spot for a lounge chair was easy. The arrival of the gay parenting sect usually meant that the Boatslip would be a nice, quiet respite. A place to escape the screaming children who invaded Commercial Street and where a person could avoid being run over by a stroller.

That was why he'd suggested they spend the afternoon here. They would be able to relax and unwind.

What an epic fail!

Rows of white lounge chairs already cluttered the expansive deck that spanned about fifty yards to the right of the front entrance. Scores of oiled-up men wearing skimpy suits lounged in those chairs. They chatted and flirted with each other while the music blared from the many speakers that lined the deck. Servers weaved through the crowd, carrying trays filled with ordered drinks. There were so many people it looked more like Twink Week or Bear Week than Family Week.

There wasn't even much space in the pool. Guys stood around the steps that descended into the usually chilly water, sizing each other up. Most likely trying to decide which one would be the flavor for the afternoon. How did he know that? Well, he'd spent his time in the pool before ultimately picking his treat.

This might not have been the best decision he'd ever made. Eric wasn't used to the sexual politics that went along with sunbathing among the gay and the restless. He'd spent the last few years married in conservative Petersham. He needed to find some place more Eric's speed.

"Two pool chairs please."

Brody turned around to find Eric talking to Bob, the tall and gruff cashier who typically manned the register. Bob wasn't unfriendly. He just always had a pissed-off look on his face. As if he constantly smelled shit and couldn't get away from it.

When Eric retrieved his wallet from his backpack, Brody trotted over to his side. What was Eric thinking? He couldn't possibly want to stay here.

"Hey, Brody," Bob said. Although his tone was friendly, his face seemed to indicate he wanted to break Brody's nose.

"How's it going, Bob?"

"Can't complain, I guess." With the sour expression that crumpled his face, it appeared as if Bob had a complaint about something.

"I can't believe how busy it is here. It's usually not like this during Family Week."

Bob nodded and laughed. When most people laughed, their eyes reflected their amusement. Not Bob. His eyes remained small and beady. If he really got angry, would anyone know the difference? "Can't explain it either," he said after abruptly cutting off his own laughter. How weird was that? It was like a laugh track dying in midplay. "Maybe the gays without kids are looking to escape the baby buggy brigade. Or maybe these are all the gay dads, and their kids are home taking a nap. Who knows and who cares? It's good for business, and that's all that matters."

Yeah, and a busy Boatslip usually made for a naughty Boatslip. "We can go somewhere else," he said to Eric. "The Provincetown Inn might be less crowded."

"I'm fine with here," Eric said as he handed Bob money. "Unless you're not."

Of course he was fine being here, but he was worried Eric's cautious and conservative feathers might get ruffled. How was Eric going to handle sitting beside a guy getting a hand job by the man in the next chair? Or what if Eric went to the restroom to find two or more guys getting it on in one of the stalls?

Then another concern hit him, harder than a Mack truck doing ninety on the interstate.

What would happen if some random drunk queen hit on Eric? That probably wouldn't go over very well. He'd already witnessed Eric's rather cool response to flirtation at the gym. The poor guy at the preacher curl station had been icily rebuffed.

A gay gym was typically a meat market. But here, the inebriated, half-dressed, and horny men turned this place into a virtual slaughterhouse.

"So what are we doing?" Eric asked.

"This place can get wild," he replied. "If you're okay with that, we can stay."

Eric shrugged. "I'm not some backward hillbilly. I've ventured into wilder waters than Petersham before."

Was Eric reading his mind or something? Now that was fucking weird.

"Okay," he said. "As long as you're sure."

Eric's nod told Brody that he was. He just hoped Eric truly meant it.

"Now that that's settled, go and see Ricardo. I'm sure you remember him," Bob said to Brody.

Fuck! Ricardo worked here now? He hadn't seen him since after their date last month. They'd gone to dinner, and he had been excited because Ricardo had potential to be the one. He was hot, met all his requirements, and had almost pounded him into next week.

But then he made the fortunate mistake of letting Ricardo sleep over.

The man snored so loudly the rafters rattled. There was no way in hell he was going to spend the rest of his life with earplugs shoved into his ears every night. Naturally, he had cut him loose and never called him again.

What would Ricardo do when they were reunited? Would he even acknowledge Brody's presence or just drop a pool chair on his head?

"Thanks," he finally said to Bob before escorting Eric through the maze of slutty sun worshippers, who peered over their sunglasses at them as they passed.

"Who's Ricardo?" Eric asked from behind him.

Brody pretended not to hear. He couldn't deal with Eric's questions right now. His mind was too preoccupied with what he was going to say to Ricardo. Would an apology work, or would that just rub salt into the wound? Maybe he could just play it off as if nothing happened. That might work. Yeah, in his dreams maybe. Dumped gay men weren't exactly known for their graciousness. Not that he could expect Ricardo to be civil. After what he had done, he deserved a concussion from a lounge-chair mishap.

He had to stop treating men as if they were tissues in a Kleenex box.

"Hey, Ricardo," Brody said when they finally made their way to him. He'd racked his brain to come up with just the right words, and the ones that escaped his mouth were "Hey, Ricardo"?

Smooth, Brody. Real smooth.

Ricardo, who had not been looking in Brody's direction, was dressed in a skimpy, almost see-through white Speedo. Brody could practically see his dark pubic hair through the fabric. The outfit most likely helped with tips. Not that Ricardo needed any assistance. His muscular body and tanned skin would make any of these boys hand over their wallet if he asked.

"Brody," he replied. His face, which had been smiling a few moments before, turned grave. Ricardo glared at him and then glanced over to Eric. After rolling his eyes, he said, "Just stand where you want your chairs. I'll bring them right there." He turned abruptly around to get the pool furniture and bent over. Could his suit be any more transparent? Brody could practically count all the hairs in his ass crack.

"How about over there?" Eric asked. He pointed to a recently vacated area along the side rail bordering the pool. It wasn't exactly an ideal location. They were too far away from the beachfront to get much of a breeze, and in this heat, a waft of wind was almost necessary. Plus they would be smack-dab in the middle of the path most people took to go to the pool or the restrooms.

He wasn't in a position to be picky, though. He just needed to put as much distance between him and Ricardo as possible. "Sure," he finally said. "That's great."

With the deck chairs over his head, Ricardo followed them over to the spot. He slammed the chairs down and then opened them up as he would for any other visitor, but the animosity in his forceful movements was apparent. It even drew the attention of some of their neighbors, who had been sleeping before Ricardo made his ruckus.

Brody glanced over at Eric. What was he grinning about?

Eric took some money out of his wallet and offered it to Ricardo as a tip. Ricardo waved it off. "Keep it," he said as he glared over at Brody. "I'm sure you'll be needing every penny." He spun around and walked back to the line of customers waiting for him to bring out their chairs.

Brody sighed as he sat down on the edge of his lounge. That could've gone better. Of course, it could have also been a lot worse.

"Bad breakup?" Eric asked. He shrugged out of his backpack and sat in the chair next to his.

"It was one date." Brody glanced up at Eric. Thankfully, there was no judgment in his eyes. But did he have to look so amused? "And you can wipe that smirk off your face. It wasn't funny."

"Maybe not to you," Eric replied. "But I found it hilarious."

If anyone needed a lounge chair dropped on his head, it was Eric. Why was Eric getting such pleasure from his pain?

"Want to talk about it?"

"Not really."

Eric nodded. "Okay. I'll let you be. For now at least. But I got to tell you, that's a story I want to hear."

"Yeah, yeah," he said as he waved Eric's comments away. "Don't you have to change or something? You're a bit overdressed in your gym attire."

Eric took his swimsuit out of his backpack before heading over to the outside restrooms that stood along the far wall, to the left of the pool. He tried to gauge what type of swimsuit Eric had brought with him, but Eric had balled it up in his hand. That meant they were definitely not board shorts.

As if running into Ricardo wasn't bad enough, now he'd have to spend the afternoon hiding a massive hard-on.

Could this day get any worse?

BRODY HAD taken off his T-shirt and his shorts, ordered drinks for him and Eric, and even applied sunscreen to his body, but Eric had yet to emerge from the restrooms. He was starting to get concerned. Had Eric eaten something that hadn't agreed with him? Or even worse—had he found someone hot in the bathroom to screw?

Guys fucking in the restroom wasn't exactly unheard of, but Eric was happily married. Not that being happily married meant monogamy. Plenty of partnered guys played well with others. Gary and Quinn, for example. They were the epitome of happiness, but that didn't stop them from sleeping with other men together or apart. And that didn't seem to affect their relationship in the least.

Yet he didn't peg Eric as a proponent of polyamory. He struck Brody as a one-man man. Something else had to be going on in the restroom.

That was when Brody spotted Dan, the guy he'd thrown out of his apartment the other day, sunning a few rows over. Wasn't that just great? Ricardo and Dan both in the same place. What were the odds?

In Provincetown, they were quite good, actually. With so many gay men visiting the same places in so small a community, running into someone familiar, whether it was a pleasant experience or not, happened a lot.

Brody turned onto his stomach. Hopefully, the move would render him invisible. He'd just be one more Speedo-covered butt among all the other butts currently facing the sun. And from this vantage, he'd be able to devour the eye candy, which was in abundance.

But as his gaze swept over the mountains of back muscle and valleys of butt crack that abounded, his cock remained unimpressed. It yawned and went back to sleep. That was new. He'd practically been walking around with a boner for the past couple of days around Eric.

Which wasn't very surprising news. Eric was quite possibly the hottest man here.

Well, he would be if he ever came out of the restroom.

"I'm back."

When Brody glanced up to where Eric stood, intelligent thought flew right out of his brain. And naturally, his cock was wide-awake and trying to bore a hole through the plastic of the deck chair.

Eric was definitely not wearing board shorts. Right now, a pair of green low-rise, square-cut trunks clung to his body as if they were a second skin, and the massive bulge in the front was breathtaking. Had he shoved a banana and two apples in his trunks?

"What took you so long?" His question came out in long pauses. He had to actually think about each word in order to sound coherent.

"Well, it's embarrassing really. But I was worried I might look ridiculous."

Was he fucking serious right now? Hot was more like it. Or maybe scrumptious was a better word. When Eric bent over to adjust his chair so that it rested at about a sixty-degree angle, Brody had to wipe the drool from his chin.

No, the word he was looking for was delicious. With Eric's toned and perky butt right in front of his face, he had to fight the urge to shove his face between Eric's cheeks.

"I think you look great," he finally said. Was he panting? It definitely sounded like panting. He had to get himself under control here.

"Thanks," Eric said. His face broke into a shy grin. It was so cute that it made Brody want to mount him right here. "Charlie bought it for me when we went to Grand Cayman a few years ago."

Well, damn. He'd forgotten all about the husband. Hell, when he first saw Eric in his swimsuit, he'd almost forgotten his own name, so he forgave himself for the lapse.

Being married, though, just saved Eric from being eaten alive and Brody from embarrassing himself. If Eric wasn't taken, he'd be running his hands across his chest, where he'd linger in the vale of chest hair that separated his taut pecs. From there, he'd follow the line of fuzz that departed hair valley to the field of dark fur across his belly. After that, well, he'd head to knob hill, where he'd definitely set up camp.

"Charlie chose well," he said.

Eric sat up in his chair. His amber eyes had darkened to copper again. Eric's mood had grown serious. What was going on? "He always did."

"Did?" Brody asked. "Don't you mean does?"

Eric shook his head.

"I don't understand."

After a huge sigh, Eric said, "Charlie's dead. He died almost two years ago."

How was that possible? Eric had told him Charlie was waiting for him back in Petersham, hadn't he?

But Eric's apologetic eyes told him that this was the real truth. And that what he'd been made to believe had been a lie.

That realization was like a punch to the gut. Maybe that was why he wanted to throw up.

Chapter Twelve

WORDS REFUSED to form on Brody's lips. He tried to respond to Eric's revelation and to his numerous pleas to forgive him, but his throat muscles had closed shut. It was like some sadist had tightened a vise around his neck. His mouth was also dry, and whatever alien had been deposited in his gut was doing somersaults.

Was this what John Hurt's character from *Alien* experienced before the chestburster exploded through his rib cage? If a tiny monster were eating its way out of him, it would serve Eric right if it chose him to be the next victim.

How could he have lied to him about Charlie? But even more important, *why* had Eric lied? That was definitely not cool. It was as far from cool as someone could get. It was, well, what the hell was the opposite of cool? Temperate? No, that was just stupid.

What Eric had done was just plain *un*cool. Was that even a word? Fuck. Why the hell did that matter right now? Uncool was the word he was going to go with. Although other words came to mind, like jackass, fuckwad, and asshole, he just couldn't bring himself to say them. The pain clearly reflected in Eric's sad, droopy eyes prevented him from unleashing a volley of completely justifiable curse words.

Never in his life had he been this pissed off at someone who wasn't either of his parents. Usually when he was this angry, he let it out. In his opinion, there was no reason not to share the rage, but Eric held some weird power over him. If Brody could throttle him and hold him at the same time, he would. What the hell was that about?

Even so, Eric was a jackass, fuckwad asshole just the same.

After all, he'd spent the last twenty-four hours or so berating himself for finding Eric so attractive. Every time he got a hard-on from looking at Eric or from the slightest contact, he had contemplated buying a baseball bat and bashing himself in the nuts.

And why not? Nothing else had seemed to be working.

But now? Well, those hours of torture had been completely unwarranted. Eric wasn't married. At least not in a legal sense. He would always be married to Charlie in his heart and in spirit, but there was no husband waiting for him at home.

If he had wanted to, he really could have done something about his attraction.

And if he'd known Eric was available, he most likely would have. He would've found some way to pawn Maddie off on someone. Most likely Van. Then there would have been dinner, dancing, and tons of making out. After that, he'd be facedown on his mattress, munching on his feathered pillow as Eric drilled his ass.

They could have had a sweaty hot time. But no! Eric had to lie about his dead husband.

Instead of getting naked, they'd gone sightseeing. Instead of mounting Eric, they mounted bikes and toured the biking trails. There was no reason for them to have been bashful about their erections on the beach. They could have taken their hard cocks in hand in the privacy of Brody's apartment.

The flirty eyes, the coy smiles, and the lingering brushes of their flesh, which had all turned him into a horny teenager, had been unnecessary. At least that was how he usually felt about those things.

He was a man, and if he wanted something or someone, he went for it. Once interest was established, there was no need for a sexual cat and mouse. Why pine for the candy bar when it was better to just rip off the packaging and eat it up?

That was how he had always approached men and every other situation in life. And that was how he'd been searching for the perfect man to call his own.

And maybe that was why it hadn't been working.

If he'd known Eric was single, he'd never have gotten to know him. He would have dismissed Eric like he'd done with Dan, or he would've been another notch on his bedpost like Ricardo.

And Maddie? Well, poor Maddie never would have stood a chance. He most likely wouldn't have acknowledged her presence. He wouldn't have talked Skynyrd with her or taken the time to recount the history of his ancestor Desire Cowing. If she'd asked him a question like she always did to those around her, he might have told her to ask her dad. He couldn't have been bothered. They wouldn't have teased each other relentlessly or laughed at inside jokes.

He'd never have grown as fond of her as he had. If he'd thought for one second that Eric was single.

What the hell did that say about him?

Well, it made *him* the jackass, fuckwad asshole, didn't it?

Eric opened his mouth, no doubt to apologize for the millionth time, but Brody held up his hand. Eric nodded and sat quietly.

His throat had opened up, and the monster in his belly had gone back to sleep. It was time to set things right.

"So," he said. "Tell me about Charlie."

WAS BRODY serious right now? Eric had just told him that he had lied about Charlie, and sure, for a while there he seemed pissed off. Okay, that might be a bit of an understatement. Had Brody been a volcano, he'd have been Mount Saint Helens about to blow sky-high.

But the eruption Eric had prepared for never happened. Just when he expected Brody to unleash a lava flow of obscenities, the rising magma stopped and reversed course.

The volcano inside Brody went dormant. Disaster had been averted.

But why?

And now, instead of asking him why he'd lied, Brody inquired about Charlie.

If Eric hadn't already been sitting on the deck chair, he would have fallen over.

"I don't understand," he finally said.

Brody leaned back in the pool chair. His green eyes, thankfully, no longer blazed with emerald fire. They were warm and kind. But why did they also appear grateful?

"Have you lost the ability to understand the English language?" Brody asked.

"What? No. Of course not."

"Then I don't understand your problem with my question."

A smile teased its way from one corner of Brody's mouth to the other. The smirking bastard was enjoying Eric's confusion. Normally he wasn't a fan of being the butt of a joke, but after what he'd done, what choice did he have? He just had to take it. And if Brody decided to punch him in the nose later, well, he wouldn't arrest him for striking a police officer.

"Why aren't you angry anymore?" he asked. "Or asking me why I lied? Hell, why aren't you punching me in the face? That was a crappy thing I did."

Brody nodded. "I'm not going to argue with you there. And if you really want me to knock you upside your head, I will." His teasing smile broadened into a full taunt.

"Why are you fucking with me right now?"

Brody arched his eyebrows. He evidently took the question far more seductively than Eric intended. Instead of answering his question, though, Brody allowed the sexual tension in the air to linger between them like an advancing warm front. Then he adjusted himself on the pool chair so that he lay on his side. The sun caught in his dirty-blond hair and turned it to gold.

Could he look any more attractive? That was what Eric had said to himself when he first exited the restroom after changing into his suit. It had actually taken him a few moments to remember how to walk. All he could do was stare at the glistening beads of sweat that coated Brody's tanned, lean body. Then when Brody turned over on his stomach, he'd had to place his hands in front of his crotch. The sight of Brody's bubble butt barely covered by his blue Speedo made him instantly hard. He had to take several deep breaths before his erection deflated.

But now, he'd never been drawn to him more. It wasn't just the sexy pose that Brody was unconsciously holding. The side of his head rested against the deck chair, and his left arm draped casually over his head and across the back of the chair. Small tufts of blond hair sprouted from the exposed armpit. What he wouldn't give to nuzzle his nose in those silky sun-like strands. Or to lick a trail from his smooth chest down to the crevices of his six-pack, where beads of perspiration collected in shallow pools.

"You're staring," Brody said with a chuckle. His laughter refocused Eric's attention.

"Sorry," he said. "Just thinking."

"Uh-huh. Sure you were." The twinkle in Brody's eyes told him that he hadn't been very convincing. He'd been caught staring, and Brody didn't seem to care. Why did that make him hard? He had to sit forward and hope that his body would hide the tenting fabric of his suit.

"So then why aren't you mad? I really want to know."

Brody sighed heavily. His green eyes, which had been sparkling, now hid underneath clouds of disappointment. Brody had seemed fine. A little too fine, actually. But maybe it was just an act. Maybe he was trying to make the best of this situation, but since Eric was pushing for answers, he was giving Brody no choice but to express his displeasure.

Perhaps Brody regretted meeting him. Or agreeing to pick him and Maddie up at the pier or showing them around town. Brody might have been trying to find a polite way of extracting himself from Eric's side, but he hadn't left Brody any other option but to say what Eric most likely didn't want to hear.

That was what he expected. And deserved.

"Will you stop that?" Brody asked. "Not everything is about you."

"What now?"

"I can see your wheels turning. You're wondering if I was just pretending to be okay or something. At least until I found some excuse to get up and leave your lying ass behind." Was Brody clairvoyant or something? "Am I right?"

Eric nodded. "Frighteningly so."

"Well, I'm not answering your question because I'm afraid what you may think of me when you hear it." Brody's knitted eyebrows revealed his concern.

"What I might think of you?" he asked. "I'm the one who's guilty of the lie of omission. Sure, I didn't outright tell you that Charlie was still alive, but when you assumed he was, I didn't correct you. I let you go on thinking what I wanted you to think because, well, because it was what I needed."

"You needed to lie to me?"

Eric shook his head. "No. It's just that I was so tired of the look people got in their eyes whenever they learned that Charlie was dead. The long-suffering sighs. Eyes filled with pity. It got so bad that I stopped venturing out of the house when I wasn't out patrolling. And even when I pulled someone over, the minute they saw me approach in their side-view mirror, their pissed-off expression about getting a speeding ticket changed. It was like, 'Oh, here comes the poor guy whose husband died.'" He realized he was rambling, but he couldn't stop himself. Not even the sideways glances from their sunning neighbors could shut him up. He'd never expressed his frustration with being a grieving husband to anyone before. Not even to Van. He'd opened the dam, and there was no holding it back now. "No matter what I'm talking about or who I'm talking to. It could be one of Maddie's teachers. Or two idiots fighting in a bar. It's always the same. They look at me as if I'm some mistreated dog they happened upon. And I'm sick of it."

When he paused to take a breath, Brody was no longer reclining in the chair. He was now sitting on the side of the lounge, facing him. He also held Eric's hands in his. When had that happened? The warmth of Brody's touch calmed him down, though. Yet again. It gave him the strength to continue.

"So when you assumed that Charlie was still alive, well, I held onto that. Because for the first time in almost two years, I'd met someone who could look at me without a crushing sadness reflected in their eyes. I don't know why, but it made me come to life. As if there was more to me than the grief that I'd been carrying around. So I embraced it. No, that's not right. I welcomed it like a vacation, and because of that, I've actually been able to have fun. I wouldn't have

132 | Jacob Z. Flores

enjoyed the Pilgrim Monument or biking to Race Point otherwise. If you'd known about Charlie and offered to show me around, I would have guessed it was out of pity. That you were showing kindness to the guy with the dead husband. And that would have been all I saw in your eyes."

Before he could stop himself, he reached out and cupped Brody's cheek with his right hand. Brody smiled and leaned into the contact. Not only did it feel natural, it felt right. "And I've preferred the way your green eyes have been looking at me instead. No sadness. No pity. Just seeing me. Eric Vasquez. Not the man Charlie Warren left behind."

"I do see you," Brody said. He placed his right hand over Eric's left, which still rested on his cheek. "But that's only because you lied to me. If you hadn't, well, you and I wouldn't be here right now."

Eric allowed his hand to drop from Brody's face. Not even the apparent disappointment reflected in Brody's expression, which made him cuter than a dog with sad puppy eyes, could make Eric resume the contact. What did Brody mean by that comment? "I don't understand."

"And that's what I was worried about admitting to you. It won't exactly paint me in a positive light."

Eric laughed. He held both of Brody's hands in his. It was his turn to be strong for Brody. "Well, I'm not exactly sparkling at the moment," he finally said. "So tell me. What did you mean?"

"Well, you remember that night at the bachelor party, when you asked me why I was alone?"

Eric remembered quite well. He'd seen such an intense sadness descend upon Brody that was quite different from the man he'd just met. He recalled wondering what that had been about. It appeared now he would get his answer. "You said you hadn't met the right man yet. That you had some pretty high standards."

"And you said that if I was looking for perfection, that I'd never find it," Brody added.

He shrugged. "Okay, so what about that?"

Brody exhaled. His shoulders slumped, and he gripped Eric's hands tightly. What did Brody fear would happen? That he would get up and run away after Brody admitted whatever he was holding back? Brody hadn't done that to him, and he was intent on returning the favor.

"I was searching for perfection, and I see that now," Brody finally said. "You see, I had this list of requirements that I was looking for in a man. If a guy I was interested in didn't meet them, I crossed him off my list and moved on. That's what happened to Ricardo," he said with a nod of his head over to the sexy pool attendant. "He's a nice guy. Kind of a catch, really. He was kind and respectful. He was never grossly inappropriate, and, well…." His face blushed, and he looked away.

"Good in bed?"

Brody nodded. Embarrassment had never looked more adorable.

"Then what was the problem?"

"He snored," Brody admitted. "And I'm talking like louder than a jumbo jet crashing into a speeding train."

Eric couldn't help the laugh that escaped his throat. He wasn't making fun of Brody, but his slanted lips clearly communicated Brody thought he was. He laughed because he'd lived with someone whose snore lifted the roof off the house. Charlie always had sinus troubles, and as a result Eric spent years sleeping next to that jet crashing into the train. "I'm sorry," he finally said between breaths. "I understand, and I'm not laughing at you. Charlie was probably worse than Ricardo, though. He sometimes woke Maddie up from two rooms away. It was awful."

Brody smiled, but it wasn't one that communicated any merriment. It conveyed disappointment. "The only difference is that you didn't kick Charlie to the curb because of it. You accepted him for who he was. You didn't let one annoying character trait turn you off from him. That's what I've been doing for the past year. If I didn't like anything about a man I dated, I cut him loose. How much of an asshole does that make me?"

How was he supposed to answer that? Honestly, it did make Brody somewhat of a prick. He'd been superficial and had most likely pissed off half the single men in Provincetown, if Ricardo was any indication. But that wasn't what concerned him right now. Brody had said if he hadn't lied, they wouldn't be here right now. That meant that there was something about him that made him unsuitable for Brody.

What could that be?

"Well, your silence indicates that I'm a great big asshole," Brody said with a frown.

Eric attempted a smile, but it died on his lips. He just had to ask. "What was your list of requirements in a man?"

Brody averted his eyes. "Don't make me say it."

"I really would like to know," he said.

When Brody finally locked eyes with him, his gaze was obviously asking him if he was certain he wanted to know. No, he wasn't. But he needed to know. So he nodded.

Brody sighed before saying, "He had to be sane, hot, single, and employed. He had to be humble and original, and he couldn't smoke, whine, or snore."

Damn. That was quite the list.

Well, he was most definitely employed, and according to his psych evaluations for work, he was sane. He didn't smoke, whine, or snore. Of course, Brody had no knowledge of that. So that couldn't have been what turned Brody off to him. He never followed what others did, which meant he was his own person, not a carbon copy of everyone else. His relationship status hadn't been the issue. Brody had believed he was married. That only left one answer: Brody didn't think he was hot.

Well, fuck.

There wasn't a damn thing he could do about that—which hurt Eric more than he'd expected. He'd finally embraced his attraction for Brody, but it wasn't reciprocated. But why would they have had dueling erections on the beach? Not only that, but Brody had leaned into his touch just a few moments ago.

Had that just been his imagination?

Maybe banging his head against the wall might help him see things clearly.

"I see," Eric finally said. He stood up. Where exactly was he going? He had no clue, but right now, he just needed to flee before he embarrassed himself further.

"But I'm not finished," Brody said. He grabbed onto Eric and tugged him back onto the pool chair. If Brody planned on telling him he was ugly, he really didn't need to hear it.

"No need," he said. "I understand. You don't think I'm hot." There. He said it before Brody did.

"Are you fucking serious?" Brody asked. His mouth hung open in what resembled surprise. "You're probably the hottest man I've ever laid eyes on. Did you not feel my boner on the beach?"

Of course he had. Now he was even more confused. Brody seemed to sense that, because he moved over to sit on Eric's chair. "Then what is it?"

"Before I get to that, I want you to know that part of my problem with you till now has been how crazy attracted I am to you. I've been scolding myself for thinking inappropriate thoughts. For popping wood when we accidentally touch. For wanting to rip you out of your clothes and ravage you until we both lose consciousness. Believe me, I think you're so hot that none of these other boys make my dick twitch even a little."

Eric couldn't help the smile that stretched wide across his lips. He had been right after all. It hadn't just been him. Brody wanted him just as badly. Okay, that sounded a bit schoolgirlish, but what did he care? He hadn't been overcome with such passion in far too long.

But he was getting ahead of himself. Brody still would have dismissed him. "So then what would have knocked me off your list?"

Brody cast his eyes downward. "Maddie."

That one-word answer stung harder than if Brody had slapped him across the face.

WELL, THAT little revelation didn't win him any brownie points. But Brody had to be honest. If Eric had the balls to man up to his lie, Brody had to confess not only his awful behavior for the past year but his previous dislike for children.

It wasn't a fact he could hide. All of his friends knew. Including Van. And why wouldn't Van tell his cousin that he was spending time with a man who had publicly expressed his dislike for kids? All it would take would be one slip of a wagging tongue, and that would be all she wrote.

But that wasn't him anymore. Spending time with Eric and getting to know Maddie had changed him. When did that happen? Well, it probably started when she'd been so excited by the Funk Van and had only grown when she'd grilled him about Lynyrd Skynyrd. After that, he'd fallen under her spell.

Maddie was quite possibly the most special little person on the planet.

"Now before you get upset—" he said. But Eric didn't let him finish. Anger flashed in his eyes. The carefree yellow tint had been purged and replaced by hard copper.

"Why would I be upset?" Eric asked. His tone was sharp enough to slice through a diamond. "You hate my daughter."

That comment caught the attention of everyone within a five-foot radius. Their eyebrows curved over their sunglass-hidden eyes as they quietly whispered to each other. If Brody had the time, he'd tell them all to shut the fuck up and mind their own business. Naturally, Ricardo had been within earshot too. He snickered as he walked by, quite pleased that someone was going to rip Brody a new asshole.

"I don't hate Maddie. I adore her."

Eric glared at him as if he were stupid. "You just said that Maddie was the reason you initially wanted nothing to do with me. How else am I supposed to take that?"

"Please, just calm down and listen," he said. He tentatively reached out to stroke Eric's forearm. His touch had been able to calm Eric before. Maybe it still could. When he made contact, Eric flinched at first. He wanted to jerk himself free from Brody, the coppery flames in his eyes expressed that quite clearly, but he didn't.

There was still something there. He hadn't ruined everything yet.

"You have five minutes," Eric said. "I owe you that for not getting angry with me about Charlie."

Thank heavens for small favors. Even though he wanted to sit next to Eric, Brody sat across from him instead. That was probably the safer choice. Eric was tense. His jaw clenched, and his chest had grown about another five inches. If Eric were a raging bull, he'd be charging.

"It wasn't Maddie. It was the fact that you had a child."

"You're not improving your situation here," Eric warned through gritted teeth. Damn. Was this what a protective parent looked like? He'd never had one, so he wasn't sure. Although the more he thought about it, the more he believed that if he suspected anyone of harming Maddie, he'd probably act the same way.

"I know," he admitted with a nod. "I just never saw myself dating someone who had a child because, well, I don't know how to deal with children. Because I never got to be one myself. My parents never really cared about me. I think they loved me, but they didn't really know what to do with me. I was more of a bother than anything else. They preferred screwing around and going on alcohol or drug binges. That is, when they weren't busy marrying or divorcing their numerous spouses. They didn't have time to take care of a kid, so I had to take care of myself."

As he spoke about his past, something he hadn't done since Teddy, in college, the veil of time lifted. He was no longer the man he was now. He was once again the boy who desperately wanted love from two people who didn't seem to give a damn. "I always figured that I was destined to screw up any kid that got too close. I am my parents' son, after all. It's in my genes, right? So I kept all kids at arm's length. Too afraid that whatever poison that had infected me from my parents might spill out onto them."

The flame of Eric's anger snuffed out, and the soothing yellow tint returned to his amber eyes. He even rose from his chair and joined Brody on his.

"That was why I'd checked you off the list. Because you were a father and you were married. I don't do adultery. Believe me when I say that my parents taught me the importance of fidelity. So it wasn't that I hated Maddie. I just don't think I'm a suitable person to be around a child. Or be any type of influence for them."

Eric's lips parted into a smile. He brushed his hand across the nape of Brody's neck before resting it between his shoulder blades. "Let me tell you what I've seen," he said. "Ever since you've met

Maddie, the two of you have hit it off like gangbusters. I've been amazed at how well you've adapted to her rather precocious ways. And Maddie, well, she's quite the handful, and not even some of her teachers can handle her. That child is just too smart for her own good. But you? You've taken it all in stride. You've never talked down to her or at her. You talk to her. That's what children need."

Was he hearing Eric correctly? No, he must be hallucinating from the sun's heat. "Are you serious?"

Eric's big smile told him he was. "You've been great with Maddie. And I think she likes you too."

Shut the fuck up! "Really?"

This time Eric laughed. "Yes, really. She's latched onto you. That doesn't happen with everyone. She's a polite and friendly young girl, but she doesn't embrace new people as she has you. Maybe it's because you've just been yourself. You haven't really been trying to impress her or win her over."

"But I have been," Brody said. "I've not wanted her to hate me. Ever since she was asking me about my favorite Lynyrd Skynyrd song. I somehow knew that question was a test."

Eric grinned. "It was. She was trying to see if you were truly a Skynyrd fan. If you hadn't been, well, you would have just been a doofus pretending to be cool."

"I knew it!" he said. His excitement drew the attention of their neighbors once again. Their eye rolls revealed they were growing annoyed with the constant disturbances. But like most gays, who had more curiosity than a herd of cats, they were also most likely wondering: what the fuck was going on over there? He had half a mind to tell them to just pull up their chairs and get a front-row seat. It wasn't like most of them weren't eavesdropping anyway.

"So see," Eric said, "you're not a bad influence. There's no poison within you that will bleed over to any child in your vicinity. I actually think you have a knack for interacting with children. And that's probably because of your parents."

If that was true, which he didn't believe at all, how the hell could his parents be responsible? "I so don't see how you arrived at that conclusion."

Eric's pursed lips told Brody he was thinking about his explanation. If he had to think that hard, who was he trying to convince? Brody or himself? "Okay," Eric finally said. "Answer this question. When I tumbled down the bike trail, Maddie was terrified that something had happened to me. She even asked you if I was okay."

"That doesn't sound like a question." Yes, he was being difficult. But why were they going down memory lane?

"Are you always this impatient?" Eric asked.

"Yes. Now hurry up." Brody flashed the broad grin he typically used to get what he wanted. Eric's even stare told him it wasn't working.

"You didn't know I wasn't hurt, but Maddie wanted to know if I was okay. You told her I was. Why was that?"

He remembered Maddie's evident distress. Her eyes were wide with fear, and she had wrung her hands in excessive worry. She had been on the verge of an emotional meltdown. "I had to keep her calm," he finally said. "There was no reason for her to worry at that time."

"And why did you make that decision?"

Suddenly, Brody was a little boy again. His mother's tour bus had veered off the road and crashed into a tree. The driver had been stoned or drunk or both. But he'd heard about it on the news while he was with his dad. He ran to the phone to call his mother, but she didn't answer. He had no clue if she was okay or dead. When he asked his father if his mom was okay, what had he said? Wasn't it something like "watch the news and find out"?

All he'd wanted was comfort. Some reassurance. Instead, he fretted for about four hours until he finally heard from his mother. No child should have to needlessly go through that, and that was what his father had done to him.

"I did it because it was the opposite of what my parents would have done."

Eric nodded. "Sometimes we learn more from bad examples than anything else."

Eric was right. Even though his parents sucked worse than Lindsay Lohan's, he had learned many lessons by their awful example. After all, he'd devoted most of his life to *not* turning into Joy or Patrick

O'Shea in so many other aspects. Why couldn't that apply to children as well?

"Thanks," he said, leaning his head against Eric's shoulder. Why did he do that? He had no answer other than it felt like the right thing to do. Eric's touch indicated he agreed. He rubbed his hand reassuringly up and down Brody's back. Although the gesture was supposed to be comforting, it sparked a fire that quickly burned across his skin.

This time, though, he didn't have to force it away. Now, he was free to embrace it.

He gazed up at Eric from his place on Eric's shoulder. Eric was looking down at him. The want reflected in his eyes made Brody speechless, and there were no amount of words to express how much he wanted him right now. How no other man, not even Teddy Miller, had ever made him feel this alive. That there was nothing in this world that he wanted more than to press his naked flesh against Eric's. To feel his soft lips against his and the hairs of his beard scratch against his neck, his cock, and his ass. To take Eric's dick in his hand and lovingly stroke it before he took him into his mouth, where he would savor every inch. And then, when Eric was ready, Eric would enter him. He would make a path inside Brody's body that no other man had made. Or ever would.

If he had the ability to speak, that was what Brody would say.

But they didn't need words. Their lingering gazes communicated what they both knew.

It was time to pack up their belongings and go.

Chapter Thirteen

THE WALK back to Eric's condo usually took him about twenty minutes, which was fast considering how far on the West End they had been. It seemed Eric's body not only pumped an insane amount of blood into his raging hard-on, but it also made his legs move faster than Speedy Gonzales from the old Bugs Bunny cartoons.

And it wasn't just him.

Brody sprinted beside him down Commercial Street. Together, they dodged strollers and screaming children. They cut off bicyclists that zipped down the street and even challenged a red trolley that took visitors on a scenic tour of Provincetown.

In half the usual time, he and Brody stood inside his condo, breathless and drenched in sweat, staring at each other. Brody stood by the couch only a few feet away. Eric wanted to go to him, to take him in his arms and bring his wildest imaginings to life.

So why weren't his feet moving?

Instead of ripping Brody's yellow tank top off and rubbing his hands down his sweat-slicked skin, he stood frozen. His eyes were certainly roaming across Brody's flesh, so why weren't his hands? His tongue should be licking a path across his chest and down his stomach, but he seemed incapable of movement. The only part of him that moved was his twitching cock.

What was he so suddenly nervous about? No more secrets lay between them. Everything was out in the open, and those revelations hadn't drenched the burning desire he had for Brody. And from what he could tell from Brody's ragged breathing and longing gaze, the feeling was mutual.

"Why are we still standing here?" Brody asked.

Hell if he knew. If he had the answer, his tongue would already be lodged down Brody's throat. "I'm not really sure."

"Do you still want to?" The fear in Brody's question was apparent. If his feet hadn't somehow been stuck in glue, he'd have crossed the distance separating them and showed Brody how much he wanted to. But his damn feet betrayed him.

"Yes, I do," he finally said. "Very much. My God, you don't know how much."

"I think I have some idea," Brody grinned. He reached down and grabbed his crotch, outlining the hard shaft hidden underneath. A low moan escaped Eric's throat. He should be on his knees in worship, not standing still like a terrified fawn.

Just what was he scared of? While it had been a long time since he'd had sex, he wasn't exactly a virgin. Or someone who didn't know how to make his partner's toes curl in mind-blowing orgasm. He was just out of practice. Maybe that was why he couldn't get his body to move in the direction his cock was pointing.

Brody's green eyes studied him. No doubt he was trying to figure out what was going on with Eric too. When he nodded and those eyes lit up, insight had finally descended. It was as if he was answering a question he had asked himself.

"What?" Eric asked. "Why the look?"

A smile broke across Brody's lips, and compassion lit up his face. "I just figured it out. That's all."

That's all? Right now, that was everything. "Are you going to enlighten me, or are we just going to stand here with our dicks in our shorts?"

Brody laughed before he crossed over to the couch and sat down. "Why don't you join me?" he asked with a pat to the fabric.

"I would if I could," Eric answered. His feet still wouldn't budge. Since when had they developed a mind of their own? "It seems I'll be standing here for a while."

Brody nodded in evident understanding, while Eric had no fucking clue what was going on. "I just want you to know," he said. "That we can move at whatever pace you want. We can talk. Watch TV. And if you're just not ready, I'll be fine. Well, maybe not fine. I'll have to run home and jerk off like a teenager, but I'll live." The smile that stretched across his face told Eric clearly that Brody meant every word he said.

But why was Brody saying them? "I am ready," Eric said. This time he pointed to the bulge in his shorts. The fabric tented outward so much that a family of four could camp out underneath it. "Or are you blind?"

"Oh, I can see," Brody said. His gaze lingered on Eric's package before he stared back at him. "Your body is ready, but is your mind?" he asked. "Or your heart?"

Before Eric could ask what that meant, realization dawned upon him. This wasn't about him or Brody. His hesitancy was about Charlie. Ever since the first time they'd shared a bed together, he'd never been with anyone but his husband. Once he got naked with Brody, that would no longer be the case.

Would he feel guilty, as if he had cheated?

Charlie might not be coming back, but that didn't keep Eric's heart from hoping he would one day wake up and find this had all been a nightmare.

"You loved Charlie very much," Brody said. "That much is obvious. So believe me, I'll understand if it's too soon."

"It's been almost two years." Without thought, he suddenly crossed the room and plopped next to Brody.

"There's no time limit on grief." Crushing sadness wasn't reflected in Brody's gaze, which was the way most people looked at him when he discussed Charlie. Instead, he appeared content. As if he could talk about Charlie all day and bask in the love they had once shared. "Everyone has to mourn at their pace. That's just part of the healing process."

"But I think I'm ready to move on," Eric said. He turned to face Brody, and their knees touched. An electrical current traveled through his body until he turned into one big live wire. As before when they'd touched, his hesitancy and fears were short-circuited. Only he and Brody remained. "And that's because of you."

He reached out to caress Brody's smooth cheek. As he brushed his fingertips across Brody's jawline and up to his lips, the charge in his body built like lightning within an approaching storm front. The winds of passion howled within him, and his breathing rumbled like thunder.

His body, which had been empty and barren since Charlie, stirred in response to the churning storm on the horizon. It anxiously awaited the first drops of rain that would replenish the spirit and wash the desolation away. But even though Eric longed for nothing more than to run out into the rain, as he used to as a child, he did not.

Why rush when he could revel in the building storm?

So Eric swept his index finger along the outline of Brody's lips, delighting in the trembling response. Brody opened his mouth and brought Eric's finger inside, where he gently nibbled it. His gnawing teeth and wet tongue sent sparks once again shooting through Eric's body until they reached his now steel-hard cock.

God. How he wanted to take Brody right here and right now. But his dick wouldn't call the shots. Yes, it would ultimately get its reward, but it had to be patient. He had to be patient, so he exhaled and then stood up.

"Where are you going?" Brody asked. His voice was almost a whisper, and his eyes, which had previously been narrow and dreamy, were now wide and apprehensive. He was clearly worried that Eric had reconsidered what they were about to do.

Brody couldn't be more wrong.

Instead of replying, Eric reached down, grabbed Brody's hands, and stood him up.

"Am I leaving?"

"Not you," he replied. "But say good-bye to your clothes." He grabbed the bottom of Brody's shirt and, very slowly, pulled it free of his body. Holy mother of God! How could he not have done this sooner? Now that Brody stood before him shirtless, the passionate winds inside him swirled into a cyclone, and the few remaining fears were ripped from their foundation.

He ran his hands gingerly up the sides of Brody's biceps, committing every curve of muscle to his memory. Around his shoulders and down his chest, he explored. He hovered over Brody's nipples, teasing them with feathery strokes that caused Brody to gasp and his body to shudder. As he slid his hands down Brody's stomach and traced the outline of each abdominal muscle, he made certain to barely skim the surface of Brody's flesh. He transferred all his desire and all his heat to just his fingertips because only the agony of barely touching his skin could communicate how badly he desired Brody.

Brody got the message. His fists clenched at his sides, and his chest heaved. He peered at Eric with eyes half-closed in longing. He would allow Eric to continue, and for now, he would refrain from touching him.

By the time Eric's fingers reached the waistband of his shorts, Brody was chewing on his lower lip. Clearly, the torture of not being taken, of not being able to return Eric's gentle caresses, was starting to take its toll. "Be patient," Eric said as he undid the button on Brody's shorts.

"I've waited for two days already," Brody replied breathlessly. "I can't hold out much longer."

"You can and you will," Eric replied before roughly unzipping the shorts to punctuate the comment. Brody nodded in begrudging agreement.

Eric slid the shorts from Brody's hips until they floated to the floor. The only item remaining was Brody's blue Speedo, the one that had briefly made him forget how to walk at the Boatslip and now barely contained the erection that stretched across his right thigh. All he had to do was remove that one piece of clothing, and all of Brody would be revealed to him.

Eric dipped his fingers underneath. Brody inhaled sharply in obvious anticipation, but instead of pulling them down immediately, Eric skirted his fingers along the waistband to the dip of Brody's back. There, his hands slipped below the fabric before he brought them down and around to the front. The movement caused the suit to flutter free of Brody's body.

Freed from its prison, Brody's cock now bobbed into view. It was a meaty seven inches, and the shaft was red. Every few seconds, Brody's dick throbbed, and with each spasm, another pearl of precum oozed from the engorged head. Eric longed to take the hardness in his hand or in his mouth, to inhale the musky scent that lingered amid the light-blond nest of hair.

But it was still too soon.

Instead, he gazed up into Brody's fiery green eyes before he fixed his stare on his bottom lip, which was red from almost being gnawed right off his face. Eric reached out and caressed Brody's lips before hooking his chin with his thumb and forefinger. Then he wrapped his free hand around Brody's waist and pressed his naked body against his own still-clothed frame.

His body sizzled upon contact, and his breathing became more labored. Now, after all this time, he finally held Brody in his arms. The weight and heat of Brody's flesh reminded him of a home he'd thought he'd never experience again.

Ever since he'd lost Charlie, he'd been adrift. He floated through life, only pretending to actually take part in the world that spun around him. Even though he wanted nothing more than for death to reunite him with his husband, he stayed strong. But that had been for Maddie. She needed him, so she became his world. While there was nothing wrong with being a devoted parent, he needed to devote just as much attention to himself.

He hadn't died. Charlie had. And Eric needed to start living once again.

Eric closed the distance between their hungry mouths. When their lips pressed together, the brewing storm finally arrived, releasing the life-giving rain that purified Eric of all the pain and all the heartache he'd experienced before this moment.

Life had once again been found, and gloom no longer resided in his world. Its overreaching shadow had been dispelled, driven back by the winds that lifted his spirit over the misery that had previously clouded his universe.

Now that he recalled what it was to feel, he wouldn't settle for anything less again. Eric's tongue shot like lightning between Brody's parted lips, drawing in the sugary nectar that Brody produced, and his hands went everywhere. He clutched at Brody's shoulders before he surfed down his back muscles. He brought his hands to the front, where he grabbed at his smooth pecs and drew crazy circles around his nipples until he'd teased them taut. He shot his hands around to Brody's ass, where he kneaded and massaged each globe of muscle before gripping them tightly. Then he forced their hips together, so their erections could once again grind against each other.

The collision of their cocks ramped up Brody, and he practically went wild. With passion crackling in his emerald eyes, he tore Eric's T-shirt from his body. The fabric ripped once before Brody yanked it free. Diving back onto Eric's lips, he spread his fingers through the chest hair that covered his torso. While they kissed, Brody pinched his nipples, twisting them between his fingers. The pain was so delicious that a groan fled from Eric's throat.

"I want you so badly," Brody said between breathy kisses.

Eric hooked his left arm underneath Brody's right and in one sweep, he cradled Brody's naked body in his arms. "Not as bad as I want you."

Brody held tightly to his neck as Eric walked them over to the couch. "Damn," Brody said in between kisses, seemingly reluctant to part lips for any longer than was necessary. "How fucking strong are you?"

"Me strong like bull," Eric answered as he lowered Brody to the couch.

Laughing, Brody pulled Eric on top of him. "Like bull, huh?"

"Yes, sir," Eric replied before resting his body between Brody's legs.

"Good. Now fuck me like one."

"I will," he answered. "But there's something I have to do first."

Brody did not look amused. His blank stare clearly revealed that. "What?"

Eric pressed his lips against Brody's before he licked a winding path from Brody's lips to his chest, over and around his nipples, and through his smooth, rippled abdominals until he arrived at the throbbing cock he'd longed to taste. He grabbed Brody's shaft at its base and gripped it tightly. "This," he finally replied.

Brody's lips parted into a perfect smile, his white teeth on display. "Well, okay then. You may proceed."

When Eric ran his tongue around the head of Brody's cock, Brody shuddered. His breathing turned ragged as Eric slurped up the milky pearls that slipped from the slit, but he practically clawed the fabric of the couch to pieces the moment Eric swallowed him whole.

With the entire length of Brody's dick lodged in his throat, Eric's nose rested in the blond nest at the base. In the air lingered a heady mixture of musk and coconut-scented sunscreen. The combination turned Eric almost feral. He feasted upon Brody, slobbering up and down his shaft. His tongue swirled around the head before he swallowed all the way back to the base. He worked so vigorously on Brody's dick that Brody's body began to tremble, and his moaning grew louder.

"Oh God," Brody called out. "I'm so close. Don't make me come. Not yet."

Eric didn't stop. He didn't want Brody to come yet either, but he wanted to take Brody to the edge and then keep him from tumbling over. So he increased his pace. He jacked the shaft up and down as he sucked and licked around the head. Brody's protests increased, but his hips thrust upward in an obvious effort to come. His mind said no, but his body said hell yes.

When Brody clutched at the sofa and his balls drew up into his body, Eric released Brody's cock from his lips and sat up. "You fucker," Brody panted, sweat covering his body. His flesh had even turned a deep red. He'd definitely been on the edge. "You did that on purpose."

Eric grinned. "Guilty."

Brody shoved him backward on the couch with his right foot, and before Eric could react, Brody landed on top of him with a huff. "Turnabout is fair play."

Eric was about to object, but Brody's lips upon his made speaking impossible. While his tongue came to life in Eric's mouth, Brody's hand reached between their bodies. It slipped beneath the waistband of his shorts until his cock was firmly in Brody's hand. When his hot, sweaty palm closed around his hardness, all breath left Eric's body. All he could concentrate on was Brody's honey kisses and the warm tugs on his dick.

After a few minutes, he was finally able to mutter, "Your hand feels so good."

"You like that, huh?"

He nodded as Brody teased precum from the head and then used it as lube to continue jacking his cock.

"Well, I've got skills too," Brody said. "Just you wait."

Brody then stood on the couch and turned away from him. He helped Eric kick his shorts free and then grinned at him from over his shoulder. "You're about to get double the pleasure while I get double the fun." He squatted over Eric's face and then lowered his ass onto Eric's already-waiting tongue.

Eric reached out and parted Brody's cheeks as Brody's blond, fuzzy center rested upon his face. When he flicked his tongue across the puckered, sweaty flesh, he was once again greeted by the musky smell from Brody's crotch. Only here it was stronger. And he became a man possessed by passion he could no longer control.

Eric lapped up the sweat on Brody's ass before gnawing on the sensitive flesh. Then he wormed his tongue inside Brody's hole before quickly withdrawing it. He repeated that process three more times before wrapping his arms around Brody's waist and shoving his ass all the way down on his intruding tongue.

Brody moaned and gyrated his hips in response. Eric continued to dart his tongue in and out of Brody while Brody rode his face. "Oh, fuck yeah," Brody gasped. He leaned over and took Eric's cock in his mouth.

This time it was his turn to gasp. Having his cock shoved in Brody's throat while he ate out Brody's ass was almost too much. The nerve endings across his body cried out in pleasure, and they required immediate release they were not yet going to get. Instead, he rocked his hips, moving his cock in and out of Brody's greedy, persistent lips while his insistent tongue continued its dance inside Brody's butt.

"All right, I can't wait any longer," Brody said as he stood. He reached over into his shorts and pulled a condom out of his wallet. "It's time for you to fuck me like the bull you say you are."

"Good," Eric growled. Brody tore open the package and rolled the condom down his shaft. "I've got you good and lubed up already."

"Now you're gonna open me up." Brody then pressed his cock against his opening and leaned back.

Damn! How tight was Brody's ass? He hadn't even pushed much past the first ring, and Brody's hole had already clamped down on his cock. Not only was it tight, but Brody had complete control over his sphincter. Without having to thrust upward once, Eric was drawn deeper and further inside until Brody's ass rested against his groin, and he was firmly planted inside.

"Oh my God, that feels great!" Brody cried before his lips parted into a delirious grin that communicated more than just pleasure. The smile told Eric that this was something Brody needed too. They had both been lost, and together, they had both been found.

With the smile still emblazoned on his face, Brody swiveled his hips. He slowly pulled almost the entirety of Eric's cock out of his ass. Just as the head was about to pop free, Brody brought his hips back, riding back down the shaft until it was once again nestled deep within.

For several breathless moments, Brody pivoted slowly back and forth. Their mouths were open wide in silent pleasure on the upswing. On the downward motion, they inhaled sharply as they both took what the other so willingly offered up.

"Shit!" Eric finally exclaimed. "It's like every muscle in your body is gripping my cock. How are you doing that?"

Brody continued to ride him, his eyes lost to the pleasure. "I know what muscles to work at the gym," he answered before surfing his hands across Eric's sweat-covered chest.

"The gym? Are you kidding me?"

Suddenly, Brody's ass clenched so tightly around his cock he almost came on the spot. "Does that feel like a joke?"

Eric shook his head, unable to answer. He was too busy trying to keep the cum from spilling out of his overstimulated cock.

Brody leaned forward, and his lips lighted upon Eric's. Eric craned up into the kiss, basking in the sweet deluge of passion that rained down upon him. When Brody's tongue pushed past his lips, he fervently welcomed it. He wrapped his tongue around Brody's, sliding and twisting them together until it was difficult to tell which tongue belonged to whom.

Then Brody abruptly broke the kiss and sat up. A devilish twinkle glinted in his eyes. It told Eric that the kiss had only been to whet his appetite and that his undulating hips had yet to fully work their magic.

Brody was about to go full throttle now.

He once again twisted Eric's nipples between the thumb and forefinger of each hand. With each slow roll, Brody's hips rocked back and forth. Every now and then, though, Brody pinched his nipples tightly, and as he did so, he impaled himself down on Eric's cock.

With each tweak of his nipples, Eric inhaled sharply. It was an intoxicating mixture of pleasure and pain, and it was one he wanted to sample more often. "You're driving me crazy," he whispered before Brody once again took his breath away by slamming himself onto Eric's dick. "Fuck! If you keep doing that, I'm going to lose control."

"I know," Brody grinned. "That's the plan."

He brought his hands, which had been clenched at his sides, to Brody's hips. "Well, as someone once told me, turnabout is fair play." When Brody slammed himself downward the next time, he met the downward thrust with an equally vigorous upthrust.

Brody's eyes glazed over in dreamy ecstasy. "Holy shit!" A feverish twinkle lit a fire in his eyes. "Do that again." So Eric did. He forced himself further inside, pounding away in Brody's guts. He turned into the bull Brody wanted him to be while Brody rode along like the fucking amazing cowboy he was.

"I'm getting so close," he muttered.

"Yes, baby. Do it," Brody said. He immediately took his hard cock in his hand and furiously jacked it. As he tried his best to match Eric's rhythmic pummeling of his ass, their grunts and groans thundered inside the condo as if a sexual thunderstorm had suddenly been unleashed within the walls.

The symphony of their lovemaking combined with the loud, wet claps of thunder their colliding bodies created took Eric right to the edge. "Fuck!" he shouted as the swirling tempest in his nuts finally broke loose.

"Yes!" Brody moaned as he no doubt felt Eric's hearty explosion inside his body. He vigorously palmed his cock, his fingers sliding up and down his sweaty shaft until at last Brody released his own eruption, which splattered in five milky spurts across Eric's hairy chest.

Spent, Brody collapsed on top of Eric, his seed and their sweat cementing their flesh together. "That was awesome," Brody said between ragged breaths.

"That was better than awesome. That was fucking fantastic."

Brody lifted his head from Eric's chest and nodded. "I won't argue with that."

"Thank you," he said. Now, why did he have to go and say something so stupid? It wasn't like he was sixteen and had just lost his virginity. It was just that he hadn't experienced a connection like that in so long. He'd almost forgotten what giving himself so intimately to another person was like. It was a bond he'd truly missed, and he owed Brody more than a ridiculous thank you for bringing that back into his life.

Brody smiled, and the sparkle in his grin reflected in his eyes. "You're welcome," he said. "And thank you too."

He rested his head back on Eric's chest and held him tight. Maybe his words weren't so ridiculous after all. Brody got the message, but more than that, he evidently felt the exact same way.

It was the perfect ending to the perfect storm they had created together.

Chapter Fourteen

BRODY COULDN'T catch his breath. His lungs burned, and stars rocketed across his field of vision. Holy fuck! When was the last time he'd been topped like that? If he couldn't remember, then it was too damn long ago.

Not only was he panting like a bulldog in ninety-degree weather, but so much sweat poured off his body, he must've looked like he'd just come in out of a downpour. And what a cloudburst it had been. His body still shook with after-tremors. That was most definitely a sign of a good orgasm.

Was that why he couldn't stop smiling?

No, it wasn't just the blissful warmth of getting off. A good come always lifted his spirits. It also made him skip up and down the street like a schoolgirl, but that wasn't the only reason he couldn't wipe the grin from his lips. He and Eric had done more than just have sex.

They had established a connection. It had been growing between them for the past forty-eight hours. He had sensed it forming. Of course, at the time he'd thought Charlie was still alive, so he'd done everything in his power to prevent it from taking hold.

He didn't have to do that anymore. They were free to explore whatever this was and follow it wherever it took them.

Would it go anywhere? He couldn't answer that. Did he hope it went somewhere? That was an easy hell yes. He'd been searching for someone for so long that he couldn't believe he'd found it in Eric. Maybe that was because he hadn't been looking.

Instead, it snuck up behind him and grabbed hold of him before he'd even realized what had happened. Who would have thought it possible? Not him, for damn sure. He'd been so set against a man with a child that he never in a million years would have entertained the idea of Eric.

But now, it was a concept he could definitely imagine. And what was more surprising than that was the fact that Maddie didn't send him running in the other direction! In fact, it made Eric that much more appealing because she had wormed her way into his heart just as covertly as Eric had.

Talk about a *what-the-fuck?* moment!

"You okay?" Eric asked. He wrapped his arms tightly around Brody. He responded by sinking into the embrace. The side of his head fell further into the down of fur covering Eric's muscular chest until the beating heart within seemed to resonate not just in Eric's body, but in his own.

"Okay?" he finally responded. "I'm great." He lifted his head off Eric's chest and gazed up at him. His amber eyes had turned a bright yellow and reminded Brody of the sun. All traces of the sadness that had lingered in his gaze when they first met had been chased away, and no frown darkened Eric's handsome features. Instead, a silly grin slid its way across his bearded face. "You seem to be doing just dandy too."

Eric laughed. "I'm better than dandy." He craned his neck down to kiss Brody's forehead. "And I've got you to thank for that."

"Is that all I get?" He pretended to be upset, forcing his face into a grimace. "You come to town all dark and brooding, and now you're all smiling and shit, and that's all I get? A kiss?"

Eric's grin slipped into an impish leer. He ran his fingers down the curve of Brody's back before they nestled along his moist center. Brody gasped as he drew increasingly smaller circles around his hole before slipping one finger inside. "You want more?" he asked. His voice deepened to a low growl. "Because I can give you more."

"Oh fuck, yes," Brody moaned in response. Eric now inserted two fingers inside his slick ass, each at least two knuckles deep. He moved his fingers in ever-widening circles until they brushed against his prostate. The contact sent electrical currents streaking through his body, and when Eric tapped his fingers across the bundle of nerves, he practically leaped out of his arms.

"You like that?" Eric asked. He now massaged the sensitive button with his fingers, rubbing over and around it.

Brody tried to answer, but only an unintelligible groan left his lips. How was he supposed to talk when Eric was finger-fucking him? As it was, he could barely remember his last name. Didn't it start with an O or something? Then, in conjunction with the fingers inside him, Eric pressed his big thumb against his taint and rubbed the prostate from outside Brody's body as well.

The pleasure was almost unbearable. His hips involuntarily moved away, trying to buck off the invading digits, but as soon as his hips got far enough away, Eric forced Brody back down on his fingers, sliding him slowly until the length of both were firmly up his butt.

"Oh, Eric," he whispered. "You're driving me crazy." He brushed his lips across Eric's, and the passionate charge from earlier crackled back to life. When was the last time he'd got fucked twice within a span of twenty minutes? He couldn't remember, but he wanted it. No, that wasn't quite right. He needed Eric lodged back inside. He longed for the sensation of Eric's throbbing cock in his ass, pushing aside all resistance and claiming his body as his own.

Because whether Eric realized it or not, Brody's body was no longer his. It belonged to Eric.

He'd never given of himself this completely to someone he'd known a relatively short time. All his other relationships, even with Teddy, had taken insistent urging on the other man's part. He had to be lured out of the corner like an abused animal being coaxed out of hiding by a piece of cheese.

It took him forever to trust. And when he did, when he finally stepped out of his comfort zone, he usually only stayed there for a short time. Something had always spooked him. Like Teddy's marriage proposal in college. Or anything that might mean he'd have to compromise himself. If he gave more than his fair share, he'd be left vulnerable. His neck would be on the chopping block, awaiting the axe.

So he always made certain he was never there when the blade ultimately fell.

He'd called it self-preservation. But he'd been deluding himself. It had been fear. Fear born from witnessing the many crappy romantic entanglements that had constantly ensnared his parents.

But none of those old feelings surfaced in response to the emotions that Eric stirred within him. No warning sirens screamed in his head. His heart didn't shudder and pull away. Instead, the door within him swung open and beckoned Eric inside.

He'd finally found him. Eric was "the one." What else could explain his complete surrender?

"I want to be inside you again," Eric growled. He now worked three fingers inside Brody. They wiggled and waved, stretching him further open and preparing the passage once again for Eric's reentrance.

"I need you inside me," he muttered. "Again."

Eric didn't need to be asked twice. He sat up on the couch while Brody grabbed the last condom out of his wallet. After this, they'd either have to stop fucking, switch to blowjobs, or go buy some more. Who was he kidding? The first choice wasn't even an option!

Once the condom was free from its plastic prison, he rolled the sheath slowly down Eric's throbbing, fat dick. When Eric was properly covered, he straddled Eric and impaled himself.

All breath immediately left his body. Even Eric gasped for air.

They sat there for a few moments with Eric's cock deep in his ass. Their hot breath blew across their sweaty faces, and their gazes locked on each other. The rest of the world spun away. All that existed at this moment was the two of them.

Eric cupped his ass in his hands, slowly lifting him up and down. Every time Eric pulled out, Brody's insides gripped him tighter, refusing to allow him to leave. When he once again rested upon Eric's pelvis, he ground himself harder into Eric, trying to force more of him inside.

"You feel so good," Eric uttered.

"Not as good as you." He once again rode Eric, slamming his ass down on his cock just as quickly as he rose off it. Eric called out in pleasure as his hands gripped his butt tight, using the leverage to once again meet Brody's downward slide with his own upthrust.

As Brody bucked, Eric glided his hands down his muscular back, clawing and grabbing at the straining muscles. Their bodies, which had been covered in beads of sweat, now trailed rivulets of perspiration. It fell from their limbs and their hair, causing their gyrating bodies to slip and slide against each other even more forcefully than before.

Eric held him close with one hand while the other continued to guide their thrusts. The strong embrace caused Brody's cock to slide between their sweat-slick bodies. The friction against his cock combined with Eric pummeling his ass quickly brought him to the edge once again. His balls churned, and he drew ragged breaths.

Eric's thrusts became more erratic, and he clawed at Brody's hip.

"You're gonna make me come," he groaned. "You're gonna fuck it right out of me."

"Shoot it," Eric commanded. "Come on me."

His cock immediately obeyed. While Eric fucked him, his cock exploded, coating Eric's chest with another volley of spunk.

"Oh fuck!" Eric cried out. He slammed himself up into Brody one final time before he shot his load deep within Brody's ass. His cock pulsed and throbbed inside him for what seemed like two minutes before the convulsions finally stopped.

Exhausted, Eric fell back onto the couch, and Brody joined him. He nuzzled into the soft down on Eric's chest and exhaled in contentment. Had he ever been this happy? Even with Teddy?

That was an easy answer, because the response was no.

It was a wonderful feeling. It filled him with more joy than he'd ever believed possible. But with that joy came an unfamiliar vulnerability.

For the first time in his life, his neck remained on the chopping block, and he had no desire to move it away or flee. He just had to hope that Eric would never let the axe fall.

"HEY, SLEEPYHEAD," a distant voice told him. "It's time to wake up."

Brody didn't want to listen. He was far too comfortable. Instead of opening his eyes, he burrowed deeper into his fuzzy pillow. Why did his pillow smell like sweat and cum? And why was his mattress so hard and lumpy? Sleeping on his plush bed was like lounging on a cloud, and whatever he was sleeping on was no cloud.

Unless clouds were now made with sculpted muscle.

His eyes immediately fluttered open. Oh shit! He'd fallen asleep on Eric.

"About time you opened your eyes, lazy butt," Eric told him. His warm amber eyes stared up at him. "I've been trying to rouse you for the past five minutes."

"Sorry," he said. He stretched out his aching muscles, but no amount of stretching could dull the low throbbing of his worn-out butt. Not that he was complaining. If they had another condom, well, he'd hop back up on that horse right this very minute. "How long have I been asleep?"

"About thirty minutes. I tried to fight it, but your low snore put me in a trance. I passed out about five minutes after you did."

Brody lifted his head off Eric's chest and glared at him. "I do *not* snore."

Eric laughed. "I beg to differ. You started sawing logs within thirty seconds of closing your eyes."

"I don't believe it." He slid off Eric and rested on his side. Eric followed suit. He turned over on the couch so they could face each other. "I've never snored in my life."

Eric rolled his eyes. "Right. Today was the first time you've ever snored. I totally believe that."

"Don't you be calling me a liar," he said as he playfully swatted Eric's chest. Of course, once he made contact with Eric, his hand developed a mind of its own. It traveled through his sweat-and-cum-matted chest hair, down to his taut stomach, and over to caress his soft, gorgeous cock. Even flaccid, Eric's dick was long and thick. Was it any wonder his ass was a little raw?

"I'm not calling you a liar," Eric replied. "I'm just thinking you might not be very aware of the fact that you snore." Then he proceeded to snort and exhale in exaggerated fashion in an annoying attempt at reproducing how he claimed Brody slept.

"I do *not* snore," he repeated. To punctuate his statement, he grabbed a hold of Eric's dick, which caused him to growl once again. Except this time the rumble was much deeper. "And even if I did, it was probably because of the lumpy mattress I passed out on. I probably drifted off at an odd angle."

"Uh-huh," Eric answered, but it was obvious from the tone and the twinkle in his eyes that Eric didn't believe him.

"It's true!"

"The only thing I know for certain at this moment is that if you don't let go of my cock, I'm gonna flip you over the side of this couch and ram your ass some more."

Fuck! He really wanted another go-round too. Especially since Eric's cock was growing harder by the second. "I'd love to," he finally said after giving Eric's dick one final loving tug. "But we're out of condoms."

"I know," Eric pouted. Then a smile stretched wide across his lips. "I think it's time for a shopping trip."

Brody laughed. He was glad Eric wanted him as much as he wanted Eric. It made his vulnerability to Eric less of a problem. There was no way someone who craved him that much could ever hurt him. "I like the way you think."

"I like the way I think too," Eric replied. "And right now, I'm thinking some pretty nasty thoughts." His lips brushed against Brody's, and his cock immediately responded. Damn, after just one kiss he was at full mast once again. And he'd just come twice already.

"Those are the best," he said after Eric pulled out of the kiss. "But if we don't stop, I might forget about being responsible and let you fuck me anyway."

Eric growled again. Damn, why did Brody find that so sexy? It had always bothered him when men he'd slept with in the past had done the same thing. It was like they suddenly devolved into Neanderthals. But with Eric, well, he could howl during sex for all he cared. He enjoyed the primal aspect of the sound. It spoke to the beast deep inside Brody, and the brute that came to life inside him roared in reply. "You really turn me on when you do that," he finally said.

"What? Growl?"

Brody nodded, and Eric nuzzled into his ear and repeated the sound. It rumbled through his body, causing his wood to turn into rock. "Fuck," he whispered. "You need to stop that."

Eric pulled away and grinned. "I will," he said. "But now that I know what effect that has on you, don't be surprised when I do it. Anytime. Anywhere."

He got up from the couch. Where the hell was he going? Brody wanted him to stop turning him on, not get off the couch. But words refused to form on his lips. Eric's naked body was beautiful, and it left him speechless. Brody also cursed himself for not having more rubbers. For the rest of his time with Eric, he'd carry around a whole damn case.

"Tease," he said as he sat up on the couch. Although he didn't want to get up, they had to. If they remained naked and alone any longer, Eric's bare cock would find its way up his ass. Surprisingly enough, though, the mere notion of barebacking with Eric didn't frighten him. He'd always used protection, but having sex with nothing between him and Eric was something he suddenly wanted more than anything else.

Just how much more vulnerable could he make himself to Eric?

"Oh, I'm not teasing." Eric pulled up his underwear and reached down for his shorts. Watching Eric put on clothes was a sad event. Why couldn't they spend the rest of the week naked in bed? Well, for one reason, Maddie stayed here too, and she would be back in a couple of hours. But other than Maddie, he couldn't come up with another reason why they couldn't have nonstop naked time. How much fun would that be? As Eric stood fully dressed before him, the answer was obvious: a whole hell of a lot of fun!

"Well, good," he said. He got up and got dressed while Eric went to the small bathroom off the kitchen. He ran the water and tried to tame his locks, made wild by their afternoon romp. When he emerged, his hair was slicked back and shiny, and he'd evidently patted his sweat-soaked skin dry with a towel.

He was just about to tell Eric how yummy he looked when he noticed Eric's features had changed. The light in his eyes flickered, and for a moment darkness once again descended. It fell across his expression like dusk descending upon the land. The shadows didn't last long. Unlike the approaching night, which always claimed dominion from the retreating sun, the light fought back. Eric shook his head and blinked the gloom away. After a few seconds, it was gone, as if it had never been there in the first place.

What had just happened? Whatever it was, Brody's gut was reacting to it. His intuition told him to run away and not look back.

But as he gazed into the soft light that now reflected off Eric's eyes, Brody's panic departed as quickly as it had come upon him. And the smile that curled the edges of Eric's lips told him that all would be well.

Perhaps it had just been his imagination. What else could it have been?

Chapter Fifteen

ERIC AND Brody departed the condo and made their way up the hill that would eventually deposit them back on Commercial Street. They had to buy more condoms for later, and Eric most definitely hoped there would be a later. It had been too long since he'd experienced the warmth of another man's body, and he didn't plan on letting too much time pass before he had Brody in his arms once again.

How could he have forgotten how much he needed that contact? He was never more alive than when he shared his body and his life with someone. He'd always been happier as part of a couple than he'd ever been alone. Eric thrived on affection and comfort. Not just in receiving it but also giving it to someone who deserved it.

And Brody deserved the comfort he willingly offered.

Brody had been just as much of a lost soul as he had been. While he had been floundering alone in the sea of life, Brody had drifted around on his boat, searching for a place to drop anchor. In just a few short days, Brody had plucked him from where he'd been drowning and deposited him on his vessel, where they'd been sailing for the past few days.

It had been wonderful. Momentous even.

So why had he briefly freaked out in the bathroom?

He'd gone in there to fix his hair, and when he gazed at his reflection in the mirror, he had to stifle a laugh. His hair had been a jumbled mess. But as he placed the nest of dark locks back in order, amazed by the shit-eating grin that had taken up a permanent residence on his lips, he grew cold. His heart, which had recently throbbed to life, grew sluggish, and a bowling ball rolled around in his gut.

Brody had noticed the shift in his mood. How could he not? When he was feeling that much unease, it was difficult for him to school his expression. Charlie had always said he had the worst poker face in the world.

Gloom descended upon him once again. It wrapped around his neck like a boa constrictor. If he didn't cast it off soon, its coils would strangle him.

Was this guilt he was feeling? He'd worried that would be how he would react at the Boatslip, when he'd finally accepted his longing for Brody. Perhaps he had set up a self-fulfilling prophecy and truly regretted what he had done and how good it made him feel.

He turned to gaze at Brody, who walked quietly by his side. He appeared to be in deep thought as well. His eyes scanned the ground before him as if he was searching for an answer amid the dirt and occasional piece of discarded trash.

Eric was about to ask him what he was thinking when they crested the hill. To the right sat the Provincetown High School, a building that reminded him of Rydell High from *Grease*. At the bottom of the hill sat Bradford Street, where cars and bicycles sped past. Just beyond Bradford was Commercial Street, where they would purchase the condoms and then be able to return to their previous activities. But instead of progressing any further to Adams Pharmacy, Brody changed direction. He headed for the grass lawn that spanned the front of the school and sat down.

"What are we doing?" he asked.

Brody smiled at him. Why did the smile communicate worry more than it did happiness? He patted the ground in front of him. "I think it's time we address the pink elephant in the room."

"Pink elephant?"

"Yes," Brody answered. "Charlie."

"How'd you know?" He didn't bother denying where his thoughts were. Why should he? Brody read him like a favorite book. To pretend he hadn't been thinking of his husband would be a disservice to Charlie's memory and to Brody's evident worry.

"I can be pretty perceptive," Brody answered as Eric sat cross-legged in the grass before him. "When I saw the darkness in your eyes had returned earlier, I tried to dismiss it. But when it came back as we were walking, I figured it was better to talk about it than ignore it." He gazed at Eric with his delightfully insightful eyes. "So tell me. What's going on?"

"I'm not entirely sure," Eric answered. And that was the God's honest truth. Brody's nodding revealed that he believed him. "All I know is that I got sad for a bit. I'd been happier than I'd been in a long time, but then all of a sudden the crushing weight that I've carried since Charlie's death just wrapped around me like a vise. I tried to play it off, but I was clearly unsuccessful."

Brody agreed. The sadness in his eyes crept down to his lips, which drew into a straight line. "Do you regret having sex with me?" Asking the question filled him with angst. His hands, which had been calmly folded in his lap, started to wring together in worry.

What kind of a jerk was he? After spending a wonderful two days with Brody and then a sexually charged afternoon, he'd managed to twist the smile Brody had worn into a frown. Why couldn't he just accept what he had right at this moment instead of dwelling in the darkness that always seemed to follow him about?

"I guess you do," Brody sighed. His hands trembled, and his eyes turned wet. After managing to blink them dry, he continued, "But that's okay. I'm a big boy. I'm just sorry that I made you feel bad."

Eric grabbed Brody's hands in his own. Brody was trembling like a rabbit hiding from a barking dog. "You misread my silence," he finally said. "I was just thinking how best to frame my response."

"Well, don't frame your response. Just answer my question. It's really easy. Yes or no."

"I wish it was that easy," Eric said.

Brody pulled his hands from his grasp. "That's as good an answer as any," he replied. "If you can't answer yes or no, then that means the answer is no. Because if you didn't regret it, you'd be able to say so."

"That's the problem," Eric finally admitted. "I don't regret a damn thing."

Well, that revelation shocked the hell out of him. Apparently out of Brody too. His jaw was almost dragging on the grass. "I don't understand," Brody said.

Neither did he. He would have guessed that the reason his doldrums returned had been in response to the smile he glimpsed in the mirror. Why else would the darkness swirl around him once again if it weren't from regret? He'd been married to Charlie for ten years. Eric loved him more than anyone else. Well, except for Maddie. It made sense that he was responding to the promise he'd broken. He had vowed to never lounge in another man's arms until death reunited him with his husband. He had accepted that he would remain alone forever. And he'd been fine with that.

Until Brody.

Now the lonely road that stretched before him wasn't quite as empty. Brody had opened up the other lanes. It was too soon to be contemplating life beyond the right here and now, but that didn't stop him from imagining a life filled with happiness once again. Would that include Brody? It might.

All that mattered was that the idea of once again including someone else in his life was no longer some impossible attainment. As improbable as it might be, it now seemed inevitable.

And Brody had brought about that change.

"I really need you to explain what's going on, then," Brody said after a few moments of silence.

He once again took Brody's hands in his. He laced their fingers together, forming a physical bond that matched the one that somehow tethered their souls. "Honestly, I worried what would happen after we... well, you know."

"Fucked each other's brains out?" Brody asked. A wry smile dangled from his lips.

He chuckled. "Yeah. I thought I might feel guilty or something. As if I had cheated on Charlie. But that's not the way I feel at all. I'm really happy. Like I've finally awoken from a slumber in the middle of a long, cold winter. And I've shaken the frost from my body. I no longer walk around numb. Pretending to live. I'm actually living. And I don't know why I stopped in the first place."

"You were sad," Brody said. He scooted closer to Eric, leaning their heads together with their knees touching in between them. "You'd lost your husband. The love of your life. Of course you withdrew." There was a brief pause and a long exhale before he continued. "How did it happen?"

Eric sighed. God, he hated to tell this story. It was like reaching down his throat and pulling out his intestines. But he couldn't run from the pain anymore. He had to confront it. Head on. It was the only way he'd ever truly move forward. Wasn't that what his therapist had told him? "He was hit by a drunk driver," he finally muttered. "On his way home from putting the final touches on an anniversary celebration he'd been planning for the two of us."

Brody no longer sat in front of him. As if sensing his need for comfort, Brody moved to sitting on top of him. He straddled his legs around Eric's waist and wrapped his arms around his neck. It was as natural as when he'd offered solace to Maddie when she was in a funk. "Is that why Maddie doesn't like to be late? Or for people to be late? Because it reminds her of when Charlie was supposed to come home but didn't?"

How the hell did Brody do that? It was like he'd read the notes Maddie's therapist had once shared with Eric. "Yes," he finally said. "I can't believe how easily you figured that out."

"Wasn't that hard, really. She's a sensitive little girl. Well, underneath her surprisingly adult exterior. But when someone is late, or when she is, it more than likely makes her remember the pain of losing her father. It probably scares her that someone else may not come home."

Even if Brody had suddenly pulled a rabbit out of thin air, he wouldn't be more amazed than he was at this moment. "For someone who claimed to not like kids, you sure are able to understand them quite well."

Brody's smile communicated how pleased he was to hear that. "I don't know if 'understand' is the right word. But I can relate to childhood pain." For a few moments, the painful memories of Brody's youth clouded his eyes. Although Brody had relayed some of his past at the Boatslip, he had most likely only shared a fraction of the story. Perhaps in time Brody would divulge more, and when he did, Eric planned on being the shoulder he needed to lean on and the strength to carry him through to the other side. Just like Brody was doing right now for him.

"I'm sorry you've been hurt too," he said. He rubbed his thumb gently across Brody's cheek. "I wish I could take that pain from you."

Brody leaned into his touch. "We've all got pain, and even though it hurts, it shapes who we are. Without my fucked-up parents, I wouldn't understand Maddie quite so well. So in a crazy way, Joy and Patrick O'Shea actually did something right. For once in their lives."

"How can you be so positive?" Eric asked. He truly marveled at how Brody seemed capable of looking on the bright side despite his hellish childhood. Eric had only ever seen the gloom and destruction death left in its wake. Maybe that was part of his problem. He failed to see what he'd had. A loving husband. Great parents. And the best sister in the world. It was more than most people enjoyed. He should see only his blessings.

Instead, he'd only focused on what he had lost.

"If I didn't learn to see the glass as half-full, I'd likely have gone insane by now," Brody admitted with a chuckle. He rested his head on Eric's shoulder and sighed. It was a sweet and simple gesture, and it was one that filled Eric's already jubilant spirit with even more joy. How was that even possible?

"I need to be more like you," he finally admitted. Even before Charlie died, he had had other losses in his life. Other tragedies that had caused him to retreat from a world that brought him nothing but pain. For most of his life, he'd been terrified to connect with other people only to have them stripped from his side by cruel fate. So instead of forging bonds, he stayed on the periphery. It was safer there. Lonely, but safer.

But maybe now, as he'd once done with Charlie, he didn't need to stand on the sidelines anymore.

"Charlie wasn't the only person I've lost."

Brody sat up in his arms. His eyes were aflame with concern. "What do you mean? Who else have you lost?"

Was he really going to recount his tales of woe? "Well, my parents died last year. That was a tough blow. They had been my rock for years. My mother died of a stroke and my father followed her six months later. They said it was natural causes. I think it was of a broken heart."

"That's so sad," Brody said. Then a smile tugged on the corners of his lips. What the hell was that for? "But as sad as that is, it's also terribly romantic. Your father loved your mother so much that he just had to be with her."

Brody's comment irked him. "Are you implying I didn't love Charlie enough to die for him? Because I did. And I would have too."

"Of course you would have," Brody replied. He gently kissed Eric's lips and caressed his face until the winds of pissy blew out of his sails. "But you had Maddie to care for. You weren't a child your father had to watch over. He knew you would be fine. He had faith in that, so he had to follow his heart to your mother on the other side."

How did Brody make death sound good? As if it was some grand romantic gesture instead of a stab wound through his heart. "But I miss them," he said. "So much."

"Of course you do. Death is hard on the living. Because we love those we've lost so much."

Why did everything that came out of Brody's mouth have to make so much sense? Thinking so positively sure made it difficult to continue the pity party he'd been throwing for himself for so long. Since Brody was able to put a positive spin on his parents' deaths, how would he handle his sister's? "What about Kimberly?"

"Your sister?" Brody asked. "You mentioned her the other day. What happened to her?"

Typically, whenever he spoke about Kimberly or any of his lost loved ones, sadness deeper than the vastness of space consumed him. While it still hurt to bring their memories to the surface, the pain was no longer debilitating.

"She was murdered during a botched robbery," he said. Brody gasped in shock and horror, but instead of interrupting him, he said nothing. "She was babysitting me while my parents went out to dinner. She was reading me my bedtime story when the front door crashed in. She made me hide, so I scrambled under my bed while she ran for the phone. One of the robbers saw her and struck her real hard with the butt of his gun. When she fell, he hit her three more times before he and his partner left with the stereo and TV."

He breathed deeply, blinking back the tears that had distorted his vision. Was he going to be able to finish telling the story? It had been so long since he'd recounted it. At least out loud. But Brody caressed the nape of his neck while he delivered a trail of feathery kisses across his cheeks and lips. All of Brody's strength immediately transferred to him. As long as Brody was by his side, he seemed capable of doing most anything. "I saw the whole thing, and I did nothing. I didn't scream for them to stop. Or call the police. I just hid. Worried more about myself than I was about my sister. How fucking selfish is that?"

Tears streamed down his face, and sobs racked his body. He hadn't broken down like this about his sister in years. He usually suppressed the pain and guilt he carried around with him. It was the only way he'd been able to cope. His parents couldn't make him feel better and neither could Charlie. The pain was too raw, too much for him to deal with. It was like trying to hold back a tsunami with a dike made of straw.

That was why he kept it inside. If he let it out, he'd drown in decades' worth of grief and misery. So why was he letting it out now? But the answer didn't matter at the moment. Brody's arms wrapped around him, and they gave him the security he needed to perhaps once and for all deal with the pain.

"You were a scared little kid," Brody said. His voice was a reassuring whisper. He ran one hand through Eric's hair reassuringly while the other stroked his face, wiping the tears from his cheeks. "There was nothing you could've done. Besides, you did exactly what your sister wanted you to do. She wanted you to be safe. She loved you so much that she made certain of that before she went for help. What happened to her wasn't your fault."

"That's what my parents used to tell me," he said in between sniffles. "And Charlie. And Van. And pretty much everyone else. But I don't buy it. I could've done something. Anything. But I did nothing." He spoke those words as if he was dooming himself to the fiery pits of hell. Wasn't that where cowards belonged?

"And each one of those people loved you so much," Brody said. "All they wanted was to take away your pain. They wanted you to see what they saw. That you were not at fault. There was no way you could be."

Eric shook his head. "Sorry. I still don't buy it." No matter how desperately he wanted to believe it.

"Then think about it this way. If someone broke into your house while you were home with Maddie, what would you do?"

Eric immediately bristled. He'd rip them to pieces before anyone had a chance to touch one hair on her head. "I'd kill them," he replied.

"But what if you couldn't?" Brody asked. "What if they got the drop on you, and Maddie was hiding. What if, God forbid, they killed you? Would you want Maddie to blame herself for what some idiots did to you?"

"Of course not," he said. "I'm her parent. It's my job to sacrifice myself for her. Anything else is not an option."

Brody nodded. "Just as anything else wasn't an option for your sister. She loved you, Eric. And she died protecting you. She gave her life so you could live. Not so you could squirrel away and hide. You had the most amazing sister in the world, and you should honor the memory of her life. And her sacrifice. Don't focus on the tragedy. Cherish her because she's still inside you. In your heart. With all the rest of your loved ones. If you think about it that way, you'll never feel lonely again."

Were Charlie and Kimberly and his parents still with him? Had he not been as alone as he'd believed he was cursed to be? Then a familiar warmth ignited in his chest. It spread throughout his body. It was as if unseen arms were holding him, caressing him, telling him they loved him.

Tears once again fell from his eyes, but they weren't tears of sadness. They were of joy. His family was with him. They were flitting about him on heavenly wings, and they were embracing him as they used to in life.

He'd never been more complete or happy in his life. And he had Brody to once again thank for that. The man who he now clung to, and the man who had given him back his family. "Thank you," he said.

Brody stared at him with knitted eyebrows. "For what?"

"For everything," he said. "I don't know how to repay you."

Brody gazed up into the sky. His index finger tapped against his temple. "Let me think. How can you repay me?"

From the amused expression on Brody's face, being serious had come to an end. It was time to be a smartass now. "Just remember I work in law enforcement, so I'm not a rich man."

Brody sighed, pretending to be completely exasperated by his lack of wealth. "How about you pay me with a kiss? I'd be happy with a million of those."

Eric couldn't help the grin that parted his lips. Brody was a man after his own heart. "I can do that," he said. He gently lowered Brody onto the cool grass and rested himself on top. "But just so you know. You won't get them all at once."

"I'm glad to hear it," Brody replied. "I never choose the one-lump-payment option when I play the lottery."

"Good. Because you're about to receive your first installment." He leaned closer to Brody, moving until their lips were only centimeters apart. Brody's hot breath swept across his face in quick, longing pants. When their lips finally touched, the few shadows of pain and misery that had hidden in the recesses of Eric's heart were forced into the light until all that remained was the warm glow.

Chapter Sixteen

WHEN BRODY first suggested they go to tea, Eric hadn't been too keen on the idea. Eric wanted to head to Adams Pharmacy, buy a few boxes of condoms, and head back to the condo for some naked time. Had he agreed to that? No. It wasn't because he didn't want to. Just the thought of Eric's cock once again slipping inside him made Brody hard, but after the serious talk they'd just had, sex wasn't what they needed at the moment.

What they required involved alcohol and dancing, both of which could be found in abundance at tea.

"I still can't believe I agreed to this," Eric said at his side. His lips stretched thin in obvious disappointment. The big baby!

"Oh, stop sulking," Brody said. He laced his fingers with Eric's as they made their way down Commercial Street toward the Boatslip, where the famous Tea Dance occurred every day from four until seven. There, among the dancing, half-naked men who crowded the pool deck and the dance floor, they would find the revelry they both needed.

"I'm not sulking," Eric replied. He held his head high as if the confident pose made him less of a whiny child. "I'm expressing my dissatisfaction. It's not like I can strip you naked in the middle of the dance floor and have my way with you. Which is exactly what I'd be doing right now if we'd gone back to my place. Like I wanted to."

Even though Brody rolled his eyes in reply, that didn't stop his lips from extending into a cheesy-ass grin. He enjoyed Eric's insatiable sexual appetite, and it was all for him. Who wouldn't smile at that? But as much as he longed to lounge in Eric's naked embrace again, he couldn't pass up the opportunity to walk into the Boatslip with a man on his arm. How many times had he witnessed happy couples strolling the deck? Far too damn many. That was for sure.

This time, though, he wouldn't be the lone single guy, traipsing behind Nino and Teddy or Zach and Van. This time, he had someone to call his own.

For now at least.

Now why did he have to go there?

Eric's imminent departure crashed upon him like a pile of bricks. The happy-go-lucky attitude he'd previously enjoyed vanished like a whistle in a windstorm. He'd have Eric until Friday evening, but come Saturday, Eric and Maddie would pack up and head back to Petersham.

He'd likely turn into a big pissy bitch—that much was certain. After all, they lived on opposite ends of the state, and he had no plans to move to Petersham. What the hell would he do there besides go absolutely batshit?

Besides, it was much too soon to even contemplate moving. Much less plan a happily ever after. They'd just met a few days ago. It didn't matter that they got along so well or that it seemed as if they'd known each other their entire lives.

After all, that had been his problem ever since he first started looking for a serious relationship. He'd been trying to make whatever man he met fit his preconceived notions of his ideal man for his perfect relationship. Life just didn't work that way.

As much as he hated the idea, he had to surrender control because, really, he had none whatsoever. If he and Eric were meant to be, it would happen.

"Where'd you go?" Eric asked. He tugged Brody to his side and placed his arm around his waist. The huge smile that greeted Brody almost made him grab Eric by the arm and head back to the condo.

"I'm right here," he answered. He mimicked Eric's gesture and slid his arm around Eric's waist. This was even better than holding hands. "Did you go momentarily blind or something?"

Eric playfully swatted him on the ass in reply. Now why couldn't Eric have done that earlier when he was naked? Spanked his butt until his cheeks flushed a deep red and a burning warmth spread across his ass. Then afterward, Eric could have coated his butt with the cream that would make it all better.

Fuck! Could he be any harder right now? They were definitely going to try that little scenario later.

"You're doing it again."

Eric's voice refocused his attention away from the fantasy of Eric jacking his big cock until he exploded all over his butt. "I'm sorry. What?"

"What's going on with you?" Eric asked. "You keep checking out on me. Everything okay?"

No, everything was not okay. He'd worked himself into another horned-up frenzy. "I was just thinking that I might need a little discipline later."

"What are you talking about?" Eric's stitched eyebrows spoke louder than the bewilderment in his voice. Was that what he looked like when he played chess with Maddie? But before Brody could explain, realization dawned upon Eric. He relaxed his arched eyebrows and wiggled them suggestively across his forehead. "Oh, discipline," he repeated as his lips hitched to the left in a seductive half grin.

"Yes, I've been a bad boy."

"Very bad," Eric agreed. He craned downward and lightly nipped at his neck. The scraping of his teeth and his beard against Brody's sensitive skin made him gasp. His cock almost ripped free of his shorts.

"Why are we going to tea again?" he asked. It was most likely the dumbest idea he'd ever had. They didn't need to drink or dance. They needed to go home and fuck.

"That was your brainstorm," Eric whispered into Brody's neck. His hot breath plumed across his skin. That was it. They were definitely going back to the condo now.

Brody stopped in the middle of the street and tugged Eric back the way they came.

"Oh no," Eric said. He clutched Brody's waist and escorted him in the direction they had been headed. "You wanted to go to tea, so tea it is."

"Fuck tea," he said.

"Brody!" Eric chided as he gestured to the families around them. What did he care if he was being too loud? He'd scream it at the top of his lungs if it produced the desired effect—him on his back with his legs spread and Eric pumping in and out of his ass.

"Fuck me instead," he whispered.

Even though Eric growled in reply, he still led Brody toward tea.

Why wasn't Eric breaking into a run, like they had earlier? After all, he hadn't wanted to go to tea in the first place. "Is that a no?"

"You wanted discipline, remember?" He winked at Brody as they drew closer to the Boatslip. "Consider this your first lesson. You'll come where I say. And when."

Damn! The sternness in Eric's voice alone almost made him jizz in his shorts. What more could he expect later? "I could get used to that."

A mischievous glint twinkled in his eyes. "Me too. So you better watch out."

Eric's words made him happier than the idea of being disciplined. While the dirty talk promised more naughty fun, it also held a slight promise that they had a future beyond Saturday.

WHEN ERIC spotted the long line of half-naked, horny men snaking out of the front entrance of the Boatslip, he questioned his previous decision. Brody had finally come around to his way of thinking and was ready to head back to the condo, but he hadn't turned tail and hauled ass back the way they came. Sure, he had been planning on teasing Brody while they were here. A grab here. A growl there. Maybe even a long make-out session along the rail overlooking the beach.

It made him hot, coming up with various ways to tantalize Brody in public.

But how was he going to accomplish any of that if they were packed into the Boatslip like sardines? Perhaps it was better to just turn around.

"Don't worry." As if reading his apprehension, Brody grabbed his hand and led him down the line marked Townie Pass. No one was in that line because it was reserved for the residents of P-town, who came to tea and got in for free. Brody might have a get-in-free card, but he didn't.

"I'm not a Townie," he whispered.

Brody shook his head and laughed. "Really? I didn't know that."

The playful sarcasm in Brody's reply told Eric not to worry. He had this covered. Still, he couldn't help but reply, "Smartass."

"I'm a terrible smartass," Brody said as he glanced over his shoulder and winked. "Just one more thing to be disciplined for."

Brody's bare butt instantly flashed in his mind. It turned cherry red as he smacked it before once again piercing Brody's flesh. It was definitely time to head back to the condo. There was no need to prolong the inevitable. Why tease and flirt in public when they could skip ahead to the good stuff? He stopped and tugged Brody backward. Brody recognized the fiery passion in his eyes because his lips parted into a big grin.

"We're here, and we're staying," Brody said as he once again urged Eric forward with a gentle tug. "But believe me, we won't be staying for long."

Eric wrapped his arms around Brody's waist and pulled him close. It still amazed him how comfortably Brody's body fit against his. "You promise?"

"I promise," Brody replied. The tender kiss he planted on Eric's lips ratified the deal.

"Fine," Eric said, finally relenting. "Let's get in and get out."

A mock grimace turned Brody's lips into a straight line. "You better not be saying that later."

Eric laughed. "I definitely won't be saying that later."

Sufficiently convinced, Brody once again grabbed his hand and on they went. They turned the corner of the Townie line and headed toward Bob, who sat behind the register. The same scowl that had greeted them earlier that afternoon still squatted on the man's hard face.

Did that guy ever smile? If he did, his face would likely crack and crumble from the strain.

"Hey, Brody. You're back." Although the welcome sounded friendly, Bob glared at them as if he hated their guts.

"Can't miss tea," Brody said before he flashed his Townie card to the cute little Brazilian twink who stood next to Bob. He slid some money out of his pocket and into Bob's waiting hand.

After examining the bill, Bob nodded toward the entrance. "Have fun."

"Oh, we plan to," Brody said as he led Eric inside.

Once they pierced the outer perimeter of the Boatslip, Eric was amazed by the transformation of the deck from earlier that afternoon. When they were here last, pool chairs spotted the entire span of the deck, which extended about fifty feet to the right of the front door. It had been packed, but even though music had been pumped through the speakers, the atmosphere had been laid-back. It might have been cruisy, but the crowd had been docile and easygoing.

That was no longer the case.

The entire pool deck, as well as the enclosed dance floor to the immediate left, was a mass of frenetic energy. Sweaty, half-naked men crowded the dance floor. They swayed back and forth like a den of snakes entranced by the music the DJ spun from within her booth. In the middle of the dance floor, some guy was twirling his flags as if he was part of a high school color guard, and around the perimeter a woman with purple hair worked her Hula-Hoop to the beat.

"That's Violet," Brody yelled in an effort to be heard over the din of the music and the buzz of conversation. "She takes that Hula-Hoop with her everywhere."

"Who's the flag boy?"

Brody shrugged. "Just some random gay. There's usually one or two of those flag-twirling guys on the dance floor at tea. It gets kinda obnoxious because they eat up half the dance floor with their private routine." Right now, the guy was twirling his flags in rapid circles to the music, and he was definitely taking up more than his fair share of the dance space. Those around him had to back up or be smacked in the face with the flags. It amazed Eric that no one told him to stop, but when he gazed into the excited expression of the man as he danced and twirled, he realized it was hard to get pissy with someone who was enjoying himself as much as flag boy was. He wasn't trying to be rude. He was clearly lost to Icona Pop's hit "I Love It." The song had become a gay anthem for the summer, and though he'd never admit it to Maddie because she'd ostracize him for days, he found the tune catchy as well. It wasn't captivating enough for Eric to choreograph an intricate flag routine, but whenever the song played on the radio, he always turned it up.

Brody's hand once again enclosed around his, and he was led away from the dance floor and flag boy and toward the bartenders who sat under a white tent on the far left side of the deck. With Tara off sailing on the catamaran with everyone else, they'd have to utilize the services of one of the many other drink slingers. According to conversation at dinner last night, she was the best bartender at the Boatslip. Who would they use in her absence?

There was an older bartender standing to the far left. He had no one in his line, so it made perfect sense to Eric that they should go to him. Instead, Brody headed for the line that had the most people. The older guy had no one waiting, and the bartender on the other side with the full head of dark hair only had a handful of customers. Why were they going to waste time and stand behind about twenty other guys?

The more popular bartender was attractive. He had a shaved head and a pair of beautiful blue eyes, but did that really qualify him as the best? "Are we really going to wait in this line?" he asked as they drew closer to the long line of customers.

"Of course not," Brody answered as they bypassed the line and went straight to the front. They shouldn't be cutting the line. Not only was it rude, but the move attracted the attention of every man waiting their turn. If their eyes could shoot daggers, he and Brody would be cut to shreds.

"Hey, Brody," the bartender said. His nametag identified him as Mitch. "The usual?" he asked as he filled four cups with vodka and then two other cups with rum.

"Yes. And a Planter's Punch for my friend."

Mitch nodded and set to making the ordered drinks.

"You realize we just cut in line, don't you?" Eric asked as he nodded to the men behind them.

Brody surveyed the line of pissed-off guys. If they had long hair, they'd be flipping their locks to the side in disdain. Instead of apologizing to them, Brody shrugged. "It all evens out in the long run."

"What does that mean?"

Brody's lips stretched into a smile before he leaned into Eric for a kiss. "You're cute when you're mortified. You know that?"

Although Eric enjoyed the kiss and the fact that Brody said he was cute, he didn't like breaking the rules. If there was a line, people were supposed to wait their turn. Maybe that was the police officer in him, but doing the right thing just came naturally to him. Cutting in front of others wasn't right. "I am mortified," he finally admitted. "We should have waited our turn or gone to the other bartender who has no one waiting."

Brody glanced over at the older bartender, who eyed Mitch's line with envy. "That's Phil. This is his first season here at the Boatslip. It'll take him a while to get the following that bartenders like Tara and Mitch have."

"What does that have to do with cutting in line?"

Brody could see his frustration. The devilish twinkle in his eye at shooting to the front of the line disappeared. "Please don't get upset. It's just the way things work around here. Bartenders like Tara and Mitch, who have worked here for years, have a dedicated following of customers. They don't go to any other bartender. Even if someone else's line is short or nonexistent. They are happy to wait in line for a chance to chat with and be served by Tara or Mitch. Think of them as Boatslip celebrities. It'll take time for someone new like Phil to build those relationships with the customers, but he will. There are new people coming to Provincetown every year. He'll make a name for himself eventually."

Eric could understand that. Having a favorite bartender wasn't exactly uncommon, but what did that have to do with cutting in line? "That still doesn't explain why we went straight to the front."

"Because there are some of us that have made a special financial arrangement with our favorite bartenders," Brody answered. "In exchange for priority service, I tip far more generously than any of the others who have to wait in line. So believe me, I pay my dues. I just don't do it waiting in line."

Brody's explanation eased Eric's guilt. There was nothing unfair about this situation. This was like getting a fast pass to one of the rides at Disney World. Except in P-town, fast passes were reserved for alcohol.

"Feel better?"

He nodded. "Tons."

"Good," Brody said as he handed Eric the drink he'd ordered for him. After he paid Mitch, Brody escorted him away from the bar and back through the gauntlet of angry eyes. Now that Eric had been clued in to the system, he didn't understand the resentment. All they had to do was pay more to get out of line. It was no one's fault but their own that they didn't.

"What's this Planter's Punch you ordered for me?"

Instead of answering, Brody grinned. "Just try it. You'll like it."

Brody's answer didn't exactly fill him with confidence. Why did he feel like he was a kid again and Van was telling him to close his eyes and hold out his hands for a big surprise? Although he didn't want to take a drink, there was no way he could deny Brody his request. His beaming smile made Eric want to see that smile get even wider, so he took a drink. Fire immediately coursed down his gullet, and a coughing spasm took control of his throat. What was this drink? Pure rum? When he finally managed to stop wheezing, Brody's laughter filled his ears. The smile had turned into a shit-eating grin.

"Asshole," he said as he cleared his throat.

"Sorry," Brody said. He wiped away the tears that had pooled in his eyes. "But it's a custom for everyone's very first tea. You get a Planter's Punch not realizing that they pour a shot of rum into the straw. After your first gulp, you'll never make that mistake again."

"You're damn right I won't. Next time I'm getting a vodka Sprite."

"Spoilsport," Brody answered. He even stuck out his tongue to indicate how displeased he was by Eric's answer.

"I've got a place for that tongue, you know?"

This time it was Brody's turn to fall into a coughing fit. Eric had managed to successfully time his suggestive reply as Brody took a drink of his Planter's Punch. Turnabout was definitely fair play.

"Bastard," Brody playfully scolded. "You did that on purpose."

"Who? Me?" he asked, feigning innocence.

A seductive smirk tugged its way across Brody's lips. He closed the distance between them and whispered in Eric's ear, "Just so you know, my tongue and your ass have a date later." He reached between them and grabbed hold of Eric's hardening cock.

Eric wrapped his free hand around Brody and pulled him close, trapping Brody's hand between them. "Let's finish these drinks and then go reintroduce my ass to your tongue."

The twinkle in Brody's eyes revealed how much he was looking forward to the introduction. "I like the way you think."

"If you were in my head right now, you'd be liking things a whole hell of a lot more."

"Why are we still here?" Brody asked.

Eric laughed. "This was your idea, remember?"

"Well, it's the worst idea I've ever had," Brody said as he once again placed his hand in Eric's. The warmth of Brody's hand in his own combined with the weight of Brody's body against his made Eric drunk. Being with Brody was more intoxicating than a dozen Planter's Punches. But even though he wanted nothing more than to go back home, get naked, and slip inside Brody once again, there was something special about being at tea with him.

It had been a long time since he'd been out as a couple with anyone. Not that he and Brody were officially a couple or anything. Still, being in public with someone reminded him how special it was to share life's moments. While he and Maddie shared many experiences, this was just a different type of special and a different type of experience. It made him feel alive and more like the man he once was when he first fell in love with Charlie.

So he really wasn't ready to head back. He had yet to experience all tea had to offer, and he wanted to do that with Brody.

"So we're here. What do we do next?" He hoped Brody wouldn't be too disappointed about his obvious desire to stay. Brody's smile indicated he wasn't. Eric firmly believed staying at tea with him was something Brody wanted to experience as well.

"Well, we have to do the customary lap around tea, and then we dance."

"Sounds good to me," he said as he followed Brody through the mobs of men, and even though they passed many groups of attractive guys who smiled at them in obvious want, he didn't give any of them a second glance. He had Brody, and that was all he wanted. The fact that Brody held onto him so tightly and constantly glanced over his shoulder at Eric told him Brody felt the same way.

IN ALL the years he had been coming to Provincetown, Brody had danced with more than his fair share of hot men at tea. Right now, though, none of them could hold a candle to Eric, who danced shirtless before him. He hadn't started that way when they first hit the floor. A remixed version of Maroon 5's "One More Night" had been playing, and though everyone else around them had long since discarded their shirts, Eric had been reluctant to do so. No matter how much Brody had begged.

For such a hot man, he was extremely shy.

It wasn't until Brody slipped off his shirt when Miley Cyrus's latest track hit the speakers that Eric had finally decided to join him. When Eric shed his shirt and tucked it in the back pocket of his shorts, Brody completely forgot how to move.

He could only stand there amid the gyrating men around him and stare at the hairy, tanned chest that now lay exposed for all to see. With each dance move, the muscles in Eric's chest and arms flexed. Brody had to fight the desire to jump his bones right there. He might have done so too, if Eric hadn't pulled him close.

Now they danced half-naked in each other's arms. He ran his hands up and down Eric's sweaty, muscular back while Eric's hands gripped his hips. He used the leverage to grind their hard cocks, which were hidden beneath their shorts, together.

Each time Eric's erection rubbed against his, he clawed at Eric's back. He imagined them back at the condo, naked, and Eric's dick just seconds away from once again charting a fiery path inside his body. God, how he wanted to experience that again! And it wasn't just the sex. It was everything that went with it. The weight of Eric's body on top of him. Their tongues swirling in each other's mouths. His hot breath rushing across his damp skin and the smell of their musk filling the room.

If it didn't happen soon, he'd likely go crazy from the anticipation.

But no matter how much he wanted to leave, being with someone special at tea was something he had wanted for so long. Now that he had it, he was reluctant to let it end.

"I love being here with you," Eric whispered in his ear before moving his hands down to Brody's butt, which he cradled in his palms. Eric's admission made Brody want him even more.

"Me too," Brody answered. He slid his hands down the sweat coating Eric's back. When they reached the waistband of his shorts, Brody dipped his fingers beneath the fabric and rested his fingertips on the swell of Eric's slick ass.

A huge grin parted Eric's lips before he delivered a slow, passionate kiss to his lips. Brody eagerly welcomed Eric's tongue inside and greeted it with his own. As they made out on the dance floor, they continued to sway and grind to the music. Their bodies, like their wrestling tongues, slid seamlessly together.

He hadn't experienced something like this in a long time. He and Eric had a connection that went beyond the physical. It was almost spiritual in the reassuring comfort that wrapped around him whenever he was in Eric's arms.

There was no trying. There was no internal argument about whether he should or shouldn't be with Eric. It had just happened. Almost from the moment they'd met on the pier.

It had confused him then, but he saw it for what it was now. This was the way it was meant to be. Otherwise, why would he have dreamed about Eric and Maddie even before he met them? Nothing else could explain that.

The universe was directing Eric to him, and it was Provincetown that had finally delivered what he sought.

That wasn't very surprising to Brody at all.

Provincetown had a way of bringing people together. It had done that for Zach and Van, Nino and Teddy, and scores of other men he knew. Why couldn't he trust the same would happen to him? Well, that was simple enough to answer. Because he'd never been given a gift like this before.

But now he experienced that offering firsthand, and as insane as it might make him sound, he'd do whatever he needed to do to make it last.

Was there really any other option?

"Break it up, ladies," a voice said to their left. It was obvious from the tone that the person speaking was pretending to be irritated. When Brody broke from the kiss to see who had spoken to them, Quinn's bearded face greeted him. A sly, knowing smile spread wide across his lips.

"Hey, Quinn," he said. He attempted to turn and face Quinn, but Eric refused to let him go. Instead, he turned around in Eric's arms and pressed his back against Eric's sweaty, furry chest.

"Don't 'hey, Quinn' me," he said. It was obvious from the mischievous glint in his eyes that Quinn was intent on torturing them with what he'd seen. "How long has this been going on?"

Not long enough, that was for damn sure. But instead of being brutally honest, he aimed for simple honesty instead. "Since today."

The blank stare in Quinn's eyes communicated his disbelief.

"It's true," Eric said.

"I'm not an idiot," Quinn said as he crossed his arms in front of his chest. It was the pose Quinn typically took when his friend believed someone was trying to pull the wool over his eyes. "I've seen the way you've been looking at each other since the bachelor party. Then you spend the whole day together yesterday, and of course you conveniently decide to *not* go sailing today. Don't tell me this wasn't all planned. Because I don't buy it. And neither will everyone else."

Did that comment mean everyone else had seen what was going on between him and Eric? That would certainly explain Nino and Teddy's behavior in front of the Lobster Pot yesterday. Nino was usually a dick anyway, so he typically dismissed whatever he said. But Teddy? Brody had wondered why Teddy had made such a big deal about their day on the town yesterday. Had that been because he had sensed what was going on? "We didn't plan anything," he finally said. "It just happened."

Quinn switched his gaze from Brody to Eric. After several moments of careful scrutiny, he finally lowered his arms and rested them at his side. Thankfully, they had passed muster. "All right. I guess you two were the only ones in the dark, then."

Well, fuck. Everyone else *had* seen what was going on. And if they had seen it, they had most likely been talking about it. His friends were incessant chatterboxes about potential new romances. Especially Gary and Tara. They were the absolute worst. Getting two people together was an obsession of theirs, and they had no doubt spent most of the day on the catamaran plotting how to bring him and Eric together.

Luckily, he and Eric beat them to the punch.

"So how long has everyone been talking about us?"

Quinn grinned. "Well, Gary and I have been talking about you two since that first night. Everyone else was clued in at dinner yesterday."

"Wait. What?" Eric asked. "Why has everyone been talking about us?" He released his arms from around Brody, and all three of them walked off the dance floor.

When they were in a quieter corner, Brody answered, "It seems that everyone knows about us."

"How's that possible?" Eric asked. "We didn't even know about us."

Quinn rolled his eyes. "That's because you two were blind. Which is pretty common for two gay men in love. Most of us don't want to see it, and we don't know it when it's happened. It was like that for Gary and me. As well as most of the others."

Okay, Quinn needed to slow down. It was way too soon to be talking about love. Eric had become someone special to him, but calling it love was a bit premature. They'd only known each other for about three days. How could two people fall in love in three days?

Still, he'd just told himself that he'd do whatever he needed to do to make things work with Eric, but that wasn't love.

Their potential relationship was going to require work and commitment. That was what he was pledging to do. After all, no one had ever made him feel this way. He'd been hot for many guys over the years, but Eric was the first man his body actually craved.

Touching Eric or simply being near him made him happy. That was for certain. He hadn't been this happy in years, but that didn't mean it was love. Even so, for the first time he'd actually contemplated changing his life for someone else instead of adhering to the insane requirements he'd once believed were so important.

Could that be called love? Well, maybe in some cases.

After all, real love was about making sacrifices, about putting someone else first.

It was in the big things people did for each other. Like Quinn's support of Gary not actively looking for a job. Nothing was more important to Quinn than Gary's happiness, even if that meant a full-time career as Penny Poison, a persona Quinn couldn't stand. Or in Van's decision to give up porn for Zach. Or even in Nino's choice to live part-time in Boston with Teddy.

But it was more specifically seen in the little things couples did for each other. In the way they constantly touched or knew what the other was feeling or thinking. It could be seen in the longing glances or in the twinkling of their eyes.

He and Eric couldn't possibly have those things yet.

When he glanced over at Eric, Brody held his breath. He was the most beautiful man he'd ever seen in his life, and the longer Brody stared at him, the more his heart swelled in his chest.

Fuck! He *was* in love with Eric Vasquez.

What the hell was he supposed to do now?

Chapter Seventeen

FROM THE pier, Eric gazed out onto the calm waters of Cape Cod Bay. The catamaran carrying his daughter would soon round the bend at Long Point, and he would once again hold her in his arms. Then he could do what he'd been doing for years. Focus all his energy on her. Forget about the crap he preferred not to deal with and withdraw into the comfortable role of a parent that kept him from remembering he was also a man.

Why would he want to live that way again anyway?

Life was easier just being a father. The other roles in his life—husband, lover, son, and brother—had ended in tragedy. Why would any sane person want to chance such crushing grief again? Especially when being a father came more naturally.

As long as he watched Maddie like a hawk and kept her safe from harm, he didn't have to worry about her being taken away. Eric certainly would never leave her. There was no one in the universe capable of wrenching him from Maddie's side, so as long as it was just the two of them, he'd never suffer the pain of loss again.

That was why he couldn't think about Quinn's foolish assumption at tea earlier. The mere thought upset the order Eric had worked so hard to achieve despite all the loved ones he had lost. There was simply no way he could allow anyone in his life again. He couldn't expose himself to the sting that eventually followed falling in love.

No. It was better for him and for Maddie to just be her Papa. It kept him strong. As her Papa, he was invincible. To add any other relationship weakened him. What would happen if he really did love Brody? It might make him happier than he'd been in years. But what if he lost Brody like he lost Charlie? What would happen to him then?

And what would become of his daughter?

It was too much of a gamble. He couldn't selfishly chance his daughter's happiness. That had to always be his primary concern. It was better to dismiss any thoughts of love and continue on this path. Alone.

He glanced to his right, where Brody stood about five feet away. He leaned against the rail, intently studying the ocean that lapped underneath the pier. Ever since Quinn's proclamation, they had both gone silent. The laughing they'd previously enjoyed ceased almost immediately, and they no longer sought out each other's touch.

They were like two boats bobbing on the ocean and drifting further apart. That was how it should be anyway. They really didn't have anything to keep them anchored together. They had enjoyed some fun flirtations and some pretty hot sex, but there was more to a relationship than good times and a few good rolls in the hay.

After all, they didn't live in the same town. By his own admission, Brody was an infamous horny bastard. He had probably dated the entire gay male population in Provincetown. As well as most of the tourists. Did he really want to expose himself to any social disease Brody might have picked up along his slutty path? Not really. There was no reason to play Russian roulette with his life and be yanked from Maddie's side because of some incurable virus. To make things worse, Brody hadn't had a long-term relationship since college, and though he claimed to love Maddie, Brody hated kids.

There was no future with a man like that.

So why was logic failing him now that he gazed over at Brody? He had to grip the rail to stop himself from crossing the distance that separated them and taking Brody in his arms. His heart practically burst free of his chest at the thought of never kissing Brody again. Of never experiencing the caress of his naked flesh against his own.

No. He couldn't think that way. He had to do what was right. For everyone.

So he released the rail and inched his way to Brody. Brody had yet to notice Eric's slow progress toward him. He still stared down into the water. The waning sun set his blond hair ablaze in a golden flame, and his fair skin glinted as if it had been covered in diamonds. Was this what a god in contemplation looked like? If not, Brody came damn close.

Just as he was about to speak, Brody glanced at him, and the words he almost gave voice to died in his throat. How could he turn this man down? He had been given a gift and was about to tell the universe "no, fucking thank you."

Brody wasn't perfect, but who was? All those circumstances he'd believed only moments ago were against them no longer seemed to matter, once he stared into Brody's emerald gaze. Distance didn't really have to be that much of a deal breaker. Zach and Van had overcome it. And Brody might have been tramping throughout town, but he'd stopped that behavior. Well, for the most part. And no matter how much sex Brody had, he'd used a condom when they were together. In fact, he'd been adamant that they buy more condoms before they had sex again.

So he'd been responsible in his irresponsible behavior.

That counted for something.

Plus, Brody did love Maddie. It was evident whenever he watched them together. No one, not even someone who professed he hated children, could fake such emotion that well.

Then why was he going to throw away the potential they had? That was fear talking, not anything else, and that wasn't the man his father brought him up to be. That wasn't the man Charlie fell in love with, and that was most definitely not the person he wanted Maddie to grow up to be.

He wanted her to embrace all aspects of life. She'd face pain and heartbreak. Perhaps even loss. But he didn't want Maddie to stop living because she might be hurt. He wanted her to laugh in the face of pain. She had to dance and sing when life told her to sit down and shut up.

If that was what he wished for his daughter, then why was he not taking his own advice?

"Just say it." Brody's voice brought him out of his thoughts, and it wasn't the carefree timbre he'd grown accustomed to hearing. His tone was sad and dejected. As if he'd been waiting for the other shoe to come crashing down upon his head.

Brody wasn't stupid. He'd intuited his feelings since almost their first meeting. Why would now be any different?

"I can't," he finally said. The green eyes that had sparkled like emeralds all day lost some of their luster, and the smile that had adorned Brody's face withdrew. It gathered into a thin line, and his lips trembled.

Brody sighed. "Then I'll say it for you. This isn't going to work. We both know it."

Eric's heart pounded in his chest, and anxiety gripped him in its steely embrace. The contents of his stomach quickly rose in his throat. He had to will the bile back down into his fluttering stomach. Brody was calling things off.

"We had a great time together, and I'll remember every moment of it. But we aren't in love, Eric. Quinn is wrong. Hell, everyone is wrong. It doesn't matter what they see or what they think. All that matters is what we feel. Right?"

Eric nodded. That was all he could muster without opening his mouth and emptying his stomach onto Brody's flip-flops.

"I mean, really? How could we be in love? It's been what? Three days? That's not how it works. We both know that. Love takes time to build and to grow. Especially the kind of love you had with Charlie. That's the kind of love you deserve. And the kind of family Maddie deserves. Like you told me earlier, when you met Charlie, there was no stopping the two of you from being together. That's not how you feel about me and that's okay." A smile forced its way across Brody's lips.

Why was Brody lying? He was not okay. The tremor in his voice gave him away and so did the glassy quality of his eyes. Were those tears he was holding back?

"You'll find that man, Eric. I know you will. When you do, nothing in the universe will stop you from being with him."

Brody then crossed the distance between them and delivered a soft peck to his cheek. The kiss spoke volumes. The shuddering lips revealed Brody's evident pain at saying good-bye. But most revealing of all was how Brody lingered upon his flesh. He didn't want to let go. The passion Brody tried to disguise as a friendly peck surged forward upon contact.

Only a man who was in love kissed like that. Only a man who was willing to sacrifice his own happiness for what he believed was better for the other person did what Brody was doing.

Brody loved him. There was no doubt in his mind.

"Stop lying," he said. He wrapped his arms around Brody's shuddering frame and pressed their bodies together. "You don't believe a word of what you're saying."

Brody sniffled. He inhaled deeply, trying to force the burgeoning tears back from where they came. "What does it matter?" He wormed his way out of Eric's embrace and took two steps backward. "You don't want this to be whatever it is. I saw that quite clearly when Quinn said we were in love. You panicked like a cat thrown into a pit of dogs. I tried to explain it away as surprise, but your mood only darkened on our way over here. You withdrew, and I could see the wheels in your brain turning. And when you finally walked over to me, I saw the answer in your eyes."

"What answer is that?"

"That you don't love me," Brody admitted. "And that's okay. It really is. If you don't feel it, you don't feel it. It's not something you can force. But I want you to know something, Eric. I have fallen in love with you. As crazy as that might sound. It doesn't make sense. I can't explain it. But I do love you, and I want you and Maddie to be happy more than anything else in this world. So please. Go and be happy."

Brody offered one final, fake smile before turning around and walking away.

Eric couldn't just stand there and let Brody walk out of his life.

"Brody, wait!" he called out. Brody stopped but did not turn around. He faced the other direction, ready to hear what Eric had to say but also ready to continue on his current path. "You're right. My wheels were turning. What Quinn said threw me for a fucking loop. I didn't understand how it was possible for two people to fall in love so quickly. It didn't make sense, and to me, these kinds of things have to make sense." As he spoke, he drew closer to Brody. If he could help it, there would be no more distance between them ever again. "I've lost so many people that I've loved in my life that the thought of possibly loving someone new scared the shit out of me. I didn't think I could handle it, and I was going to tell you just that."

Eric reached out and turned Brody around, tears streamed down his face. He brought his hands to Brody's cheeks and wiped them away with his thumbs. "But then I looked at you. And I realized I was deluding myself. I was letting fear control my life. Hell, I've been letting fear drive my actions for most of my life. But I can't do that anymore. It's not good for Maddie. Or me. Because if I let my fears have their way, then I lose you." He pulled Brody close enough to rest their foreheads together. "The man that I've fallen head over heels in love with."

Brody's wet eyes blinked three times. He no doubt believed he heard Eric incorrectly. "What did you say?"

"I love you, Brody O'Shea. Is it crazy? Hell yes. Do I care? Not one fucking bit."

The warm smile that spread wide across Brody's face quickly dried the tears in his eyes. "Are you serious?"

Eric laughed. "How many times do I have to say it before you'll believe it?"

"At least a million."

"I can do that," he said with a nod. "But that means you're going to have to stay awhile to hear them all. That okay with you?"

Brody pressed his lips against Eric's as they clutched each other for dear life. It was quite possibly the best yes he'd ever received.

How long had they stood on the pier in each other's arms? From Eric's perspective, only a few minutes had passed since he and Brody had declared their love for each other. They embraced, and they kissed. Hell, they even shamelessly fondled each other.

Eric didn't care one bit.

It had been too long since the warm flame of love had sparked for him, and he intended to fan that spark into a roaring fire. So he held Brody tight, memorizing every curve of muscle or dip of flesh with both his eyes and his hands. When their tongues jostled back and forth from Brody's mouth to his, he drank in the ambrosia, and Eric couldn't get enough. And the faint odor of musk, sweat, and aftershave that wafted from Brody made him drunk. He inhaled deeply until his lungs could hold no more. Then he'd reluctantly exhaled and started the process all over again.

"I could so devour you right now," he growled.

Brody's eyes half closed in evident ecstasy. Eric's growl turned Brody on badly, but in conjunction with his words, it was obvious Brody was ready to strip naked and get fucked right there. "I wish you were eating me," he finally managed in a breathless whisper.

Eric kissed his way from Brody's lips to his neck, where he nibbled and nipped. He then rubbed his prickly face against Brody's smooth skin. In response, a whimper escaped from Brody's throat, and he clawed at Eric's T-shirt.

There was no doubt about it. Had they been alone, Brody would have already impaled himself on his cock. Damn! Why were they still standing on this pier again when they could be getting naked and sweaty at home?

Well, because Maddie and everyone else were due back soon.

Shit! They had to get a hold of themselves. How would Maddie react to seeing her Papa making out with Brody? She'd only ever seen him kiss Charlie. Although she'd have to get used to seeing him and Brody together, he didn't want to unnecessarily rush things for his daughter. They would have to move at whatever pace was comfortable for her.

This wasn't about just him and Brody. This was about Maddie too.

"I know," Brody sighed. "We need to stop before Maddie gets here." Although the crazed passion from a few moments before no longer blazed in his emerald eyes, it hadn't died out completely. Brody's desire sizzled in the corners of his eyes and in the mischievous upturn of his smile.

Eric returned the smile. "I just love that you're able to read my thoughts so well. How do you do that?"

"I'm a mind reader."

"Really? Then what am I thinking right now?"

A wide grin spread across his face. "I don't need to be a mind reader to know that one," Brody said with a chuckle. He grabbed Eric's hard cock, which tented his shorts. "Not when the answer is out there for the world to see."

Eric growled again and once more fell upon Brody's lips. He couldn't get enough of him, especially when Brody was stroking his cock the way he was now. Did they have time to sneak behind one of the many shops that lined the pier? If so, they might be able to get in a quick romp before the catamaran docked.

"And no, we don't have time for a quickie," Brody answered. How the hell did Brody do that? "The catamaran's pulling up now."

"What?" he asked as he turned around to see the vessel carrying his daughter and their friends inch closer to the pier. They were about fifty yards away from where the catamaran was docking, so their public display of affection was most likely not seen by anyone. But what if Maddie had spotted them?

"Stop being a worrywart," Brody said. He grabbed Eric's hand and tugged him toward the boat. "Everyone's on the back deck. They didn't see a thing."

"You're starting to scare me," Eric admitted as he followed Brody. "You've got to tell me: how do you do that?"

"It's a gift," Brody shrugged. "One of many that I'll introduce you to." This time it was Brody's turn to growl, which caused an electrical current to pulse through Eric's cock. His erection turned harder than steel. In fact, it could probably cut through diamond right about now.

"I can't wait," he finally uttered.

Instead of answering, Brody smiled knowingly. As if he had plans for him that Eric couldn't even fathom. Damn, that was hot!

By the time they made it to the gangway, they only had to wait about five minutes for everyone to disembark. Eric used that time to will his erection flaccid and fix his hair. He couldn't very well greet his daughter looking as if he'd just been rolling around on the floor with Brody.

Brody took several deep inhalations, most likely to get *his* hard-on under control, and he gazed at his reflection in one of the storefront windows to make sure that every strand of hair was in place and that he was presentable.

"There they are," Van's voice said from behind them. He carried Zach's niece Sophia in his arms. The little one was passed out and drooling. How cute was that? "When we pulled up and didn't see you, I thought you guys might have been otherwise engaged."

The smirk on his lips revealed what Eric had already guessed. His friends had been talking about him and Brody for part, if not most, of the trip.

"I told them you wouldn't be late," Maddie announced. Her head was held high in triumph.

"I'd never be late to get you," Eric said as he swept Maddie into his arms. She giggled as he rained kisses upon her cheek and forehead. Although she wasn't a fan of her dad going all mushy on her, it appeared she was letting it slide this once. She had missed him as much as he had missed her.

"Okay, that's enough," she said. She placed both her hands on either side of his face to stop the assault. "I get it. You missed me."

"I did."

A tiny smile worked its way across her lips. "I missed you too, Papa." She then hugged him tight once more before requesting he put her down.

Reluctantly, he did as Maddie asked. When he looked up from his daughter's sun-kissed face, the smiling, tanned faces of his new friends greeted him. Well, except for Zach. He was lobster red. "Didn't you put on sunscreen?"

Zach frowned. "I did. SPF one million. A fat lot of good that did me."

"I told you to sit in the shade," Van complained. His cousin didn't appear amused. He gazed askance at Zach the same way he used to glare at Eric when they were kids and Van had been pissed off about whatever Eric had done to rile him up.

Zach plainly realized he was on Van's list. He sauntered over to Van's side and wrapped his arms around his man. "I didn't have a choice," he said. "I had to be wherever you were."

Tara oohed the comment while Nino pretended to vomit.

"Stop that!" Teddy scolded. "That was sweet."

"I know," Nino said. "Saccharine enough to send any diabetic into a coma right about now."

"And an obvious attempt to derail my righteous anger," Van said in pretend irritation. His jovial tone gave him away. And so did his posture. He leaned into Zach's embrace. "It was not the look I was going for for the wedding pictures."

"It'll be fine," Gil said as he inspected his son's sunburn. "We'll buy some aloe, and it should clear it right up."

"Ooh," Zach said. His voice filled with excitement. "That's one ointment we haven't tried yet."

Zach's family grimaced in disgust.

"Zach, please," his mother begged.

Sami swatted her brother upside the head. "You're gross, you know that." She then gestured to Maddie. "There are little ears around here, ya know."

"I think my ears are average for my age," Maddie replied. "They're not little at all."

Everyone broke out into laughter, and the hitch of Maddie's lips told Eric she was pleased with herself, even though she wasn't exactly sure why people were laughing. Thank God she was still young and innocent. What would he do when she grew up enough to catch a double entendre?

"Did you have fun?" Brody asked from his side. Although he hadn't forgotten that Brody was beside him, Eric attempted to act nonchalant. It was either that or freak out his daughter by acting like a lovesick schoolboy. That wouldn't go over too well at all.

But instead of answering Brody's question, Maddie stared at him. Her green eyes carefully scrutinized. She then switched her gaze to him and proceeded to examine something she clearly found very interesting. Did she know?

"Something's changed between the two of you," she finally said. "I can see it."

From behind Maddie, Gary sniffed the air. "Yes it has," he nodded. "I can smell it."

Oh God! Did they smell like sweat and cum? They hadn't showered after having sex at the condo. They most likely reeked of man stank. If they did, he'd die of embarrassment. And if he had a bat, he'd bop Gary over the head with it. It would serve Gary right for the smug expression he now proudly wore.

To make matters worse, everyone else snickered at the comment. They sure as hell seemed to know too. Teddy was grinning as if he'd never been happier, and Tara and Irene's eyes were practically beaming. Even Donna Kelly appeared amused. She hid her smile beneath the back of her hand.

Maddie's voice dragged him out of his internal meltdown. "Well, I don't know what you smell, Uncle Gary." Uncle Gary? When did that happen? "But something's definitely different." She crossed her arms and gave him her typical look of inquiry. Her lips hooked up to the left, and her right eyebrow arched. Whenever Maddie took on this stance, she wouldn't stop asking questions until she had a suitable answer.

He opened his mouth to speak, but no sound issued forth. A quick glance over at Brody revealed that he was in a similar state of shock. The two of them were at the mercy of a nine-year-old with deductive skills that rivaled Sherlock Holmes. How were they going to get out of this?

"Lighten up, Papa," Maddie said. The exasperation in her voice was very apparent. She even rolled her eyes at him and shook her tiny head. "I'm nine, not three."

"I don't understand," he finally mumbled.

She walked over to Eric and hugged him. Then she reached out to Brody and grabbed his hand. She smiled up at him as if he were a present under the Christmas tree. "I'll save the both of you from yourselves, then," she said. "I take it you both finally realized you like each other?"

What the hell?

"You knew?" Brody asked. His tone revealed how surprised he was too. Brody's intuition paled in comparison to Maddie's insight.

"Of course I did," she said. She turned to stare at everyone else. When she rolled her eyes again, they all laughed. "We've *all* seen it. Why do you think I kept bringing up Brody's ancestor Desire Cowing? Or insist you and Brody sit together at dinner? Or why I wanted you to hang out with Brody while I was with everyone else today? I was hoping you'd both finally buy a vowel and solve the puzzle."

How much more incredible could his daughter be? She was not only smarter than her father, but she'd been scheming to get him and Brody together from the start. That could only mean one thing. "You're okay with me and Brody?"

Maddie gazed up at him as if he were a grinning idiot. "Of course I am." She then turned to smile at Brody. "Brody's a good guy. Even if he likes Britney Spears."

Brody scooped Maddie in his arms and delivered a great big hug. Naturally, Maddie complained. She even wiggled around in Brody's arms in an attempt at escape, but Brody wasn't going to let her go. The gesture made Eric love him even more.

"You're awesome," Brody said once he finally returned Maddie to the pavement.

She straightened out her wrinkled Led Zeppelin T-shirt and shot Brody a pretend grimace. "If I have to endure double the public affection, I might have to rethink my stance on the two of you."

He caught Brody's eye, and they smiled at each other. They didn't need intuition to tell them what was next. The two of them lifted her up once again, and Maddie found herself in the middle of a big group hug.

"The two of you are going to kill me," she complained as they squashed her between them. Eventually, though, she gave in and wrapped her arms around both their necks. She switched her gaze from Brody to him before she said, "I'm just glad you're happy, Papa."

Tears quickly filled up his vision, and before he had a chance to stop them, they fell across his cheeks. "I am," he said. "But you always made me happy. I hope you know that."

"Well, duh," she said, once again feigning irritation. "But you're a different kind of happy now. I can see it." She then kissed Brody on his cheek. "Thank you for making my Papa happy, Brody."

Now, it was Brody's turn to tear up. "He's made me happy too, kiddo."

She nodded. "Can you both put me down now? Sheesh!"

After they returned Maddie's feet to the pier, she took both their hands in hers and launched into telling them about her adventures on the open water. Eric didn't hear a word she said. His heart was too full.

He had a family again.

Chapter Eighteen

BRODY WAS dressed and ready for the wedding. Now all he had to do was wait for Eric to get out of the bathroom so they could make their way over to Flyer's Boat Rental. Gary had rented a private ferry to carry all the guests over to Long Point Beach, where the ceremony was to take place.

It was a romantic locale that had everything. Windswept dunes, abundant sunshine, and the soothing crash of the surf upon the shore. It promised to be spectacular.

If they made it.

"We need to be leaving soon," he called down the hall to the closed bathroom door. He didn't get a response. Not even the flush of a toilet. What the hell was taking Eric so long? The shower turned off at least twenty minutes ago, but Eric still hadn't emerged. If Eric didn't hurry up, Gary would be banging on the front door demanding they get their asses in gear.

He most certainly didn't want to face Gary's wrath. Ever since he'd gotten back from his day off on the catamaran a few days ago, Gary had become even more unbearable. There was much that still needed to be done. He barked orders and set people to task with even more severity than he'd expressed for the bachelor party.

Gary had gone from Hitler to Genghis Khan at neck-breaking speed. If Gary had carried around a mace as he commanded his troops about, Brody wouldn't have been surprised.

"Is he still in there?" Maddie stood at the top of the stairs. She was already dressed in her flower-girl dress. The white, tailored sash cinched her waist, and it highlighted the sea-foam color of the fabric perfectly. With her hair done up and ringlets hanging on either side of her face, she was the picture of a pretty, pretty princess. How was it possible that a little girl, who had to fit that sleeveless dress over her up-do, and a gay man like Brody, who prided himself on looking damn fine wherever he went, were ready before Eric? He was the one person Brody knew who didn't have to try to look good. It came naturally and quite easily to Eric.

"Yes," he finally responded. "I don't know what's going on in there."

She stared at him as if he should know better. "He's stalling."

Stalling? But before he had a chance to vocalize his confusion, he realized what Maddie was referring to. They would be crossing the bay in a small ferry, and Eric was terrified of the ocean. He walked over to the door and lightly rapped on it. "Eric, honey. It's going to be okay. The ocean is calm, and the ride over to Long Point takes maybe twenty minutes. If that long. There's really nothing to worry about."

"You and Maddie go ahead," Eric said from the other side of the door. The trepidation in his voice was extremely apparent. He wasn't the big, strong sheriff's deputy right now. He was a frightened child being asked to confront a serious phobia. "I'll join you guys at Flyer's when I'm done."

"We're not leaving here without you," he replied. He was doing his best to sound as composed as possible. Being irritated would get him nowhere. But he was far from cool or collected. A tempest of butterflies flitted around in his stomach. In a few minutes, Gary would arrive to drive them over to Flyer's. If Eric wasn't out of the bathroom and ready to go, Gary would no doubt use a battering ram on the bathroom door. "So why don't you open the door and let me help you finish getting ready?"

"No" was all he received in reply. If he didn't love Eric so much, he'd be throwing a bitch fit.

"You're Van's family, remember? What's Van going to say if you're not there?"

"He'll live. Besides, Nino's practically his brother. He won't even miss me."

"Do you really want to disappoint Van like that?" he asked. "We both know how important family is to you."

A barely audible sigh emanated from the bathroom. Brody was making progress. Thank God.

"I know how much you hate the ocean, but I'll be right there with you." He glanced down at his side to see Maddie's green eyes gazing up at him. "And so will Maddie."

"That's right, Papa. We'll hold your hands the whole time."

Even though this scene reminded him of some insane sitcom skit, Brody couldn't have been happier than he was right now. It was silly that a grown man had locked himself in the bathroom to avoid taking a short ferry ride across the bay, but there was no place he'd rather be.

If anyone had told him last month or even last week that he'd be here, he'd have told them they were out of their fucking minds. But now he considered himself the luckiest man in the world.

How fucking great was that?

"All right," Brody finally said. "You win."

"What?" Maddie asked. "Are you serious?"

"Of course I am," he announced to the door, but then he shook his head at Maddie, who realized what he was doing. She grinned in obvious appreciation of his deceitfulness. "I'll call Van and tell him we can't make it." He grabbed Maddie's hand and walked her back to the bedroom he and Eric had been sharing for the past few nights.

After picking up his phone and pretending to call Van, he placed his cell to his ear and started the fake conversation. "Hey, Van. How are you?" He waited a few seconds before continuing the charade. "Yeah, I bet you're excited. But listen. I have some bad news. We won't be able to make it. Eric's not feeling too good. He hasn't been able to get away from the toilet for more than a few seconds." He covered his mouth and laughed silently. Maddie was doing the same thing. She even gave him a thumbs-up sign. "It does suck, and I know you're disappointed. But what can we do? He's not feeling good. Maybe we'll see you at the reception later if Eric hasn't exploded by then. You should hear the sounds coming out of that bathroom. It isn't pretty." Maddie was wiping tears from her eyes and clutching her stomach. If she didn't get control, she was going to clue Eric in on what they were doing. "I'll see if Gary has any Pepto. Maybe that will work, but I—"

"You can hang up on your pretend phone call now. I'm out." Eric's voice drew his and Maddie's attention away from their silent hysterics. Eric's stitched eyebrows and crossed arms revealed he was displeased by their little performance, but damn if he didn't look fine. Eric was hot enough in a muscle shirt and shorts. Dressed in a tuxedo, he was fucking delectable. If Maddie wasn't with them, he'd have already ripped Eric out of his fancy duds.

"Feeling better?" Brody asked.

Eric replied with a roll of his eyes. "You're good, O'Shea. I'll give you that. Pouring on the guilt and the embarrassing toilet humor to get me to do your bidding."

"Good?" he asked. "I'm freaking excellent."

"Yes, you are," Eric said with a nod. He crossed over to them, took both of their hands, and sighed. "But I'm going to make you both keep your promise of holding my hand."

He and Maddie glanced at each other before replying, "No problem."

The three of them then walked hand in hand down the stairs and out the door just as Gary and Quinn were exiting their condo. Their timing couldn't have been any more perfect, but right now, all he knew about perfection was having Eric and Maddie at his side.

BRODY HAD been thankful that most of the ferry ride to Long Point had been uneventful. It certainly didn't start out that way.

The misery on Eric's face when he initially boarded the vessel made him doubt Eric would be able to survive the voyage. Nino, being the complete jerk that he was, teased Eric mercilessly. Teddy had fortunately made Nino stop. Luckily for him. He'd been about two seconds away from tossing that curly-haired motherfucker overboard.

When they finally got under way, Eric held onto his hand in a death grip. He winced and almost called out in pain at least half a dozen times. Thankfully, Maddie escaped the torture. Even though Eric held her hand too, he had only been squeezing the shit out of Brody's hand.

That had been good for Maddie but bad for him. Especially since Eric almost broke a finger or two out of sheer terror.

But then a miracle happened.

About a quarter of a way to Long Point, Eric relaxed. Whether it was the soothing movement of the boat, the calm waters, or the gentle breeze that wrapped around them, Eric loosened his grip. He had released the tension and most likely finally accepted he was not going to suffer a muddy death.

Brody's fingers couldn't have been more grateful.

When they reached Long Point, Eric was a completely different man. Instead of scrambling off the boat, he stood to help the ladies off and was actually the last man to exit the vessel. What the hell had happened? Even though Brody was dying to know, he decided not to look a gift horse in the mouth and simply be grateful.

He joined the others—except Zach and Van, who would be making a grand entrance on horseback later—as they traversed the path through the sea grass. After a few hundred feet, the trail opened up to an exquisite expanse of beach that had been wonderfully decorated in pristine detail. Gary might have driven them homicidal, but no one could argue with the results.

A makeshift aisle had been finely carved into the beach. Instead of the usual waves of sand that typically adorned Long Point, the aisle had been paved as flat as a sidewalk. On either side of the passageway sat rows of white chairs. Blue sashes had been tied around the seat backs, and each sash sported a tiny bouquet of blue and white stephanotis.

At the end of the aisle, about twenty feet from the shore, stood a wooden archway, the one he and Quinn had been charged with building yesterday. Today, the wooden structure was covered with white silk that had been carefully draped around the posts. The fabric had been so excellently arranged it appeared as if the fabric stood entirely on its own. It was magical.

To complete the look, garlands of blue begonias interspersed with white roses hung at the corners of the arch.

Was he at Long Point, or had he stepped onto a movie set?

"It's beautiful, Gary," he said. Everyone else echoed his compliment. "You outdid yourself."

"I know," Gary replied. The smug satisfaction currently etched onto his expression was well deserved. That was why no one, not even Quinn, told him to wipe the smirk from his face. If it was possible, Quinn appeared just as proud of Gary as Gary was of himself. He sported a grin that practically mimicked the one Gary wore.

"Aren't you looking for a job?"

Maddie's question caused the oohs and ahhs over Gary's masterpiece to immediately cease. Everyone in attendance stared uncomfortably at Gary, whose proud countenance disappeared completely.

The only one to move was Eric. After smacking his forehead with his palm, he bent down and said, "Madison, now is not the time for such a conversation."

"I disagree," she said. She crossed over to Gary and gazed up at him with her big green eyes. Before speaking, she waved her hand at all Gary had accomplished. "Look at this place, Uncle Gary. It's probably the most stunning beach wedding I've ever seen. Of course, I've never been to another beach wedding before. I'm only nine after all, so I'm limited on life experiences. But I've seen such weddings on TV. This beats them all hands down. Have you considered making this your new career?"

A light bulb went on in Gary's brain, and his eyes swept the crowd. They all nodded their heads in agreement with Maddie's proposal. How the hell did she see things no one else saw?

"You know, she's right," Quinn finally said. He put his arm around his partner. "You'd be great at this."

"You really think so?" Gary asked. On his face warred excitement and fear, as evidenced by the fire in his eyes and the uncertain smile sliding across his lips.

Maddie answered, "Why else would we say it?"

Gary glanced down at Maddie. Fat tears sat in the corners of his eyes, and when he smiled at her, they streaked down his face. "Thank you, Madison. I think it's a great idea."

"A great idea?" she asked. "It's fantastic. With so many same-sex couples coming to the Cape to get married, you'd have quite the business. Plus, you could even work Penny Poison into it somehow."

Quinn groaned. "Maddie! Why did you have to go and ruin such a good idea?"

"Ruin it? I've made it better. What other wedding planning business has a drag queen as its spokesperson?"

The smile that now graced Gary's face appeared wider than the Cheshire cat. "This girl is a genius!"

"I'd say 'well, duh,' but I hate repeating myself."

While everyone laughed, Brody and Eric walked over to Maddie and once again lifted her between them. "Aw, man, not again!"

"Yes, again," they both said in unison. They both kissed her rosy cheeks before setting her back on the beach.

She gazed up at them, warily. She was apparently making sure they were done embarrassing her. "Now that that's over," she said while pointing to two riders on horseback making their way toward them, "let's get this wedding started. Zach and Uncle Van are here."

Everyone cheered when they spotted the two figures and then took their seats.

Before following Eric and Maddie down the aisle, Brody stood still for a moment, silently taking everything in. It was finally time to celebrate the wedding of his two friends. As he stared after the man he loved and the little girl who'd stolen his heart, he'd never been more thankful in his life.

"You coming?" Eric asked. He stopped halfway down the aisle and held his hand out to Brody. Maybe one day, Gary would be planning their wedding.

"Of course," he finally answered. Nothing in this world was capable of standing between him and Eric. While it was too soon to plan their wedding, he had no doubt that one day they would.

BRODY TRIED to fight the tears that welled up in his eyes, but it was a losing battle. It was impossible not to cry watching Zach and Van declare their undying love for each other. Who would have ever thought that a former porn star and a bumbling author would tie the knot? Not him, that was for sure.

But this was Provincetown. When love comes to town, anything and everything was possible. How else could he explain Teddy and Nino? There simply was no explanation for someone as sweet as Teddy winding up with an asshole like Nino.

The same could be said for him and Eric. Anywhere else, they wouldn't have had a chance. But in Provincetown, anything and everything was possible. Even love between a former horndog and a grieving widower.

Provincetown brought these couples together.

Eric rested his hand over his, and the contact made the tears he'd been fighting course freely down his cheek. He extended his arm around Brody's shoulders and drew him close. The gesture was so sweet and loving, the only thing he could do was rest his head on the broad shoulder Eric offered in comfort.

"I love you," Eric whispered before planting a kiss on top of his head.

He gazed up into Eric's warm amber eyes. How could he have gone his entire life without this man? "I love you too." He kissed Eric's tender lips before they smiled at each other.

"If the two of you are done with all the mushy stuff," Maddie whispered, "how about you pay attention? It's almost over."

He and Eric grinned at Maddie, who pretended to be disgusted by their affection. But Brody could see the truth in her eyes. She was happy for all of them.

"Do you, Evan Harding Pierce," said the pastor from the Universalist church, who was at the head of the aisle, "take this man, Zachary Aidan Kelly, as your husband, to love him and to honor him, to nurture, serve, and support him, in times of joy and in times of difficulty? Do you promise to remain by his side regardless of what trouble befalls you, and in the presence of temptation not to forsake this love? Do you promise to remain steadfast and true? Do you promise with all of your heart and your soul to honor this vow till death do you part?"

With tears in his eyes, Van answered. "I do." Zach then slipped the wedding band onto Van's finger.

The officiant then turned to Zach. "Do you, Zachary Aidan Kelly, take this man, Evan Harding Pierce, as your husband, to love him and to honor him, to nurture, serve, and support him, in times of joy and in times of difficulty? Do you promise to remain by his side regardless of what trouble befalls you, and in the presence of temptation not to forsake this love? Do you promise to remain steadfast and true? Do you promise with all of your heart and your soul to honor this vow till death do you part?"

"You bet my life I do," Zach answered. The tears that streamed from his eyes couldn't douse the smile that stretched across his face. Van then placed the ring on Zach's finger.

The pastor spread his arms wide as he addressed the guests. "Then by the power vested in me by the great state of Massachusetts, I pronounce you now and forever as a married couple. Husbands in life and forever more. You may now seal your vows with a kiss."

When Zach and Van's lips touched, Brody, Eric, and Maddie, as well as everyone else, stood up and cheered.

The pastor smiled in evident appreciation at the assembled joy. "May I now present for the first time, Mr. and Mr. Pierce-Kelly."

As Zach and Van made their way down the aisle, Brody wiped the tears from his eyes and clapped louder than he'd ever clapped in his life. Eric wrapped his arms around him.

"It was a beautiful ceremony," Eric whispered.

Brody was too choked up to speak. He simply nodded in reply. It was beautiful. Zach and Van were now legally married in the eyes of the state and the country. But what made Brody the happiest was the wellspring of hope that bubbled up from within.

One day, it would be him and Eric up there. He didn't need his intuition to tell him that.

Chapter Nineteen

BRODY WAS exhausted. It was after midnight, and they had danced most of the night away on the grounds of the Pilgrim Monument, where the reception had been held. It had been a wonderful party, even though they had played "The Chicken Dance." He and Maddie hated that song, but that sure as hell didn't stop them from shaking their tail feathers.

They were having too good of a time. He even managed to get Maddie on the dance floor for a Britney Spears song. She hated it from the track's beginning till its end, but she grinned and bore it for him. How sweet was that?

Now, though, all he wanted was to die in place, but that wasn't going to happen.

It was his and Eric's last night together. Tomorrow, Eric and Maddie would make their way back to Petersham.

It was going to be hard to see them go, but it wouldn't be forever. He and Eric already had plans to see each other again in a couple of weeks, when he would head over to the western side of the state. Eric promised to show him all the sights. The only place he wanted to visit, though, was Eric's bed. Where else did he really need to go?

The door to the bedroom opened, and Eric came through the doorway. He closed the door quietly behind him and leaned against it. "Oh my God, I'm beat."

"Is Maddie asleep?"

Eric nodded. "She was long gone before her head hit the pillow."

"Good," Brody said as he rose from the bed. He'd already shed his tuxedo and most of his clothes. All he still had on was his underwear. That meant Eric was far too overdressed. So he crossed the length of the room and undid Eric's bowtie and tossed it to the floor. He made short work of the buttons and slid the shirt from Eric's torso.

He'd never seen a more beautiful chest in his life. It wasn't the strength it housed or the manly fur that coated the taut pecs or dusted his muscled stomach. It was the heart that beat inside Eric that he'd fallen for. "You're so beautiful."

"Are you looking in the mirror again?" Eric asked as he rested his hands on Brody's hips.

"Most definitely not," he answered. "I'm looking at you."

He closed the distance between them until their lips brushed together. The familiar spark of passion once again crackled between them. Whenever they kissed, it was like standing in front of a live wire, and it was an energy he never wanted to subside.

Instead, he wanted to own it. To plug himself directly into the source. And the only way to do that was to get Eric out of his clothes. So he undid the button on Eric's pants and forced the zipper open. He yanked the trousers and underwear from Eric's hips. When his hard, thick cock bobbed into view, Brody took the erection in his hand and returned his lips to Eric's.

"God, you feel so good," he muttered between kisses. As he wormed his tongue inside Eric's mouth, Brody teased his cock. He fluttered his fingers around the base before drawing circles around the engorged head. Eric moaned and thrust his hips harder into Brody's grip in response.

Eric enjoyed being teased. The tiny drops of precum that coated the head of his dick revealed that clearly. Brody wasn't about to let those pearly drops of pleasure go to waste. He ran his fingers through the liquid and then stuck his fingers in his mouth. The sweet nectar danced upon his tongue. One helping was definitely not going to be enough. "You taste good too."

"Fuck, you're driving me crazy," Eric gasped before shoving Brody's briefs from his body. He backed Brody up to the bed, their lips still touching, Brody's hand still jacking his cock. When they made it to the bed, Eric guided Brody onto the mattress and then lowered himself on top.

What was he going to do when he wasn't sharing a bed with Eric tomorrow night? He'd grown accustomed to his naked flesh pressed against his. The strong arm that pulled him close in the middle of the night. The hot mouth that milked the cum from his balls. The throbbing cock that pierced his flesh. And the loving kisses that he'd subsisted on for the past few days.

How would he handle Eric's absence?

"Stop thinking about tomorrow," Eric said. He positioned himself between Brody's open legs before caressing his cheek and running his hands through Brody's hair. "We still have tonight."

"Now who's becoming intuitive all of a sudden?"

Eric grinned down at him. God, he was going to miss that big, beautiful smile. "I've learned from the best."

Brody nodded. "I won't argue with that."

"But seriously," Eric said. He delivered a long, slow, passionate kiss that made Brody's toes curl. When he finally broke away, he continued. "Distance isn't going to change anything between us. It's going to be hard, sure. But it's not permanent. I know that. You know that too, right?"

That he did. There was no other man for him in this world, and there was no other little girl he longed to see grow into a young lady. As far as he was concerned, it would be the three of them against the world. It was going to be hard, and he was going to pout like a little bitch when Eric and Maddie departed on the ferry. But it wouldn't change how fast his heart beat whenever he saw Eric again. Or extinguish the urge that burned through his body whenever they touched. What he'd found was special, and he loved Eric and Maddie more than he imagined was possible. "I do know that," he finally answered. "But I don't have to like being away from you."

"I won't like it either," Eric said with a grin. "But it won't be good-bye. I could never say those words to you."

"Good," he said. "Because I'd never let you say them. Does that sound like a deal to you?"

Eric nodded. "Of course it does."

He wrapped his legs around Eric's waist. Eric's hard cock nestled against his crack, and right now, he needed Eric inside him to seal the deal they'd just made. Only Eric's flesh pushing inside him could accomplish that, and since they'd abandoned using condoms a couple of nights ago, the spilling of Eric's seed inside his body would bind them together. Forever.

"Make love to me," he whispered before pressing his lips against Eric's.

Eric leaned into the kiss, forcing his tongue inside Brody's mouth. As their tongues twined together, Eric glided his hands from Brody's chest down to his ass. He squeezed them tightly and said, "Nothing would make me happier." Then he reached into the nightstand, pulled out the bottle of lube, and applied it to his hard cock and Brody's twitching hole.

Eric slid the liquid around his ass, teasing his center with wide circles before tapping on the opening. When he slipped a finger inside, Brody gasped. He clutched onto the arm Eric used to support himself on the bed and bit his lip. He desperately wanted to cry out in pleasure, but he couldn't wake Maddie.

She no doubt already knew they were intimate. They'd been sleeping together since Maddie returned from her catamaran voyage around the Cape. She had no trouble with the sleepovers when they'd talked to her about it. She had simply shrugged and told them that as long as her Papa was happy, she was happy. That was all that mattered to her.

Still, she definitely didn't need to hear the two of them in the throes of ecstasy. So while Eric worked one, then two fingers inside him, he whimpered as quietly as possible. He even shoved his fist in his mouth, but his moans still managed to escape.

"I love watching you squirm," Eric whispered before sliding a third finger inside. Brody almost passed out. Especially when Eric began to fan his fingers inside him. When Eric lowered his mouth to take Brody's hardness down his throat, the world spun around him. How was he supposed to remain quiet when Eric was finger-fucking him and bobbing up and down on his cock?

He grabbed Eric's shoulders, clawing at his tanned, muscular flesh. He used the leverage to pump his cock in and out of Eric's mouth while also grinding his ass further onto Eric's intruding fingers. When Eric found the bundle of nerves nestled deep within, Brody almost came off the bed. Eric gently rubbed his prostate, and Brody's eyes rolled to the back of his head. If Eric didn't stop what he was doing, Brody was going to blow his load down his throat.

"You need to stop," he whined. "You're gonna make me come."

Eric allowed his cock to slip from his lips. "I know. I'm not going to sleep tonight till you fill my belly."

"Oh fuck," he said. "That's hot!"

Eric grinned. "That's what I'm saying."

"Okay, then," Brody nodded. "Let's do it. I'll be as quiet as I can."

Eric gobbled his cock back into his mouth and increased his suction. He slid quickly up and down his shaft. His spit dripped from his mouth and matted Brody's blond pubic hair. While Eric sucked, he flicked his tongue around the ridges of the head. Fuck! He was already closely approaching the edge of his impending orgasm.

He thrust his hips upward, forcing himself further inside Eric's greedy mouth. With each motion of his hips, he teetered further and further over the edge. His breath caught in his throat, and beads of sweat burst from his skin.

When Eric once again started working his fingers inside his ass and massaging his prostate in quick, urgent circles, Brody finally fell over to the other side. As he came, he brought the pillow to his face and covered his mouth as he cried out into the cushion. His entire body convulsed as he ejected his sperm inside Eric's mouth. Eric slurped up his juices, moaning in pleasure as he swallowed each jet of spunk.

"Good God!" he panted. "I've never come like that before."

Eric sat on his haunches and chuckled while he wiped his saliva from his chin. "Well, I'll do my best to top that performance real soon."

Brody grabbed his knees and brought them to his chest, exposing his hungry hole to Eric. "Well, real soon has just arrived," he said. "It's time for you to top me. Because if you think I'm going to bed without my ass full of you, then you're crazy."

"I'm definitely not crazy," Eric said as he stroked his cock. "And I definitely want to be inside you."

"Then do it," he panted. "Do me."

Without further invitation, Eric aimed his cock at his center and gently nudged himself inside. Brody's body opened up completely and dragged Eric all the way in past the second ring of muscles. "Oh God, yes."

"I love being inside you," Eric said once his groin rested against Brody's ass. He slowly began to work his cock in and out of his butt. Pulling his dick almost completely out of him, until only the head remained inside, and then slowly returning his cock all the way back up his ass.

He reached up and pulled Eric down to him. He skimmed his fingers around Eric's lips before hooking his chin. "And I love you being inside me," he said. He brought their lips together once again, and they resumed their passionate kisses. Eric's breath smelled of musk, sweat, cock, and cum. It was a heady mixture that drove him crazy. He shoved his tongue further inside Eric's mouth, trying to savor every last flavor while Eric increased the speed of his thrusts.

As Eric pummeled him, his balls slapped against his ass. He forced himself harder and faster inside. His breathing turned ragged, and sweat poured down his face. Brody wiped the sweat from Eric's eyes before lacing his fingers around Eric's neck. He used the leverage to slam himself upward, meeting Eric's savage thrusts with his own. The moist collisions of their bodies, and Eric's frenzied swiveling-hip motions once again brought him back to the edge he'd previously tumbled over.

His cock was rock hard and slid between their writhing bodies. The familiar pressure was once again building in his balls, and his dick began to twitch. "Oh, Eric," he uttered. "You're getting me close again."

"I'm almost there," Eric panted. "I want to come inside you so badly."

"And I want your cum so badly," he grunted.

"It's yours," Eric said as he kissed Brody. "All yours."

He rested his head against Eric's sweat-coated chest and listened to the thunderous beat of his heart. It raced like a thoroughbred's, and a low moan escaped from his throat. This was it. Eric was on the verge, so Brody reached between their bodies. He furiously jacked his cock while Eric's thrusts turned as ragged as the breath that fled his lungs.

"Fuck!" Eric mumbled. "Here it comes." And with one final thrust, Eric's cock spasmed, spraying his seed inside. As he came, Eric's cock pulsed and increased in girth.

The sensation shoved Brody back over the precipice. "Me too," he cried out as he blasted both of their bodies with his spunk.

Eric then collapsed on top of him. Their bodies were covered in sweat, and Brody's cum coated both their bellies. "That was awesome."

"That's not a lie," he answered.

After Eric's hardness withdrew from his body, Eric turned on his side and slid off Brody. He put his arms around him and drew him close. "I'm going to miss you," he said with a sigh. "Real bad."

"I know. I'm going to miss you too." Brody gazed up into Eric's stunning amber eyes. "But it's only for a few weeks. We have a deal, remember?"

Eric nodded. "I do." He hugged Brody tightly before inhaling deeply at the top of his head.

"What was that for?"

"Just committing everything about you to memory," Eric answered. "It's got to hold me over for the next couple of weeks."

He climbed on top of Eric and straddled him. "Don't worry. I plan on making this a night you won't soon forget." He swiveled his hips on top of Eric's already-hardening cock. "Does that sound like a deal to you?"

Eric nodded vigorously. "Hell, yeah."

"Good. Because it's time to seal the deal. Again."

"I just love making deals with you."

Brody chuckled. "Hey, me too!"

"Want to know what I love even more than that?"

Brody shook his head. "Nope."

"What?" Eric asked. He grabbed Brody's shoulders and turned over on his side. The move caused Brody to fall onto the mattress, where Eric pinned him underneath his hard body. A fake sneer curled his upper lip. "Why not?"

"Because I already know," he answered smugly.

Eric smiled down at him before gingerly kissing his lips. "There's that intuition again."

Brody nodded.

"What else does your intuition tell you about us?"

"It tells me you're just going to have to wait and find out."

"I can live with that," Eric answered with a kiss.

Brody cupped Eric's cheek in his hand. "Me too."

Epilogue

HOW HAD one year already gone by? Brody sure as hell didn't have the answer. It seemed like just yesterday that he'd first picked up Eric and Maddie at the pier. Time had sped by so fast it was sometimes hard for him to handle all the changes that had occurred.

A week after Eric and Maddie left, he managed to snag the lead in Brian Long's *Poke-a-hunkus*. Brian had been so impressed by his performance that he'd landed another lead role in Brian's next summer production *Booty and the Bear*. How fucking awesome was that?

It still blew his mind to see his name and picture on the marquee outside the Provincetown Theater. He'd never get rich, but he was happy. Besides, he was lucky enough to land a permanent paying gig with Gary's new wedding-planner business. Naturally, he called it "Penny's Perfect Day." While it wasn't easy working for Genghis Khan, it paid the bills of the new condo that he and Eric had purchased together a few months ago.

Eric and Maddie had moved to Provincetown shortly after Eric applied for and got a job with the P-town Police Department. Now they all lived together, and Maddie, who had spent the past two-and-a-half years with only her father, now had a whole mess of people to call family. And boy, were they sometimes a mess!

But what family was perfect?

While his intuition had told him last year that the three of them would be together, nothing had prepared him for the latest shocker in their lives.

Nino and Teddy were getting married.

It had sure as hell shocked the shit out of Brody when Teddy told him Nino had proposed. He hadn't seen that one coming. Sure, they loved each other, but Nino getting married was too absurd an idea to ever consider.

Yet here he was. Standing in front of the breakwater with the gang while Gary, who was dressed as Penny Poison, discussed the specifics of Nino and Teddy's impending nuptials. He should have been paying attention to the details, but no one else was. They had all zoned out too. Quinn chatted with Tara and Irene, to the side. Zach and Van, who seemed to be on a perennial honeymoon, made out against the fence a few feet away, and Maddie and Eric sat on a bench a few feet away over at the small park most everyone called Pilgrim's Landing.

Eric held something in his hand, and Maddie was jumping up and down in joy. Had he just given her a gift? It wasn't Maddie's birthday. She had turned ten three months ago. What were the two of them up to over there?

"Brody O'Shea, are you paying attention?"

Gary's irritated voice pulled him back to the conversation at hand. "Of course," he lied.

"Good," Gary said with a nod. The bangs of Penny's green wig bobbed across his forehead. "There'll be a quiz later."

Well, fuck! Not another damn quiz. Why did Gary find it necessary to quiz his employees about client meetings? It wasn't like Gary didn't memorize every damn piece of information.

He'd be in trouble with Gary later, but oh well! It wasn't the first time, and it wouldn't be the last time either. Besides, it wasn't like anything was going to come from this meeting. Nino was being too hardheaded for there to be any progress on the subject.

How many times had Gary gone over this already? It had to be a hundred. At least.

It was impossible to build any kind of archway on the rocky wall. Nino didn't understand why. Yes, the breakwater was important to him and Teddy. After all, the two of them fell in love on the rocky structure that extended from the Provincetown Inn, where most straight visitors stayed, and reached all the way to Long Point at the furthest tip of the Cape. But just because the spot was special for them didn't mean that Gary could work a miracle.

The tide constantly swallowed up huge parts of the breakwater. Even if constructing a temporary structure on the breakwater were allowed, anything built on it wouldn't outlast the tide.

Yet Nino still argued with Gary.

"Come on, Gary, there's got to be some way." If Nino were any more like a whining child, he'd be stomping his foot.

"There's not," Gary said. "I can create an exquisite ceremony at the Provincetown Inn. They have a beautiful lawn that overlooks the breakwater."

"No," Nino replied with a firm shake of his head. "It has to be on the breakwater."

"Gary said it can't be done," Teddy said. Although Teddy was far more reasonable, it was easy to see how badly he wanted their wedding to take place on the breakwater as well.

He could understand that. If he and Eric ever got married, he would want it to be some place special too. Like the Pilgrim Monument, or the Boatslip. Or better yet, the pier. That was where they'd first professed their love for each other. It wasn't the most romantic spot in P-town, but to him, that pier was magical.

"But that's where we first let our guard down around each other," Nino said. "Under the stars. In the middle of the ocean. With no one else, not even ourselves, standing in our way."

Teddy nodded. "I know, but if it can't be done, it can't be done."

"Oh my God!" Brody said. How fucking brilliant was he? He rushed over to Teddy and Nino and grabbed their hands. "I think I've got it."

Teddy stared at him with hope in his eyes. Nino was only annoyed.

The excitement in his voice, however, drew everyone's attention. They all gathered around. Even Eric and Maddie strolled over from the park to listen in.

"Got what?" Nino asked. Now that Brody and Eric were an item, Nino had fewer problems with him. He was no longer seen as a rival. But it still didn't stop Nino from being a great big asshole on occasion.

"We can't construct anything on the breakwater, but what if we don't have to?"

Teddy's previously hopeful eyes narrowed in confusion. "What are you talking about?"

"The two of you don't need this fabulous archway. Or anything like that. Your story's far simpler, and your wedding should reflect that."

Gary beamed. "I agree."

Nino glanced from Gary to Brody. "Would one of you tell me what the hell you're talking about?"

"A midnight wedding," Gary said with a flourish of his hands. "To commemorate the time you fell in love. All your guests dressed in white, holding candles while the two of you stand on the spot where you fell in love. That will be where you exchange your vows." He crossed his hands over his chest and jutted out his chin to express he was pleased with the brainstorm Brody had jump-started. "What do you think?"

Nino and Teddy stared into each other's eyes for a few seconds before replying in unison. "It sounds perfect."

"Hallelujah!" Gary exclaimed while everyone else cheered. He patted Brody on the back. "Thanks for that. I was worried I was going to have to beat Humberto senseless with my sensible pumps."

Well, shit! If he'd known that was a possibility, he might not have said a thing. Who wouldn't want to see Nino getting a Penny Poison beat down? "Just part of my job."

"Sounds like someone deserves a raise," Quinn said with a wink to Brody.

Gary gasped. "Bobby Quinn, you hush!"

"I think you're right, Quinn. I deserve a commission at least."

Gary smacked Quinn on the shoulder. "See what you've started. Now you've got Miss Thing over here thinking she's something special."

"He is something special," Eric said. He took Brody's hand and kissed it. "He's the man that I love."

"No. That would be you," Brody replied before returning a kiss. Except he delivered his on Eric's velvety lips.

"Now that all this has been decided, can we go home?" Van asked from within his husband's embrace. "Zach and I have some,"—he paused and giggled—"things to do."

Irene rolled her eyes. "Can't you two keep it in your pants for longer than half an hour?"

"Irene!" Tara scolded. She nodded to Maddie.

"Hey, I'm not the one practically getting it on in front of her," Irene replied.

"Well, before you all leave, I have something I want to say."

Eric's words stopped all conversation. Why did Maddie look like she was about to pee her pants in excitement?

"What is it?" Brody asked.

Everyone gathered around them, forming a half circle. Why did he feel as if this had been planned?

"Brody, meeting you has been one of the greatest gifts I've ever received. You came into my life at just the right moment. I'd been coasting through existence on autopilot. Not really living and not really feeling anything for anyone but my daughter. It was easier that way. And safer. How could I lose someone if I never let anyone back inside my heart? But my heart opened up for you. Not because I wanted it. Or willed it. But because my heart saw the man you were. My soul sensed the missing piece of myself that you carried around with you. And I fell in love with you. Like you once told Maddie and me last year: 'To fall in love once is a blessing. To have it twice in a lifetime is a miracle.'"

When Eric bent down on one knee, Brody almost passed out. Was this really about to happen? After reaching into his back pocket, Eric pulled out a black felt box and held it open for all to see.

"Brody O'Shea, I love you, and I want to spend the rest of this lifetime with you. Will you do me the honor of being my husband?"

Brody knelt down beside Eric. Tears streamed down his face. Even though he'd known this day would come, now that it was here, he was almost speechless. "Yes," he said, finally forcing the words past the sob of happiness lodged in his throat. "Of course I will. Yes."

Eric slipped the ring over his finger and delivered the most powerful kiss Brody had ever received in his life. It wasn't just their love the kiss celebrated. It was their future.

When their lips finally parted, the thunderous applause of their friends filled their ears. But none of them were happier than Maddie. She squealed in glee.

"We did it, Papa!" she exclaimed. "We're going to officially be a family again."

"We've already been a family," he told Maddie as he pulled her into an embrace. He gazed around at Zach and Van, Nino and Teddy, Gary and Quinn, and Tara and Irene. "All of us."

"Most definitely," Zach agreed.

Van beamed as he once again leaned into Zach's embrace. "Happy and dysfunctional, just like everyone else."

Nino nodded. "As much as I hate to admit it, Brody's right."

"Of course he's right," Teddy said with a playful swat. "Who else but all of us would put up with all of us?"

"That's the God's honest truth," Irene added.

Tara rolled her eyes. "You're always so full of joy, my love, aren't you?"

"She wouldn't be Irene if she wasn't," Quinn chuckled as he hugged Tara and Irene.

"We are all who we are," Gary said proudly. "I wouldn't have it any other way."

Maddie squeezed Eric and Brody around the neck. It was quite possibly the strongest hug she'd ever given before. "Me neither."

"We're a perfect family," Eric said before he kissed Brody.

Brody smiled. "Who could ask for anything more?"

"How about a happily ever after for all of us?" Zach asked.

Eric grinned as he stared at the ring on Brody's finger. "Now that sounds like a perfect ending."

Brody couldn't agree more. "It does to me too."

JACOB Z. FLORES lives a double life. During the day, he is a respected college English professor and midlevel administrator. At night and during his summer vacation, he loosens the tie and tosses aside the trendy sports coat to write man-on-man fiction, where the hardass assessor of freshmen level composition turns his attention to the firm posteriors and other rigid appendages of the characters in his fictional world.

Summers in Provincetown, Massachusetts, provide Jacob with inspiration for his fiction. The abundance of barely clothed man flesh and daily debauchery stimulates his personal muse. When he isn't stroking the keyboard, Jacob spends time with his husband, Bruce, their three children, and two dogs, who represent a bright blue blip in an otherwise predominantly red swath in south Texas.

You can follow Jacob's musings on his blog at http://jacobzflores.com or become a part of his social media network by visiting http://www.facebook.com/jacob.flores2 or http://twitter.com/#!/JacobZFlores.

The Provincetown Series from JACOB Z. FLORES

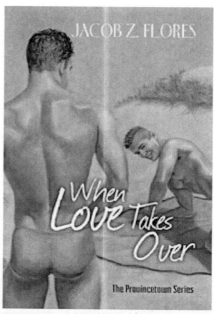

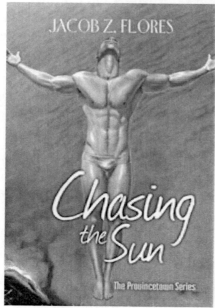

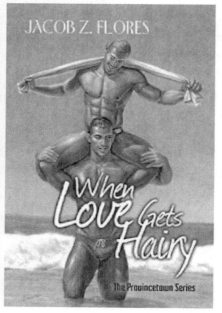

http://www.dreamspinnerpress.com

Also from JACOB Z. FLORES

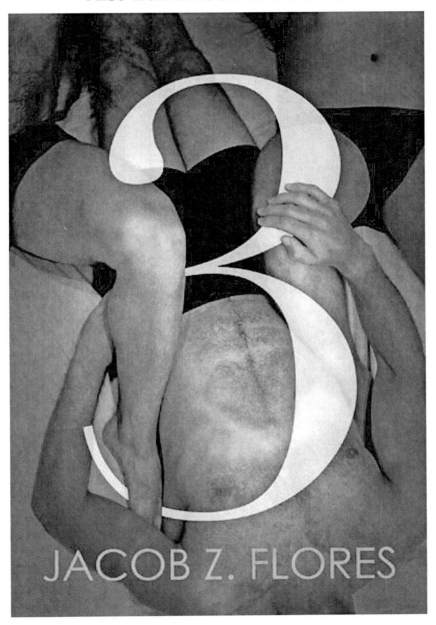

JACOB Z. FLORES

http://www.dreamspinnerpress.com

Also from JACOB Z. FLORES

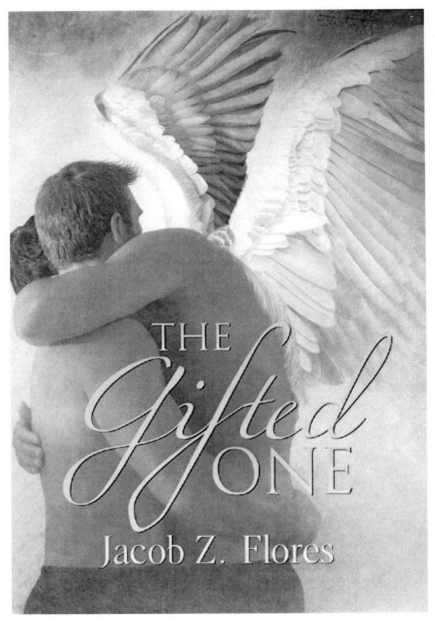

http://www.dreamspinnerpress.com

Also from DREAMSPINNER PRESS

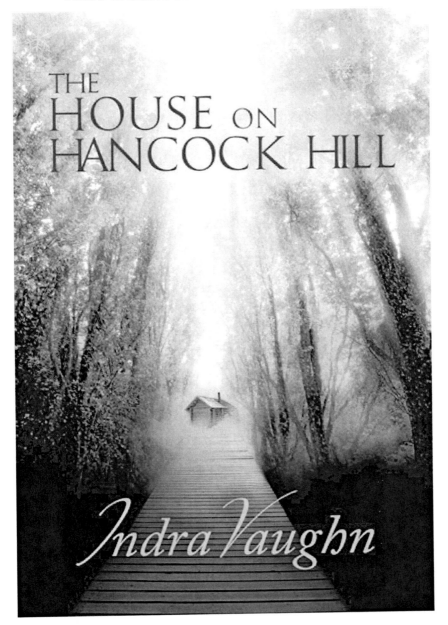

THE
HOUSE ON
HANCOCK HILL

Indra Vaughn

http://www.dreamspinnerpress.com

For more of the
best M/M romance,
visit

Dreamspinner Press

www.dreamspinnerpress.com